Hidden
BLOSSOM

SKYLINE MANSION BOOK TWO

NOLA LI BARR

Tapioca Press

Edited by Corina Douglas
Cover design by The Red Leaf Book Design / www.redleafbookdesign.com

ISBN 978-1-7327814-5-0 (ebook)
ISBN 978-1-7327814-6-7 (paperback)
ISBN 978-1-956919-02-8 (hardback)

www.nolalibarr.com

The Lin Family

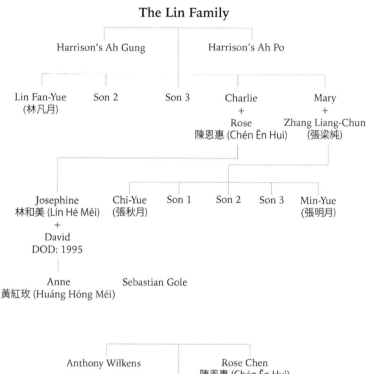

Harrison's Ah Gung — Harrison's Ah Po

Lin Fan-Yue (林凡月)　Son 2　Son 3　Charlie + Rose 陳恩惠 (Chén Ēn Huì)　Mary + Zhang Liang-Chun (張梁純)

Josephine 林和美 (Lín Hé Měi) + David DOD: 1995　Chi-Yue (張秋月)　Son 1　Son 2　Son 3　Min-Yue (張明月)

Anne 黃紅玫 (Huáng Hóng Méi)　Sebastian Gole

Anthony Wilkens — Rose Chen 陳恩惠 (Chén Ēn Huì)

Harrison 林飛鴻 (Lín Fēi Hóng) + Grace

The Wilkens Family

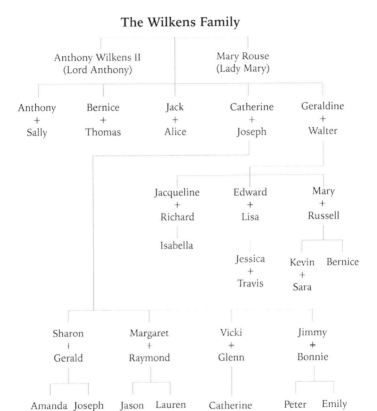

ABOUT THIS BOOK

A second journal falls into Anne's lap just as she is accepting her inheritance and her grandmother's secret. This time, an old photo of her mother with a mixed-race boy and an unknown woman comes with it. When she finds out the boy is her long-lost uncle—someone whom her mother has never mentioned—she promises to find him.

Anne embarks on a new journey to Taiwan with her mother and boyfriend, Sebastian, where her Taiwanese American culture hinders more than helps. She must navigate a culture and a complex extended family that is at once familiar and foreign. Family bonds and relationships are tested as she hopes to locate her lost uncle, but the most tested relationship is the one she holds with Sebastian.

CHAPTER 1

One month of being pampered by Mom after my car was blown up.

One month of peace since Andy passed away at the end of February.

Now, it's the end of March and I still haven't ventured beyond the boundary of my new property. But Lady has been keeping me company. Sebastian insisted that I get a dog since I wasn't venturing outside much. I tried to push back because I had the best of intentions to travel again, but right after Andy's funeral, Sebastian arrived carrying a cocker spaniel with a big red bow around her neck. I instantly bonded with Lady. I could talk to her and she wouldn't talk back. I could hug her and know that I was loved without any complications.

My days had become simple and unimaginative. I woke up at ten o'clock every morning. As I lay in bed, I would wonder what I'd do with myself that day. I would try to type up a travel blog post about a trip I had done in the past, but inspiration just wouldn't come.

Cook would have brunch ready for me by the time I

meandered downstairs, and it ranged from congee to eggs and sausage. My favorite was the thin waffles with cottage cheese and peaches on top. Ben would meet me at the brunch table to see if there was anything I needed for the day. My answer was always no; Andy had trained him well—he came back every morning without fail. By noon, I was in the library reading one of the many books on the shelves and was currently working my way through the *Count of Monte Cristo*. I had read it in high school, but there was something about reading an old version in a classy library that made the story come to life. I'd read till dinner, at times taking a break to wander through the garden.

Sebastian sent me fresh roses once a week. Life was wonderful. The stress of everyday living had evaporated given there was no need for me to earn money—well, as long as I didn't go out and spend all my billions at once, which was impossible for me. Life was pretty much perfect except for one nagging thought in the back of my mind . . .

Andy's letter about my uncle would sneak into my thoughts once a day, leading me to concentrate even more on my book or venture outside for a walk. I often reminded myself that I had everything I wanted or needed. There was no need to go stirring up the past again. I had done enough of that, and it had ended with me in the hospital after someone intentionally blew up my car. We still didn't know who was behind it, but I had my suspicions.

Nope, I had no desire to look into it. And yet . . . the thought never left my mind. The piece of paper that had come with my uncle's letter had included a phone number and an address for a woman called Mary, who apparently was my Ah Gung's sister. I had tucked the note and the letter safely in my desk drawer and never touched it again, not even mentioning it to Mom.

I still couldn't believe it—my mom had a half brother. A

half brother she didn't know existed. I had no idea how to bring up the subject. Maybe she did know and had never told me? It wouldn't be the first time Mom had kept something from me. I quickly shooed that thought from my mind, chastising myself for thinking ill of Mom.

It was at this moment that Lady decided to jump into my lap and make herself comfortable, kicking me out of my thoughts.

"Look, Miss Anne, she loves you," Ben said.

Andy had done such a terrific job of training Ben that life had gone on seamlessly. I'd like to think that Andy would have been proud of him. Of course, Cook could be heard every once in a while, chastising Ben for something or another, mostly for setting foot in her kitchen when he had no need to. I had tried to tell Cook that she'd worked so hard all these years that I wouldn't mind if she wanted to retire. After all, her daughter had been working in the kitchen with her for years now and would gladly take over. That incident cost me a week of burnt meals. Suffice to say, I never brought the subject up again.

"I love her too," I said, giving Lady a snuggle.

"Where's my love?" Victoria asked, still in her nightgown as she joined us on the porch.

"Good morning," I answered, waving Lady's paw at her in greeting.

"Is that sausages I smell?"

"Yup. Help yourself. Cook made way too many for us."

I watched as Victoria shoveled sausages into her mouth. It was amusing to watch because it looked like she hadn't eaten in days when just last night we had eaten at Adina, my favorite tapas restaurant in Portland.

Victoria had stayed in Portland after Andy's funeral. She'd mentioned something about wanting to spend more time with me, but I think my car accident had spooked her. She had taken me out dancing. We'd eaten at restaurants neither one of us had previously been able to afford, and she never left my side unless we were at home. Even then, when she stayed over, she insisted on taking the room next to mine despite the fact that I had set up a nice guest room for her facing the back of the house where she could see the garden. However, I really didn't mind. Having Victoria here—a real friend—made me feel less alone, and with the addition of Lady, I felt quite content.

"Where's Sebastian?" asked Victoria, having moved onto the eggs Lavender had just brought out.

"He's working."

"On a Saturday?"

"You know how he is with work. Apparently, there's this big case that's going on right now," I said while playing fetch with Lady. "He can't talk about it," I added before Victoria could ask.

Victoria hadn't quite warmed up to Sebastian, and was suspicious of him still working with Isabella's family. The thought had crossed my mind, but Sebastian had been so attentive and I really liked him. He was nothing like Brian, and the more time that passed, the sting of Sebastian's betrayal began to mellow.

"Maybe the three of us should all go out for dinner one night? I don't want my best friend and boyfriend holding a grudge."

"You know how I feel . . . ."

"Yes, but let's give it a try. I think we can all be civil."

There was silence for a few seconds before Victoria finally said, "Fine. But I get to wear one of your dresses in your closet."

"One of the vintage ones?"

"No, your red qipao from your Ah Po."

I must have given her the most surprised look because

next thing I knew, she was laughing so hard that she had to cover her mouth so she wouldn't spit her food out.

"Yes, of course, one of the vintage ones! I couldn't fit in your Ah Po's qipao even if I wanted to—which I don't."

"When did you get into vintage clothes? You were always very . . . non-conservative."

"Oh, you know me. I like to mix things up a bit from time to time," Victoria said, not looking me in the eye.

"You've met someone," I said, feeling my smile grow bigger at the thought of Victoria having met someone who wasn't just a temporary standby.

"I . . ."

"Come on! Spit it out."

"Let's go to your room. I don't want to broadcast this to the world."

I turned to my cocker spaniel. "Lady, come here. We need to go to our secret spot so Victoria can spill the beans on her new beau." At this, Victoria gave me a shove so hard that I fell over. But I was laughing so much that I could have fallen over without her assistance.

We made our way to my room and as soon as I shut the door, she dragged me into my closet.

"What are we doing in here?"

"I'm so embarrassed and you know how servants talk."

I had never seen Victoria so nervous. "You've been watching way too much Downton Abbey."

"I love that show and don't you dare diss it."

"All right. All right," I said with raised hands. "What's the big secret?"

"I was minding my own business—"

"You? You were minding your own business?"

Victoria put her hands on her hips. "Are you going to let me tell the story or not? If you're going to be this way—"

"Okay. Okay. I won't say another word."

Victoria stared at me for a minute and I could almost see the thoughts churning in her mind. I had never seen her like this about a guy. It was usually the other way around—the male species couldn't help but fawn all over her.

"I was minding my own business"—she gave me a look and I made sure my face was featureless as she added—"in the library."

She was giving me the stink eye and I was already having a hard time keeping a straight face. Victoria was not known to set foot in a library unless absolutely necessary, but I managed to straighten my features enough for her to continue with, "I'll have you know that in the last month I got a job at an ad agency."

"How come I'm just hearing about this now?"

"Because you were going through all your hullabaloo and I didn't want you worrying about me."

"Why would I worry? This is great news!"

"Anyways, part of my job is to go look up past ads, and what better place to look than the library? I do venture there when I need to, you know."

She seemed hurt that I would question her, so I reached over and gave her a hug. She seemed appeased and continued, "I was minding my own business when a guy came up behind me and asked if I was using the other books on the table."

"Who?" I demanded.

"His name is Paul, and Anne, he is *so* cute! He has Harry Potter glasses and a chubby nose, but his eyes are the softest, kindest eyes I've ever seen. I don't know how to describe him —he's just him. Nothing more. He's not trying to be someone he's not."

"Look at you! You're totally smitten."

She flushed. "I know!"

"So, what's wrong? Have you seen him again?"

All she did was nod.

"And?"

"I've been seeing him every day since we met," she confessed. "Usually at the library because he's a postdoctoral fellow. He's studying something about electrons and photons and producing light. I don't know. He's so smart and I'm . . . I'm me."

"And there's nothing wrong with you!"

"You're only saying that because you're my best friend. You know me, Anne. I'm not someone who falls in love. I just like to play around."

"I do know you, Victoria, and I know you want to fall in love. You want to find *the one* and all those other boys have not been good for you. What are you so worried about with Paul? He sounds perfect!"

"I'm worried that I'm going to mess things up. He wants me to be his plus one at a family friend's wedding this weekend and I'm so nervous."

She had whispered the last part so low that I wasn't sure if I had heard her correctly. "You're nervous?" And he was already taking her to a wedding where she'll meet his family? Sebastian hadn't even mentioned meeting his parents yet, and Brian didn't introduce me to his parents until we'd been dating for a year. I suddenly wondered how Brian was doing. Then I stopped myself. *Why was I thinking about Brian?*

"Yes, I, Victoria, am nervous," she said. "There, I said it! I'm worried that his family won't like me."

"They'll love you!"

She shook her head slowly. "No . . . I didn't mention that I overheard him talking to his sister one day. She didn't—she didn't seem too impressed by me," she stuttered.

I couldn't believe it. My best friend who was gorgeous and smart—not bookish smart, but smart everywhere else—was in tears in front of me because she wanted approval from her boyfriend's family. This was not the Victoria I knew, but I was also super happy that she might finally have found someone who cared about her. I opened my arms and she moved into them. We stood like that for a while with her tears running down my shirt.

"Is this why you want to borrow the dress?" I eventually asked. I felt her nodding against my chest. "You shouldn't change yourself. This guy likes you for who you are."

I could feel her shaking her head now.

Victoria said in a muffled voice against my chest, "I really think he does, but he loves his family. They're really tight-knit. I can tell by the way he talks about them all the time. He mentioned once that his parents still dressed like they were in the fifties, and I thought, well, I could wear one of your outfits and try to win them over."

"Victoria, you can borrow any clothes you want out of my closet," I replied softly. "I'm going to be able to meet him one day, right?"

"Of course! Just not yet. And Anne . . . thank you."

We spent the rest of the morning and afternoon trying on dresses. I had found some more in a closet down the hall and by the end of the day, Victoria had three really nice dresses that she loved. A part of me was getting a little worried that she was going to permanently change her style. I loved Victoria for who she was, and I didn't want her to be forced to become someone she wasn't, but I had never seen her so infatuated with a guy before. This guy had to be something.

At that moment, Lady growled. I turned to look and found her staring at Ah Po's trunk. Her paws were set as if she was ready to pounce. Why would she be growling at Ah Po's trunk? But the question remained unanswered as both mine and Victoria's stomachs rumbled, and we left in search of some food.

CHAPTER 2

COOK HAD MADE US A DELICIOUS CAPRESE SALAD telling us she didn't want us ruining our dinner. I had to admit, I was starting to get used to my new life. I worried that I was still taking all this for granted, but at those times, I reminded myself that I knew what it was like to live unceremoniously. And yes, I had started having debates with myself. Never aloud though; I didn't want others to think I was crazy.

"You have that look on your face again," Victoria said, having just swallowed a big mouthful of salad.

"What look?"

"The 'I'm going into my own world because it's more interesting than the world I'm living in' look."

"What?"

"Don't 'what' me. Besides your mom, I know you better than anyone else—who I invited over tonight, by the way."

She said this in the most nonchalant way possible. I almost didn't even notice and was about to nod my head in agreement when what she said hit me. Did she just say that she'd invited Mom over for dinner?

"You—?"

"And Sebastian too."

"Why?" I exclaimed, having lost interest in my snack. "I thought you and I were having bonding time given we are finally able to spend time together for more than a week or so."

"You haven't left this house since you moved back in two months ago! Sebastian is working way too many hours on whatever new cases he has, your mom has a new art gig she is starting work on, and I have a new job. I've pretty much exhausted your whole list of family and friends."

"There's . . . there's . . .?" I looked at Victoria who was bringing up small bites of cheese to her mouth. Methodical movements that would have had me hypnotized if it weren't for the expectant look in her unmoving eyes. I detected a hint of amusement there too. "Fine. You win. There's no one else."

"I don't want to win. I want you to be happy. You were the one I looked up to. The one who traveled all over the world."

"So you staged an intervention?"

"No, I absolutely did not."

Now it was my turn to give her the look.

"Fine, but it's for your own good," she conceded.

I laughed under my breath and turned my attention back to my salad, thinking that I was loved enough to have a staged intervention.

Mom came right on time, as usual. I could see the worry written on her face as soon as she stepped into the foyer. She enveloped me in such a tight hug that I wanted to cry. I had missed her so much.

We settled into the library sofas and caught up on the last

month. It wasn't until Lavender came to tell us that dinner was ready that I realized Sebastian still hadn't shown up.

"I thought you had invited Sebastian too?" I said, turning to Victoria who had a scowl on her face while shooting daggers at her phone.

"I did," she huffed. "Apparently he's running late and is trying his best to make it as soon as he can. I tell you, Anne, if you didn't love the man as much as you do, and if I didn't see how much he takes care of you, I would go to his office right now and give him an earful about his negligence as a boyfriend."

"I know you would, and I love you for it," I laughed, giving Victoria a hug.

I had to laugh. Sebastian was barely here these days. His roses were always on time each week, but the person himself was lagging a bit. I couldn't say I didn't feel a bit upset, but it was Sebastian, and I was trying to keep an open mind because I couldn't have gotten through the last few months if not for him. Plus, Anthony had told me to not give up on him. I had a little chuckle at the thought. Who knew I'd ever be in this position? Part of me still wished I was traveling the world, meeting new people, sharing my experience with total strangers on the internet, and not having a thought for my future. Brian would have appreciated this a lot more than me. He always liked the finer things in life. I wondered if he would have left me if he knew I would be inheriting all this money. I'd like to think otherwise given he had integrity, and he had always been generous.

It was a beautiful chill day. Spring was right around the corner, but for now there was still that bite in the morning air. I had the food served on the balcony with extra thick blankets so that we could enjoy the fresh air. The gardener had just finished pruning the maze and I could see tools set to the side so that they were ready to mow the lawn tomorrow. This was the life. To be able to sit on my own porch and look out at a lawn that stretched for miles. There was no one else in sight and I could pretty much be guaranteed to never have to see anyone I didn't want to if I just stayed put. That in itself was causing me a bit of a problem because I was starting to think that wasn't such a bad idea after all.

I could see why Victoria was worried about me, because it was possible that she would visit me one day, and I would have become a recluse with only cats and dogs keeping me company. I shuddered at the thought. It would be the complete opposite of who I was before my inheritance.

The three of us ate our dinner in peace, each one of us absorbed in our own thoughts. No doubt the two of them had agreed that this was a good time to hold my intervention. I laughed inside at the thought and felt loved.

"I guess Sebastian isn't joining us for dinner," Victoria said.

She asked Ben to take the food back to the kitchen. I was able to stop him and add that Cook should save it for Sebastian, because I was pretty sure he wouldn't have eaten yet. Victoria gave me a scowl, but I didn't care. Sebastian was working hard and I wanted to make sure that he knew I cared.

"How are you and Sebastian getting along?" Mom asked.

"We're great. He sends me roses every week. He hasn't been around a lot, maybe once a week or so, but I know he's working on a big case right now and I don't want to bother him. Plus, I'm enjoying my own time right now. I'm lapping up the fact that I literally don't have anything to worry about at this time."

Both Mom and Victoria stared at me like I was mad. What was with them? Just because I hadn't left the house these last two months didn't mean I wasn't doing okay.

"Why don't we head to the sitting room?" Victoria said,

standing up with Mom in tow.

"Why are you two being so silent? I thought this was an intervention," I said with a laugh.

"It is, but to tell you the truth we couldn't come up with a good idea on how to get you out of the house," Mom said. "We thought if all three of us were here we'd come up with something, but you look so content. I'm starting to think that maybe this quiet pace is what you need right now."

"No!" Victoria snapped.

I looked over to find her head between her hands.

"The last thing she needs is to be left where she is right now," Victoria continued. "I know you, Anne. And Mrs. Lin —no disrespect, but she's not my daughter, she's my friend and I don't need to be nice to her at a time like this. Anne, you have to get out of this house. You need to go out and explore again; see and meet other people. I can't bear to see you get complacent. That's how you became with Brian—just following him around and doing what he wanted."

"Now that's just unfair," I said, a bit shocked she would bring Brian up. He was long gone. *Was she capable of reading my thoughts?*

"I'm worried about you, Anne," Victoria said with tears in her eyes.

"I appreciate that but there's no need to." I was starting to get a bit heated. There was no reason for her to drag Brian into the conversation, and saying I was complacent? Now that was just . . . I didn't even know what to say.

"Now girls, that's enough. You two are best friends." Mom turned to face me, her features firm. "Victoria and I are very worried about you, Anne. We just want the best for you."

I gave a sigh. "I know, Mom. I do."

Mom smiled and moved closer to put an arm around us both. "Well then, why don't we watch that new movie you've been wanting me to watch?" she said, already steering us into the sitting room on the other side of the foyer.

"Eat Pray Love? You want to watch that now?" I asked.

"Why not? It's as good a time as any," Mom said, already turning on the TV.

I hadn't been in this room a lot. It was quite comfy now that I was seated on the sofa between Mom and Victoria. I remembered thinking it was stuffy when I first moved in. A fireplace was situated at the far wall and there used to be an exceptionally large family portrait of Lord Anthony, Lady Mary, and their children over the mantelpiece. It was so foreboding that I hadn't gone back into this room for weeks, but after Andy passed away, I'd thought it was time for me to make this place my own.

I felt bad making too many changes all at once, so I did little things here and there. One was to take down the big painting and replace it with a TV. A nice seventy-five-inch flat screen. It was a thousand times better than any television I had ever owned. I also repainted the walls with a fresh coat of paint, keeping with the cream color that matched the rest of the house. I loved the original wooden floors and had the whole first floor refinished, and then got some new throw blankets that were a lighter shade of cream and gold to complement the dark leather sofa, which I imagined had been there for decades. The original throw rug remained in its different shades of muted red. It was quite worn around the sides where the coffee table hadn't covered it. I could only imagine all the foot traffic that had come through here. I hoped to one day have it restored but for the time being that could wait.

"Shall we begin?" Mom asked.

"Begin what?" a voice said from behind me.

I leaped across the back of the sofa at the sound. Next thing I knew, I was enveloped in Sebastian's arms with my head on his chest. Lady was so happy to see him, she had started running circles around us.

"I'm so glad you're here. It's been a while since I've seen you," I said.

"Yeah, Brian never spent so much time away from you," I heard Victoria mumble. What was up with her bringing up Brian today? I sent a glare her way and hoped Sebastian hadn't heard her.

"I know. I'm so sorry. This case is eating away at me. I'm thinking of asking for some time off so I can breathe for a little bit."

"Is there anyone who can help you if you take days off?"

"Yes. Samuel is good. He's been on the case with me since the beginning, but it's my case and I'd like to be there through the whole thing."

"What are you two talking about?" Victoria piped in. "The movie is starting without you, Anne, if you still want to watch it. Sebastian, glad to see you finally made it," she added, not even glancing at him.

"Victoria," was all Sebastian said while he rubbed his face. I heard a sigh escape his mouth.

"Do you want to join us?" I asked.

"Did they already do the intervention?" Sebastian whispered in my ear. His arms were still around me and he had buried his face into my hair. I wanted to stay like this forever. Just the two of us.

"I think it's postponed. We decided to watch a movie," I whispered back.

We both let go at the sound of a throat clearing, which to my surprise was from Mom. Reluctantly, we joined the others on the couch. This time I was sandwiched between Sebastian and Mom. All my favorite people were here and I was happy, but I still didn't know why they'd had the crazy idea to stage an intervention.

15

CHAPTER 3

WHEN I WOKE UP, I WAS SNUGGLED AGAINST Sebastian on the sofa, with my head in the crook of his arm. Mom was sleeping, too, and Victoria was nowhere to be seen. She must have taken herself to bed. The screen was blank, but the on button showed it was still on. I slowly lifted myself into a sitting position, carefully untangled the remote from Mom's hands, and closed the TV. At that moment, the clock in the hallway cuckooed twice. I flinched as it broke the silence, and Sebastian woke up.

He rubbed his face and ran a hand through his hair. His eyes met mine and before he could say anything, I planted a kiss on his lips. His arms tightened around me and he held me close, deepening the kiss. Then without speaking, he helped me up off the sofa and quietly watched as I tucked Mom in before we sneaked like teenagers up to my room.

Now, at two in the morning you wouldn't expect anyone or anything to distract you from your handsome boyfriend— who had already tried multiple times to envelop you in his arms before you even made it to the door. But as soon as I set one foot in my room, I heard incessant whining, followed by silence, and then a low growl.

` "Is that Lady?" Sebastian asked, already heading to the closet where the noise was coming from. "Do you keep her in there at night?"

"No, of course not. She has a perfectly good pad at the foot of our bed."

Sebastian flipped on the lights before I could stop him. I was momentarily blinded but I saw Lady sitting in front of the trunk, just like she had been before when Victoria and I were talking in the closet. She seemed quite irritated.

I was protesting the injustice of blinding someone when Sebastian said, "Anne, come here."

"As soon as I can see again."

"Oh, stop complaining, your eyes will adjust. Just walk over here. You're going to want to see this."

I walked toward him with my hands shading my eyes and felt my way to the floor beside Sebastian. Lady snuggled onto my lap. At first, I didn't realize what I was looking at. The trunk had become as familiar to me as all of my personal belongings. I knew it front to back. Every nick had been rubbed over by my fingers knowing this was once my grandmother's, my Ah Po's. The journals that it protected introduced me to Ah Po—a woman who I knew nothing about except that we were related. Her past actions had caused me to inherit billions four months ago, all because she had a relationship with Sir Anthony Wilkens—someone outside of her social and cultural class. Inheriting billions might seem like the best thing that could happen to anyone, but it threw me into a completely foreign world with people who didn't look or act like me. People who were used to money. People who had 'earned' it.

Even the servants had taken a while to warm up to me. I cringed at the memory of meeting the household staff for the first time. I'd had no authority, no desire to be here, and I'd been clueless on how to run a household. Thank goodness for Andy and Cook. They and Sebastian had kept me afloat.

"I know, it's a big surprise to me too," Sebastian said, knocking me out of my thoughts.

What was he talking about?

I refocused on the trunk and what I saw made me gasp. A secret compartment at the very bottom of the trunk had popped open. How in the world had I not noticed that before? Inside the compartment was a journal tied with a red ribbon and a picture in a simple metal frame of a mixed-race boy standing next to Ah Po and my mom. There was another lady with them, but I didn't know who she was.

I stared at the picture. Was this my uncle? It was obvious that Mom knew of his existence. How could she not have told me? After everything we went through and her promising to never keep secrets from me again . . . .

I felt tears start to fall. Thank goodness Sebastian was here. He took the picture and put it back in the drawer, and I heard a distinct click as it closed. Next thing I knew, I was being carried to bed and securely enclosed in strong arms who held me while tears streamed down my face.

I awoke to moist air on my cheek and pried my eyes open to find Lady looking at me with her food bowl in her mouth. Cook had been incredulous when I denied her the right to feed Lady the first week the dog had arrived. I had made a point that I would be the sole caregiver for Lady. That meant she needed to wait for me to wake up to eat, which was one of the only reasons I got up most mornings. This morning, however, I was deeply regretting my decision.

"Okay, Lady, I'm awake," I whispered, trying not to wake Sebastian up. "Just give me a minute."

Lady just sat there, not budging an inch. Groaning, I walked in a semi-straight line to the bathroom, Lady following the whole way. When I finally made it down to the kitchen, Lady was whining and I could hear her stomach rumbling—or maybe that was mine. We ate our breakfast in silence. Snippets of last night were starting to creep into my head and they were coming so fast I wanted to put my head down and go back to sleep. How could there be another journal in that trunk? If this was more information about my uncle, there was no way I was going to start another family hunt. I'd already had a grandmother thrown at me earlier this year and I didn't want anything more to do with family at the moment. I just needed some peace and quiet.

"Good morning," Victoria said, quite chipper as she entered the kitchen.

I looked at her with a raised brow. "What makes you so happy and bouncy? You're never a morning person."

"Paul wrote me a letter," she said with a goofy grin on her face.

"When did he do that? We were together the whole day yesterday."

"Oh, I've had it since yesterday morning. I snuck out of the room once you three fell asleep so I could read his letter in private."

"Are you going to tell me what's in it?" I asked with my spoon halfway to my mouth.

"Of course I will. I just wanted to read it first."

"Well . . .?"

She placed a bright purple envelope into my hand that smelled like . . . was that freesia? A man sent Victoria a bright purple envelope smelling like freesia? I was impressed. I didn't think Victoria was a freesia type of person, but I did know she didn't like things to be normal. This was not normal. He had written on the whole page in neat block letters. It was like he had taken a ruler and written each letter perfectly aligned to the straight edge. I even held it up to the light to make sure it was written in ink and not a printout. The whole letter was a love letter. I almost cried because he was so sweet. He told her how much he liked her. How he enjoyed spending time with her. How he hoped she realized that he genuinely cared about her. At the bottom he had signed his name in larger block letters and drawn a bunch of hearts in lieu of flowers in a bouquet.

"That is the sweetest letter."

"Isn't it? He's the best." Victoria looked at the letter for a few seconds longer before tucking it into her bra. "But enough about me. You look like you need a pep talk."

"Oh, I don't know about a pep talk. It's just that I found something last night that I really wish I hadn't found. It's brought up a lot of questions."

"And?"

"And nothing. I don't want to talk about it."

"Yeah right, like I'm going to let you get away with that. Spill!"

I looked at Victoria, who by this point was sitting across from me with a bowl of Fruit Loops, chomping away while maintaining eye contact. If there was anything I knew about Victoria, she was tenacious. She would never back down until I told her what was going on. So I said, "Sebastian and I were headed to bed last night when we heard Lady in the closet. We found her growling at the bottom of the trunk again, but this time a secret bottom compartment had popped open."

Victoria gasped and I thought she was going to choke.

"You mean it was there under the trunk this whole time?"

"Yes."

"Well, what did you find in there?" she cried.

"There was a journal and a picture."

"Did you read it? Who was in the picture? You sure there wasn't anything else? Please tell me you started reading the journal."

"Chill," I said, laughing. If I didn't know any better, I would have thought she had a more vested interest in what we'd found than I did.

Victoria's eyes were bulging, and she had all but forgotten about her Fruit Loops. Her hands grasped mine tightly in her excitement, and I was glad it had been Victoria who walked in first this morning and not Mom. A sense of guilt followed that thought, knowing that Mom would have meant well, but I would have been put in the position of asking her if she had known about the little boy in the picture.

I said to Victoria, "Keep eating. Neither one of us does well on an empty stomach. Besides, there's really not much to tell. I didn't touch anything but the picture. It showed Rose standing next to a half-Asian boy, who was standing next to a younger version of my mom. There was another lady there who seemed similar in age to Rose, but I have no idea who she is."

"Do you think—?"

"I know it's him. I just do. But why was it hidden in the bottom of the trunk, and what will I find in the journal?"

"Let's go find out," Victoria said, already halfway out of her chair, breakfast long forgotten.

"Hold on, Sebastian is still sleeping."

She paused. "Well, at least tell me this. Do you want to go and find him?"

"No . . . Yes . . . I have no idea." I groaned. "We just got through Rose's history."

"You could use the momentum to keep unraveling this new mystery."

"I'm a bit wary about finding out more about my family. It

didn't exactly end well with Rose. Part of me wishes that I was still off frolicking all over the world meeting new people, sharing my experience with total strangers on the internet, and not having a thought for my future."

"Well, why can't you still do that? It's just what you need. You need to travel again; get out there in the world."

"It's easier said than done. I have a—"

"A job? A position? Being a rich Taiwanese lady? Anne, really, you don't even have to work for your money. You have a board to help you take care of the business—not that you really understand what it was Anthony did anyway. I know I don't."

"I was going to say that I have a home now."

"That can take care of itself!"

"You're incorrigible."

Victoria smiled. "That's why you love me."

CHAPTER 4

"I HAVE A BROTHER?" MOM WHISPERED, STARING AT me with her eggs halfway to her mouth.

I looked at Victoria and Sebastian, who were sitting at the breakfast table with us. They appeared to be holding their breath just as much as I was. "Yeah."

"And you knew about this a month ago?"

"Yes . . ." I didn't like how this was going. "At Andy's funeral, Sebastian gave me a letter from Andy. It listed a phone number and an address for a person called Mary. In the letter, Andy said that Mary is Ah Gung's sister, my great aunt. How come I've never heard of her?"

At this, Mom's eyes opened wide. But I took her silence to mean that she wasn't going to share anything at the moment. "I didn't want to worry you until I had found out some more information. I thought I'd see if there was anything else in Ah Po's journals that I'd missed. I fully intended to tell you as soon as I knew more." A little white lie never hurt anyone, right?

"Well, what have you found out?"

As she continued eating, I went on to tell her that I had

found a journal and a picture. I handed her the photo and she stared at it for what felt like an eternity, food all but forgotten. I went to take her eggs because I was starving, but she slapped my hands away, turning to look at me with what looked like the beginning of tears forming at the corner of her eyes.

"You found this picture? Where?"

"Lady found it in a secret compartment at the bottom of the trunk. The drawer must have popped out when she was playing with it," I said in a rush, waiting for Mom to say something, but she just went back to looking at the picture. "Mom, do you know who the other people in the picture are? I think the boy is your brother—or half brother—and I know Ah Po, but who's the other lady?"

"Mary." It came out as a whisper.

At this point, Victoria and Sebastian had scooted so close to me that I felt a little bit claustrophobic.

Mom continued, "She showed me more love than my mom ever did, and she used to send me the most beautiful, handcrafted birthday cards."

"You mean the ones that are framed and hanging in your room?"

"Yes," was all she said. Nothing more.

Sebastian and Victoria went back to their seats, and I eventually went back to eating too. Mom just continued to stare at the picture.

Over the course of the next few days, Victoria somehow convinced Sebastian to take two weeks off so that he and I could go to Taiwan to search for this lady named Mary. Mom became more talkative after that first day and insisted that she come along. I wasn't going to stop her, but she made a big ado that she was the only one who had met Mary.

We dialed Mary's number together. Mary answered and welcomed us across the ocean with open arms. And just like that, we were all on our way to Taiwan to find my long-lost uncle. Mom warned me that she couldn't stay with me for more than a few days because she had to come back to finish some pieces for her art show, but I dived right in. I figured that if I was going to upturn my life again, I might as well go full speed ahead. I was excited to travel again, see new places, meet new people. My luggage was already half packed.

"Anne, I've been thinking," Sebastian said, coming into the room.

"That's a dangerous pastime for you."

"Ha, ha. But really, I don't think I should take the two weeks off. This case I'm on is really important. I have to get it right."

"Sebastian, I'm not asking for much. You haven't taken time off for years and you deserve at least two weeks. We've already gone over the fact that you can still work in Taiwan. It's not like you're going to be completely disconnected. Plus, I already bought tickets."

"You did?" Sebastian looked incredulous, probably because we had only discussed flights this morning.

"You should be proud of me, I remembered that I'm rich. I'm embracing my new norm as you keep reminding me. You and Mom both said that you'd prefer to leave and come back as soon as possible because you have important projects to finish. So I thought, why not leave this weekend then, and I bought first-class tickets."

"Well, I can't argue with that."

Sebastian actually looked sad, which made me irritated. He sat on my bed, his body slumped with both of his hands in his hair and his elbows on his knees.

What could be more important than spending some time with me? I had barely seen him. Even Victoria was having better odds in the relationship department these days.

I continued, "It'll be fun. We can explore Taiwan while we're there. Maybe even do a road trip around the island. It's not that big of a place. I've heard the food there is super delicious." I trailed off because Sebastian now looked even sadder than before. "What's going on? I feel like this isn't just about the Taiwan trip."

"I . . . I heard what Victoria said the other day."

"Victoria says a lot of things," I said with a laugh, trying to lighten the mood.

"You know what I'm talking about. You tensed up when she mentioned his name."

I didn't want to be talking about this. Why was Brian messing with my life when he wasn't even in it anymore?

"Brian and I were together for a long time. He's also Taiwanese American and knew things I didn't have to explain. But he—"

"He was a better boyfriend than me," Sebastian cut in sharply. "He'd be a better companion to go to Taiwan with."

"What I was going to say," I said pointedly, "is that he was a lousy human being who never knew how good he had it. Sebastian, Brian means nothing to me. You've had girlfriends in the past. You should understand."

"Yeah, and you're super jealous of my last one," he said, raising an eyebrow at me. A faint smile crossed his lips.

I sure was jealous of Isabella, but it was nice to see him smiling again. This was a good sign. He pulled me onto his lap and gave me a deep, long kiss. He smelled so good. I wanted to stay in his arms forever.

"I'm sorry, Anne. I really do want to be there with you on this trip. I know how important it is to you. I just feel very inadequate. I haven't been there, I don't speak the language, and I won't be able to help out as much as I'd like to."

"You're going to be a fantastic support for me, and it's going to be a lot of fun. I promise. I know I've been tense since this uncle thing popped up, and I don't even know if it's worth it to go and search for him. He could be a crazy person, someone who we're better off never meeting."

"Well, you won't know until you find him."

"Who even knows if he's still alive, though?"

"We'll find out together. I'm going to come with you, and your mom will be there too. Let's treat this like a vacation."

I smiled. "I like the sound of that. A vacation."

Sebastian enveloped me into his arms, and if not for the grumbling of my stomach, we could have stayed like that for the rest of the day.

CHAPTER 5

"ANNE, I CAN'T BELIEVE YOU MADE ME EAT THIS! The smell alone!" Sebastian exclaimed.

"I love it. You did say you wanted to try something you've never had before."

"But this? Why couldn't I have tried hot pot or xiao long bao? You keep raving about them, but you take me to eat this?"

"I had a craving," I said, trying to hold back my laughter. Secretly, I had just wanted to see his reaction and it was all worth it.

We'd arrived in Taipei, bright and early yesterday morning. Sebastian had been so proud of himself for eating everything I'd put in front of him that I'd needed to rock his boat a bit. Fried stinky tofu was something I had always associated with Taiwan. Even though I had never been, my mom had learned to make it herself because she loved it so much. Apparently, it was one of Ah Po's favorite foods and hers as well. I was happy to not be disappointed.

"Can we please go find something to drink? I need to

wash this foul taste from my mouth and get away from this smell."

"Yes, Sebastian," I said, this time not bothering to cover up my laugh. "I told Mom we'd meet her at Taipei 101. Are you going to be able to make it there?"

He nodded eagerly. "Anything to get away from here."

"Mister Dramatic."

He gave me a stare and walked off with me chasing after him.

I was so happy that Mom had decided to join us on the trip to Taiwan as it wouldn't have been the same without her. She kept remarking that Taipei had changed. Everything was a lot cleaner than she remembered. Last time she'd visited, there had been litter everywhere and an unpleasant odor. Now, not only were the streets cleaner but there were also no trash cans in sight. As a result, we had to throw our trash in bins inside our hotel or at a restaurant. Here, everything was rinsed and sorted. The garbage truck came every night playing *Fur Elise*, and then you'd see masses of people walk their trash and recycling toward them. Sebastian and I got all excited the first time we heard the song. We ran around the corner thinking it was the ice cream truck, and wham! We were hit with the smell of garbage truck fumes.

Even though there was no trash on the roads, everything still had a certain grunginess to it. There was a layer of rust and oil on the roads, and the buildings had cracked facades. The air was filled with fumes from what seemed like millions of scooters going in every direction. We were tentative about crossing the streets but there were tunnels at certain intersections so we could walk underground. I wondered how there weren't accidents every single day.

As we approached Taipei 101, Taiwan's iconic skyscraper, Mom was standing at the entrance looking up at the stature of the building. It's 101 floors towered above all the other buildings, making everything else seem small when they were actually large in their own right. This part of the city was very modern, accommodating the most Western looking architecture with wide open spaces, conference centers, hotels, and fancy cheeseburgers.

"Hi Mom."

"Oh, hi Anne."

"Oh, hi Anne?" I repeated, staring at her. "Were you that mesmerized by the tower?"

"I was just thinking about how much everything has changed here. I've seen old pictures of Taiwan, and my memory of this city is nothing like I remember. Everything here is shiny and big and Westernized. I don't know if I like it. I was expecting something more traditional and—"

"Old-school?"

"Yes."

"Maybe we will find more of that once we venture out of Taipei. You know, like the difference between Portland and Astoria."

"When did you become the mom?"

I laughed. "Come on, Mom. Let's see if we can go to the top."

When we walked in, we were stunned. It looked exactly like the Lloyd Center, and top end stores like Ferragamo, Lindt, Gucci, and Apple popped out immediately. Everywhere we looked there were stores that you'd see in the States. The ticket booth was by the elevators, which took you to the very top of the building. We enquired if there were any tickets available to get to the top, but the next ride was sold out, so we went to sit in the middle of the mall eating Haagen-Dazs . . . because that's what you do in Taiwan. *Groan*. I wanted to get away from Westernized things when I traveled and become fully immersed in the local culture. Sebastian, on the other hand, looked comfortable for the first time. This was a place he could relate to. That in itself made me feel more relaxed, because seeing him so tense all the time was tiring. He had traveled in the States, yes, but not internationally. He couldn't understand anything, the customs were all new, and he was struggling to stay awake.

"I'm not big on going shopping," said Mom.

Well, there went my thought of window shopping. I loved looking at all the finery and for the first time in my life, I could actually afford whatever I wanted.

Our turn to go up the elevator couldn't come fast enough given I could only do so much people watching. Thank goodness the elevator ride was amazing. It never seemed to end; every time we thought we were at the top, it kept on going. I gasped when the doors finally opened. I hadn't been at the top of a skyscraper since the Twin Towers in the eighties, and had forgotten what an amazing view they afforded.

Taking Sebastian's hand, we walked out of the elevator directly toward the closest window. Along the way, I couldn't help but be amazed at how spacious the viewing platform was. There was probably twenty feet between the elevator and the windows, and it was even more impressive because the observation deck took up the whole eighty-ninth floor, forming a circle around the core that gave you a three-hundred-and-sixty degree view of Taipei. There was probably thirty people milling about in the area we were standing in. I didn't feel claustrophobic and I could hear my own voice when we were conversing. Beside us were big placards depicting the building of the tower, and thank goodness it was translated into English. Anything to make Sebastian feel less awkward.

I walked right up to the windows that spanned from floor

to ceiling. It felt like I was flying over the city. There wasn't a cloud in sight and we could see all of Taipei. "It's beautiful."

"If you like concrete and lights," my mother said from beside me.

"Mom, can't you see the majesty of it all? How everything works together?"

"I miss my trees, but those mountains are pretty impressive. Since I'm in tourist central, Abi said there's a high-end jewelry store with the prettiest coral necklaces here. I thought I might get one for her."

"They have jewelry stores up here?" Sebastian asked.

"Well, there's that convenience store too," I said, pointing behind me.

"Yeah, a convenient store to trap tourists for postcards, trinkets, and miscellaneous things you don't need. But a high-end jewelry store?"

"They cater to all tastes," I said dismissively. "Mom, let me know what you think." I still didn't dress like I was a billionaire, but I didn't say no to fine things anymore.

"Well, I'm going to see if I can find something to eat," said Sebastian.

"You do know we're eighty-nine floors up, right?" I asked.

"I do, but you said so yourself that 'they cater to all tastes.' And they have postcards there," he said, giving me a wink.

I loved postcards. It was the best way to share my trip with family and friends, and most importantly, they were small enough to collect. My collection was starting to get a bit out of hand though and I needed to figure out how to manage them. "I'm going to stay here and enjoy the view a bit before losing myself in that store."

As Sebastian and Mom went their separate ways for food and jewelry, I found a nook by the window and stared out across the city, lost in thought. Here I was, traveling once again, but this time I could stay, eat, and play wherever I wanted. All I had to do was wave my money and everything would be taken care of. Only five months ago I'd been traveling the world with not a care for the future, sleeping on people's sofas, guest rooms, even the floor. I'd eaten at hole in the walls—which are still my favorite places to eat—and backpacked through cities because flying had been a luxury. Now, I lived in the world of luxury, and I'd also managed to land myself the best boyfriend in the world. True, he and Isabella were a thing for a long time, and I still held a grudge that he had been contemplating marrying her when we dated, but he had stuck with me after the accident and was still here by my side.

My mind went back to Isabella. I couldn't shake her from my thoughts no matter how hard I tried. According to her, I didn't belong. It had to be her who blew up my car. Who else could it be? She had a vendetta against me—she wanted her family's money and property, and she wanted Sebastian back.

The woman irked me, and yet, I had a nagging feeling that Isabella was not my biggest problem, that it wasn't really her who had placed the bomb in my car . . . . But it had to be her. She'd tried to get me out of the house for weeks, including manipulating Sebastian behind my back. Anyone with that kind of tenacity had to be crazy.

I looked down at my hands, which were clenched so tight I could see red marks forming in my palm. Willing my breathing to regulate, I looked back at the city below me again before slowly prying my fingers open one by one. I still felt hatred toward Isabella, which surprised me because I had never truly hated anyone before. Brian maybe, but that didn't compare to what I felt for Isabella.

"What are you contemplating so hard?" Sebastian asked, giving me such a fright that I fell out of the nook.

"That wasn't funny."

"That was *so* funny. You were like a cat caught unawares who had fallen off her perch. You should have seen the look on your face!"

"You didn't have to sneak up on me like that," I said, trying to hold onto some dignity. The place was filled with tourists, a lot of whom were from China, but I heard European accents here as well. Did he have to embarrass me in public?

"Well, you deserved it after making me eat that nasty tofu thing earlier," he replied.

"Oh, it's not like it would have killed you."

"You don't know that," he said, standing so close to me that I couldn't help but forget what to say next.

He was running his hand up and down my back and he smelled so good. I hugged him close and enjoyed the feel of his arms around me. I was so glad I wasn't mad anymore about his past mess with the Wilkens family. I was still annoyed, yes, but not mad. Especially because he stayed by my side after the accident. That earned him major brownie points.

"What were you thinking about that had you in such a trance?" Sebastian asked.

"I was just thinking about how my life's changed."

"It's been quite a journey," he agreed, trailing light kisses across my forehead. "I'm glad I came. I hope you know that." He held my face in his hands as he added, "What do you say we try to do a road trip around Taiwan? I looked it up and it's not that big of a country. We could easily do it in two weeks."

Before I could contemplate what he was asking, I saw Mom coming toward us with a huge smile on her face, arms laden with three shopping bags.

"What are you two love birds talking about?" asked Mom.

"Oh, you know, pondering life and its many twists and turns," Sebastian said, but I could see Mom hadn't really cared what we were doing; she was already unpacking one of the bags.

"Look at what I got. Abi is going to love it." She pulled out a beautiful red coral necklace that had three strands of coral on one latch. Each strand contained detail carvings of about fifty roses. I immediately thought of Anthony's carvings in the mansion.

"I think she'll love it," I said.

"Yeah, I love it so much I got myself one."

"You did?" Sebastian and I said together.

"Don't sound so surprised. Your mom likes fine things every once in a while too. Well, now I can afford them."

"I'm glad you're enjoying yourself," I said with no hint of sarcasm because I really was glad.

"I got you one too," Mom added.

At first, my mouth dropped, but then I smiled. "Actually, thank you. I did want one."

"I know," she said with a big knowing smile. "We should get going. We don't want to keep your great aunt Mary waiting. She's invited us to one of the most famous restaurants here in Taiwan: Din Tai Fung. They're known for their xiao long bao."

"I'm game. I'm finally going to sink my teeth into these delicacies you two keep talking about," Sebastian said already walking to the elevator.

"Always traveling on your stomach," I laughed.

"Well, Taiwan is supposed to have delicious food everywhere. I have to try as much as I can while I'm here."

"True that," I said, joining him at the elevator.

CHAPTER 6

TAIPEI REMINDED ME OF A MINI NEW YORK CITY. Taxis, buses, and subways were abundant here. We didn't have to drive and that made me super happy. Therefore, we took the subway from Taipei 101 to Xinyi Road, then walked to the original Din Tai Fung Taiwanese restaurant that skyrocketed the brand to international success. When we arrived, we found lines of people at the door even though it was only one o'clock in the afternoon. Thank goodness we had made a reservation.

We were ushered to the third floor. The stairwell wasn't all that big. Each floor ended at one door, which looked into a room with about six tables in it, and the third floor wasn't any different. I was a bit surprised as dining areas in the States had sprawling open spaces, but I couldn't focus on that difference for too long because next thing I knew, I was looking at Mary.

As she stood up I immediately went into full Taiwanese mode. Every nerve and muscle in my body remembered all the lessons Mom had given me directly or indirectly about maintaining my manners around older people. I could feel every fiber of my being tingling with nervousness; I was so fearful that I would mess up. I wondered if Mom felt like she might screw up, too, even though she had spent more time with the Taiwanese community than I ever had.

"She looks nice," Sebastian said from behind me.

I leaned close and whispered, "Let my mom speak to her first. And don't stick your hand out for a handshake or a hug. Just say hi and stand there politely. Answer her if she asks you any questions."

"Yes ma'am," he laughed. "I know how to deal with people."

"Yes, but you don't know how to deal with older Taiwanese people."

"I'm sure it'll be fine. I can hold my own."

I gave him a look. Sometimes, you just can't talk sense into a lawyer—they always have a counter response.

We approached the table and even before Mary had said a word, I immediately liked her.

"Sit. Sit. It's very nice to finally meet all of you," Mary said in perfect English. It took us by surprise as Mom had only spoken to her in Mandarin on the phone.

"Wow, you speak fantastic English. I don't remember that," Mom said.

Mary smiled. "Well, I did live in the States for a couple of years."

"That's fascinating. I would love to hear more of your story when we have time," I said.

"You must be Anne," she said, placing her hands on mine and looking me straight in the eye. But her next words were addressed to my mom. "She looks like a good girl."

She let go of my hands and turned to my boyfriend. "And you must be Sebastian," Mary said, sticking out her hand.

"I am. It's very nice to meet you, Ms. Lin." He accepted her hand and shook it.

I could see Sebastian about to turn and give me a knowing smile, when Mary asked, "What do you do for a living, Sebastian?"

"I'm a lawyer."

"Do you make a lot of money?"

Sebastian's brow raised. "Um, yes . . ."

"Good. Good. Then are you the kind that cheats people out of their money or the kind that actually helps others?"

Sebastian flushed and looked sideways at me before slowly replying, "I... help?"

Mary smiled. "Well, when you're sure, let me know. But you seem like a nice enough guy to be with my family."

I sighed with relief that Mary had responded just like any other older Taiwanese person would—straight up asking about money and family. However, Sebastian was looking at her like a dog caught with a torn-up sofa.

"Welcome to being Taiwanese," I said, nudging him into his seat.

"Uh huh." He didn't say another word as he took his allocated place.

Mary turned to my mother as the rest of us took our own seats. "It's been a long time since I've seen you, Josephine."

"I know. Mama never wanted to come back. I'm not sure why."

Mary asked, "Did you receive the birthday cards I sent you?"

"I did. They came till I was fourteen. You're the reason I wanted to become an artist."

I didn't know that. I think my mouth had dropped open because Sebastian was elbowing me in the waist.

Mary looked surprised and pleased. "I was, was I? Let's not live in the past, Josephine. Please, tell me why you are in Taiwan. Are you on vacation? In sudden need to see family? I would love to introduce you to my daughter. The timing is perfect as her daughter is getting married this Saturday. You should come. I'll let her know to add three more people to the guest list."

"Goo Goo. Can I call you that?" Mom asked.

"Of course you can. You are my niece."

"Goo Goo. Thank you for the invitation, but I'll be leaving in two days. Sebastian and Anne would love to attend though," Mom said, looking over at me. I nodded in agreement. "Goo Goo. Could you tell me why you stopped sending those birthday cards?"

"I promised your mama a long time ago to let the past be the past."

"That's what she always said." Mom looked disappointed.

"Sometimes there is good reason. Don't go digging up something that should be left alone."

"The problem is we received Ah Po's journals last year. We now know her past and want to learn more," I piped in.

"What do you mean you received her journals?" Mary said, looking a bit startled. This unsettled me because I was hoping that she would be open in sharing what she knew.

"Well, this man named Sir Anthony Wilkens—"

"Sir Anthony Wilkens? Whatever would you have to do with him?" Mary interrupted.

Why was she so flustered? Did she know him? "Um . . . I inherited his house and all his fortune," I said, trying hard to breathe normally. I wasn't sure if I had said something wrong.

"Well . . . I do have to say the past really doesn't like to stay in the past," Mary finally replied. "It looks like this meeting of ours is not so simple. All of you will come back to my place. My daughter, Ming-Yue, who you will call Ah Yi, is home with her grandkids. They had an errand to do otherwise they would have come to lunch as well. It'll be nice for the whole family to be back together again. For now, let's just have a nice lunch. Let's eat. Eat. Their xiao long bao are the best. Thin skin and juicy."

We held polite conversation through lunch and didn't touch on the subject of why we were here again. I was a ball of nerves by the end of the meal and wanted to get to Mary's house so we could continue our conversation.

We didn't have to go far after lunch. Her house was a few blocks over. The walk was quick and we cut through public space and people's backyards. On the way, Sebastian and I started lagging behind.

"That was really rude of her to ask me those questions. I felt like I was in an inquisition," Sebastian said.

"It wasn't rude. Those questions are just what older generation Taiwanese ask us younger folks. Mary was just concerned about my well-being and they like to cut to the chase. At least that's what Mom says. You'll get used to it."

"Well, I still think it's rude. Money is a private matter."

"Then you're going to have a very difficult time here."

"I just think people should be considerate."

"They are, but you're not in the States anymore. Being considerate means a totally different thing here."

"But . . ."

I took in a deep breath. "Look, I know you're upset. I totally get it. Trust me and just try to accept Mary's questioning for what it was."

Luckily, we arrived at Mary's place right then. She squeezed us into the tiniest elevator ever. There was only four of us and I was getting claustrophobic. Five floors seemed like the entirety of Taipei 101 and we were deposited on a floor mat that was covered in shoes of various shapes and sizes. The hallway couldn't have been more than four feet deep. The neighbor's door was probably ten feet away. That's when I saw the stairs hidden behind the elevator. Next time I was going to take the stairs. Five floors of walking were better than getting in that elevator again.

A big metal door opened and a couple of little faces greeted Mary—or Ah Tai. Mary gave them a hug and a kiss, something that took me by surprise because Taiwanese people didn't usually give hugs or kisses.

Mary pulled back and gestured at the assembled people. "This is Ming-Yue, my youngest child. And these two little ones are her grandkids." The youngest peeked out behind Ming-Yue's legs, looking at Sebastian with big round eyes. The other kid got brave and popped out too. I couldn't help laughing while Sebastian looked at me a bit lost, but to give him credit, he recovered fast.

"Hi, I'm Sebastian. What's your name?" he asked, kneeling to their level. They hid behind Ming-Yue's legs again. A lot of giggling ensued, then the children popped out from hiding, walked over, and started rubbing his hair while talking about his eyes, all round fascinated by his pale skin and blue eyes. Mom and I just stood to the side like bystanders.

"That's enough. Go in. Go in," Mary said, shooing everyone inside. "Sit. Sit. Ming-Yue, make some tea. I have a feeling we will be here for a while. Josephine, you sit here, and Anne, you sit on the other side of me. Sebastian, you sit next to Anne. There we go."

The kids were still pointing out Sebastian's features, running close and then running away, all while giggling. It was so cute to see and Sebastian was soaking up the attention. I hadn't known he was good with kids. I softened toward him even more at the thought.

"Ming-Yue's second daughter is getting married this Saturday, so we are holding a big engagement party. She studied English, so Sebastian, you can converse with her as you and Anne will be joining us on Saturday. My oldest is in Australia and she'll be the death of me. She keeps wanting me to come over, but all those spiders and snakes." Her nose scrunched up in disgust. "Plus, I'm the mama. *She* should be flying to see *me*."

"Mama, we agreed to not talk about Da Jie," Ming-Yue scolded. "And she's here for the wedding."

"Yes. Yes. Well, in between the two girls, I had three boys. Two of them are in Taipei. The youngest is in London. Now, London is a place I have gone to visit. That's a fun city."

"Mama."

"Fine. Fine. He-Mei here, is your cousin. She also goes by Josephine. It's too bad none of us could afford to travel to see each other. I remember growing up with my cousins. What fun we had and the mischief we would get into. I remember—"

"Mama."

Mary glared at her daughter. "I'm allowed to reminisce in my old age! Anne here, is Josephine's daughter, and this young man is Anne's boyfriend, Sebastian. He's a lawyer. Makes good money."

"It's really nice to meet all of you," Mom said.

"He-Mei brought some much-needed vitamins for me, some beef jerky for you guys, and some M&Ms for the kids." At Mary's statement, the kids clambered over again before disappearing with their treats back to their play area.

"No one's used my Mandarin name since Mama died," Mom said, looking a bit startled and moved at the same time.

"You should use it. It's your name," Mary answered, and that was that.

"Instead of sitting here, I can take you guys around Taipei," Ming-Yue offered.

"Oh, that's awfully nice of you. We would love to," I said.

"Ming-Yue, take Sebastian," Mary said. "I'm sure he would love to see more sights. He-Mei, Hong-Mei, and I have some things to talk about."

Because Mom rarely called me by my Taiwanese name, at first, I just stared at Mary before realizing she was also talking about me.

"Shouldn't I stay?" Sebastian asked.

"No. No. You are not family. Go and have fun. There's no need for you to be dragged into this."

Oh, if she only knew.

"Great. Sebastian, let's go," Ming-Yue said, already heading out the door.

We stared at each other on the sofa and I was getting very uncomfortable. Why was everything so tense between us? We were supposed to be here to explore the past. Rather, I felt just like Sebastian had said—that we were in an inquisition.

"So, tell me more about this inheritance you received," Mary finally said to me. "How much about your Ah Po do you know?"

Well, she got to the point pretty quickly.

"Mama never wanted to talk about her past," Mom began.

Mary lifted a hand, effectively halting Mom. "We'll get to Rose in a little bit. I want to know how much Anne knows."

"I know what she wrote in her journals," I said with faux confidence. Mary had a knack for making me feel very small.

"And how did you come upon these journals? And what were in them?"

"Why all the questions?" I asked.

"Anne, there is history that your grandmother wished to

43

hide, and I have always respected her wishes as I hope your mama has too."

"See, that's the thing. Her journals told me everything. She was seventeen when she moved to the States and got a job at the Wilkens. They hired her as a seamstress and used her in the kitchen as a maid if they needed her there too. She did fantastic work." I took a breath and added in a rush, "Unfortunately, the boss's son, Anthony, started showing interest in her and she ended up falling in love with him."

"Hmph," Mary said, giving me an annoyed look that I wasn't sure was directed at me, my mom, or because I had just said Anthony's name.

I said hesitantly, "Um . . . their love was discovered, and through the process of running away, she hurt herself and ended up in the hospital where she found out she was pregnant. That was the only instance of it because she never mentions the pregnancy again in the journals." I paused, my eyes on Mary. "Are you okay, Ah Goo?"

"I'm fine. Keep going," she snapped, but I swear that she was holding her breath. I hoped she didn't faint on us.

"She was kicked out of the house and ended up at a bakery with a lady called, Josephine, who Mom's named after." And who was currently wringing her hands together. I was getting nervous just watching her. "She ended up meeting Charlie, your brother, and they moved to Astoria where we currently still live."

"Well, that is quite a lot you've learned, but you still have not answered my first question," Mary said sharply. "I want to know about the inheritance that you received."

I swallowed and said, "I got a letter from the Wilkens lawyer, Sebastian."

At this, Mary's eyebrows raised and I saw her hands clench.

"I was requested to attend a will reading, and that's

where I met Anthony's siblings, their kids, and some of the grandkids. It was there that I learned I had inherited billions of dollars and three houses, one of them here in Taiwan."

Mary seemed to sit up straighter at my revelation of the Taiwan house. Did she know about it?

But instead, she asked, "If you have all this money, why are you here digging up the past?"

"I want to know my family. Ah Po's journals made me realize that I don't know anything about our history, and I think it's important to learn. Plus, that isn't all."

"No?"

"Andy, the butler who was working at the Wilkens at the same time as Ah Po, sent me and Sebastian a letter before he passed away. He said Ah Po never had an abortion. He said that she had the baby. Andy provided me with your name and contact information in the letter. He said you could help us find Ah Po's son."

"And where did he think this baby was?"

"So, there is a baby?"

"Isn't that what you just said?" said Mary, turning the question back on me.

"Well, yes, but we weren't sure if it was true."

A dead silence filled the room, and I could feel sweat starting to form at the top of my forehead.

Mary turned to my mother. "Josephine, what have you shared with Anne?"

"I've shared my side of the story. That Andy found me and hired me to do art for the family. They showed me the journals, too, but I wanted nothing to do with them. However, I did end up reading them before I gave them back."

"That is all?" Mary pushed, giving Mom a stare that she had clearly mastered over the generations.

"Ah Goo, we would love to learn more about our family," I interrupted.

"Is that all?" Mary asked again, this time more sternly.

"Yes. Yes. That was all," Mom said.

"Ah Goo . . ." I tried again.

"I do not understand you Americans and your need to dig into family history. If it wasn't passed down, don't you think it should stay hidden?"

"No, I don't," Mom replied.

I looked at Mom, surprised. I felt so proud of her. It had taken a lot for her to stand up to Ah Goo.

"Josephine Lin! I know your mama raised you to not meddle in stuff you shouldn't."

"She did, and it's precisely that reason I don't agree with anymore. Anne has shown me how important it is to know your own history, to know where you came from, and why your family is the way it is. I agree with her now, and I think it was wrong to have raised her without knowing our history. I also think it was wrong of my mom to have hidden her past from me."

"Josephine—"

"I'm not done yet," Mom said.

I heard a sharp intake of breath from Mary, and I could feel goosebumps crawling up my arms as I threatened to turn as red as a beet. My mom standing up to an elder was something I hadn't seen before.

"I could have understood her a lot better if she had shared her past with me," Mom continued. "She was my mom. I loved her and still do. It would have brought us closer if she had. Instead, I felt like there were too many secrets between us. That we would never be close. That's not how a mother and daughter relationship should be," she finished, looking at me.

I didn't know what to say, and clearly, neither did Mary.

Mom continued, "Anne, being here has brought back some memories of your uncle—"

"Josephine Lin, you stop right there! You are not allowed to say anything more. You know your mama would be so upset with you."

"Well, Mama is no longer here," Mom returned, "and Anne has had to learn her past in the worst way possible—from someone she didn't know and who wasn't even family. She deserves to know the rest of the story."

Mary turned to me, her face set. "Anne, I need to talk to your mom alone."

"Mom?"

"Anne, I'll be okay. Just give us a few minutes."

"Okay . . ."

I was suddenly left alone in the living room while Mom and Mary went to one of the bedrooms. Leaving me there quickly became awkward. I saw little heads popping back and forth from the doorway of the other bedroom. Clearly, they had heard the yelling and were trying not to say anything or look at me but were failing miserably. After about ten agonizing minutes, Mom reappeared. She actually had a smile on her face. Aunt Mary followed close behind not looking very happy . . . but was that relief she was showing?

"Anne, it's time to go. Say thank you to Ah Goo."

I stood immediately and did as I was told. "Ah Goo, it was really nice to meet you."

Mary looked at us for a long while before shaking her head. "The past should be left in the past, but you two seem to have an unhealthy urge to dig it up. I will not disclose my secrets. He-Mei will show you what I've given her, but remember this, if you hurt anyone on this discovery of yours, don't say I didn't warn you."

CHAPTER 7

WE WALKED OUT IN SILENCE, UNACCOMPANIED, which in itself was unusual as my mom's friends always walked us out where a long conversation would ensue on the driveway before we finally left.

Mom and I stood on the sidewalk and I could see that she was lost in her thoughts. I didn't want to disturb her, so I started looking around at my surroundings. So much of it reminded me of New York City—the skyscrapers, neon lights, people everywhere, taxi cabs, buses, and subways. The only differences were the abundance of motorcycles and the fact that there were only Taiwanese people around. Occasionally, a foreigner of European descent would walk by and it would be all I could do to not stare. I was a foreigner, yet I blended in so well here that no one knew that until I talked in Mandarin for more than ten seconds. My mash of Mandarin and English would come out and it was obvious to all that this wasn't my home country.

My phone rang and when I saw who it was, a stab of guilt went through me. I had totally forgotten about Sebastian. I pushed accept and held it up to my ear.

"Hey Anne. Just checking in on where I should meet you. Ah Yi took me to the night market, and I've eaten so much that I could go to sleep right now. Did you know that people here eat pigs blood? Ah Yi made me try one and I have to say that if it wasn't for the peanut powder and cilantro on the outside, I would have gagged on the first bite. I can't believe you Taiwanese people eat this sort of stuff."

I was trying so hard to not be offended. It still bothered me that he clumped me and every Taiwanese person into one person, like we all thought and did the same things. He sounded like he'd had a fun night though, rather than being stuck with us upstairs, so I let it slide.

"Glad you had fun. I personally don't like pigs blood either so I'm glad Ah Yi was the one who had you try it."

"We also had mango over shaved ice with tons of sweet-condensed milk poured all over it. Now, that was amazing. Why couldn't you have taken me to eat that instead?"

"I can still take you." I paused, my thoughts returning to the present, and said, "Sebastian, let's meet back at the hotel. I'll see you there soon."

"Oh, okay. I'm up for staying out longer if you want?"

"No, I have a feeling my mom needs to talk to me in private."

"Tell Sebastian that I want him to be there too," Mom said, leaning her head closer so that Sebastian could also hear her. "You're going to need support through this new journey of yours."

"What's happened? What did I miss?" Sebastian asked, a tinge of worry in his voice.

"You missed a lot," I replied.

"What is that supposed to mean?"

"Oh, I don't know. My mind is all over the place. We'll see you back at the hotel, okay?"

"Okay, see you there."

We were staying at the Sheraton. It wasn't fancy, but the entire hotel reminded me of every Sheraton I had stayed at in the States with the only difference being that the staff were so attentive here. There was someone there to greet and assist us before we even knew we needed the help, whereas in the States, we'd have had to find someone for help. I'm not sure if I preferred all the attentiveness.

Sebastian had said we should stay at my house seeing that I owned it, but I just couldn't make myself visit it yet. I wanted to start our visit to Taipei on neutral ground, and it wasn't like I didn't have the money to stay at a hotel anyway.

Sebastian and I both sat across from Mom in the hotel restaurant. I was getting really nervous at this point because Mom hadn't said a word all the way back. She seemed to be lost in her own world even though she was the one who wanted us to be all together when she shared what she'd learned about my uncle and Ah Po. I was dreading what she had to say and yet super curious at the same time. Why would she have come out of that room with a smile on her face? It just didn't make sense.

"You two must have a ton of questions but if I may, I want to ask the two of you to hold off on asking me anything until I'm done. And Anne, please do not think I kept this secret because I wanted to. I have questioned my own memory about my first Taiwan trip my whole life because Mom never wanted to talk about it. It seemed like a dream. Your Ah Goo reprimanded me for letting you find out as much as you have, but I can tell she also wants to share the news. She has kept these secrets for so long that it's hard for her to suddenly tell us what she knows. However, I persuaded her to share something with you, and if you find out further information all by yourself, then she will feel guilt free."

I didn't know what to say so I simply watched in silence as Mom pulled out a box from within her purse. She opened it and inside it there was an ordinary key.

"What does this have to do with your half brother?" I finally asked.

"Remember, questions after," Mom chided. She held up the key and said, "This key fits a safety deposit box here in Taipei. Inside it are items that belonged to my half brother because your Ah Goo didn't want them in the house anymore. I couldn't tell you why. Now, here is where I don't want you to be upset with me. I did remember more from that picture you found back at the estate, and Ah Goo confirmed my suspicions when we were talking privately."

"Mom—"

"No, I've kept secrets from you long enough."

Sebastian, looking a little uncomfortable, suddenly said, "Ms. Lin, maybe I shouldn't be here. This information should be privy to just you and Anne."

"No, Anne needs support through this. And yes, before you ask, Anne, I will always support you, but I think you need someone who is not emotionally involved to help you through this. So, back to the picture you showed me.

"Mama took me to Taiwan once when I was eight. When we arrived in Taiwan, I could tell Mama was so much happier. Happier than I had ever seen her before. I, on the other hand, was in shock. Having grown up with no other family besides my mama and baba, there were suddenly a lot of aunts, uncles, cousins, and many elders. They were so intimate with each other and I was awkward around them. Thank goodness Mama and Baba had always talked to me in Mandarin, but it took a while to adjust. One boy in particular made me feel at home. He had green eyes."

"Green eyes?" I asked, leaning toward Mom.

"Yes, green eyes. Let me finish. He was lighter skinned

than everyone else, his hair was a distinct brown instead of jet black, and he had the greenest eyes. Many were jealous that he had natural highlights, which I remember people always commenting about. My most distinct memory of him was that he felt out of place, lonely, and shy. He didn't associate with anyone, so he was glad when I showed up and we instantly took to each other. He would take me to eat at all the local eateries, such as to the shaved ice store, or out for sao bing, yu tao, and fried stinky tofu—which is where I started my love for stinky tofu by the way. You name it, he took me everywhere. We'd go swimming in the ocean and collect rocks off the beach, much to my Ah Po's chagrin. Our whole family is Buddhist. I know we don't practice it, but Ah Po would always remind me that the rocks had souls and God would be mad at me.

"I felt guilty but I really wanted to bring something back with me from the trip. I still have them. They're in a box in the closet somewhere. I tried pig intestine with thin noodles, hot pot, and many more dishes. My Ah Po, your grandpa Charlie and great aunt Mary's mom, was a good cook. They had lived in Hong Kong for about a year, so she had picked up some Cantonese dishes as well, although, most of the food she made was Hakka meals. I do miss them. Your Ah Po was a great cook too. She would make the dishes when she felt like it, and it would always be a treat. I cooked some of them for you too."

"I would also like to learn how to cook them," I said softly.

"I always wanted you to, but you were always busy with something else."

"Well, now I have time."

"Ladies, we are in the middle of a riveting story. Enough about food already," Sebastian interrupted. "I for one would like to hear more about this green-eyed boy."

I smiled and snuggled into Sebastian, and he put his arm around me. Mom was right. I felt glad Sebastian was around for this.

"Yes, the green-eyed boy. We were in Taiwan for a couple of months. Mama really wanted me to meet my family, and she later told me that she hoped it had sunk in that I had a network that wasn't just her and Baba. But to tell you the truth it never sunk in. I was eight for goodness sakes. I had no appreciation for other family members who I hardly knew. As far as I was concerned everyone was a stranger and it was fun while it lasted, but they didn't mean anything to me. At least, when I went back to the States that's how I felt. But when I was in Taiwan, it was a different story. I loved having all these people around and it felt like we belonged together. There was Mama, Mary, and Mary's two older brothers."

"Was Grandpa Charlie there?"

"Your Ah Gung stayed in the States. He couldn't take the time off."

"He didn't want to see his family?"

"Anne, it is never that easy. Of course he wanted to see his family. He missed them terribly. I remember my parents staying up late at night discussing how they were going to pay the bills. Mind you, we weren't poor, but we didn't have extra money to spend. They saved for a long time before they had the money to fly one person to Taiwan. Following one of my fights with Mama, Josephine—who I'm named after—told me that she lent money to them so that they could go back sooner, and she was the one who persuaded them to take me too. I felt a lot of guilt when I was old enough to comprehend all the sacrifices my parents had made for me, but I digress.

"Harrison, as the green-eyed boy was called, was my new best friend. It never occurred to me to ask him why he looked different from everyone else, but there was no getting around it. Wherever we went, someone would comment on him. It seemed like everyone wanted to touch his hair or look into his green eyes. Our other cousins were no better. Mama was very protective of him; she doted on him. She never said I couldn't go out with him, and she always told the other kids to leave him alone. She'd buy treats for him, have him sit next to her during meals, and take us to the beach. I thought it was because she knew what it was like to look different in a foreign country. But by the end of the trip, I was jealous of all the time she spent with him and not me that I was so happy to be heading home because I would have Mama all to myself again.

"But Mama didn't say a word on the trip home. I swore she was crying the whole time we were on the plane. After a while, life went back to normal and we never went back to Taiwan. Aunt Mary came and visited us once, and that was that. I never thought of my family outside of the States again. Even Mama's parents came to meet me only once. It wasn't until high school that I learned who the green-eyed boy was. Someone had started spreading a rumor that there once was a boy born into a rich family who lived here. I brought it up at dinner one night and Mama flipped. She started going off about people not being able to let the past be the past. It was all Baba could do to calm her down. Josephine had to come over and help. Mama made Baba promise not to tell me, so I never got an answer. But I was so scared by Mama's reaction that I didn't want to know anymore. I know now, though, that that one time in Taiwan was the last time she got to see her son. Two months. That was it. I can't even imagine being able to only see you for two months, Anne."

"Oh Mom!" I went to give her a hug. I held Mom for a bit while Sebastian ordered a round of drinks.

Mom pulled away and said softly, "Anne, I'm sorry to have kept this a secret from you too. Today, your Ah Goo made it very clear that this was never to be mentioned. I know that after last year, I should share family matters with you. And even though your Ah Goo did not want me to share it, I told her that I was going to with or without her permission."

"Mom, it's okay. Part of me wants to be mad at you for not sharing this with me, especially after we found out Ah Po's son was still around. But I get it. Not everything's black and white, right?"

"Right. And I have something for you that will help with your journey." She picked up the key again.

"As I said before, this is a key to a safe deposit box that contains some items owned by my half brother. Ah Goo was willing to give it to you after much persuasion. Her only stipulation is that you are not allowed to share this information and whatever else you find with anyone but me or Sebastian."

I nodded and said firmly, "First thing in the morning, we'll head to the bank." Yet, my curiosity was taking over and I wanted to go now.

"You don't have any questions? Any thoughts?"

"After what I went through last year, I'm trying to just take it as it goes."

Mom and Sebastian shared a look but I wasn't worried. What was one more surprise on top of all the others this last year?

CHAPTER 8

THE BANK WAS IN A NONDESCRIPT AREA. WE COULD have been on the other side of town and it would still all look the same. There were old cement buildings butted up right next to each other with signs over doors, sticking so far out that they overhung the sidewalk. Everything was in different colors so there wasn't a theme to any neighborhood and yet, it all just fit. Nothing seemed out of place.

There were also vehicles and people everywhere. Walking across the street when there were mopeds making left turns scared us. Even though they always missed, it was unnerving.

We walked into the bank and found tellers behind glass walls. They looked like they were behind a movie theater ticket window, the ones where you slid your money through a hole and hoped they could hear you on the other side of the glass as you confirmed your movie. We stood in line, and I was glad that we weren't outside where it was nippy. The wind was blowing so strong that I had bought an extra pair of gloves, a scarf, and a hat.

Great Aunt Mary had told us to ask for a specific manager, and when he showed up it was obvious that he'd been educated in the States. He shook all our hands, immediately told us he'd went to Penn State for grad school in finance, and that he lived there for eight years before moving back to Taiwan. American culture just wasn't for him. Plus, all his family were here. They wanted him to come home, marry someone local, and live near his parents. He was the oldest, so he needed to take care of them. And all we had said was "Hi."

By the time he'd finished giving us his life history, we had walked to the back of the bank, and he was pulling out another set of keys as he turned to face us. "Mrs. Lin said only Anne was to come in with me."

"Oh . . ." Mom and Sebastian said simultaneously. It wasn't awkward at all, but Mom gave my arm a squeeze and Sebastian gave me a hug.

"It makes sense you're going in alone," Sebastian murmured in my ear. "It sounds like she's guarding this secret as much as she can. Maybe she thinks it'll be easier for you to say no to looking at the contents if we weren't there with you. I know your mom is standing up to her and I'm just plain curious."

I whispered back, "I'm curious too. I don't think I'm going to be saying no to anything though."

I pulled back and gave them both a last look before turning to follow the manager into the room. He inserted his key into the largest safe deposit box in the wall. I joined him, inserted my key, and we both turned the lock. When the box clicked, my heart raced. What was I getting myself into again? Was I ready for another mystery? Learning about Ah Po's history opened up secrets that even I wasn't sure should have been exposed. But battling Isabella, and almost getting killed over the inheritance—those I could have done without. However, the adventurous side of me wanted to proceed and I was too curious to stop.

The manager pulled out the box and set it on the table in the middle of the room. He left me alone and all I could do was stare at it at first. There was nothing here to distract me. I was seated at a metal table big enough to hold four people. Three walls were covered in safe deposit boxes and behind me was the door.

I remembered how excited I was when I had found Ah Po's trunk. I was so naive back then. In hindsight, given my recent inheritance, I should have expected that someone in my family had been in a relationship with the Wilkens family, but the thought never crossed my mind. Probably because I didn't know my own family well enough to have any such suspicion.

I loved that with the journals I got to know Ah Po through her own words; and because the boss's son fell in love with her, I inherited Skyline Mansion. At times, I still wondered if it was worth it. What if Harrison was greedy and wanted to fight me for the inheritance? Or tried to blackmail me for money? Not that there was anything to blackmail me with. And there was also the fact that I'd be happy to split the inheritance with him . . . or would I? Mom and I had a happy life. Why was I so interested in digging up the past? Was I ready to do it all over again?

I rubbed my hands across the top of the box and felt the cold metal seep into my palms. It would be so easy to just say no, to leave here without opening the box. I could go and find my multi-million-dollar house in Taipei, and enjoy the rest of my vacation with Mom and Sebastian . . . . But then I might regret never knowing what was inside it.

Darn my curiosity! Why were there so many secrets in my family, and why was I the one who had to dig them up? What was wrong with traveling and minding my own business? I was a good girl. I visited my mom, kept in touch with her regularly, did my work, did well in school, and always listened to my elders. Why then, was I so determined to unearth the past that everyone was trying to keep hidden?

I shook myself. I needed to commit to my decision. To do this or leave, and to make that decision now. Mind firm, I picked up the key and poised it over the keyhole. My hands were shaking a little but I told myself it couldn't be as bad as before, and I had a right to know my family. My mom also had a right to know her brother—well, half brother, but still her own flesh and blood.

I wondered what it would have been like to grow up with an uncle and maybe cousins. Cousins that would be like brothers and sisters to me. And a doting grandmother because she would have raised both her kids and never have had to give one away. What a different life that would have been.

I quickly opened the box before I could change my mind.

As soon as the lid was raised, a rush of mustiness came wafting out. I caught sight of a teddy bear not more than five inches tall. One of its eyes was missing and there were a couple of places where its fur had rubbed off.

Below the bear were pictures. Old, yellowed pictures. The sepia-colored photographs had the feel of a time long past. There was a family photo and one of a mixed-race boy standing next to an adult bicycle. He was maybe ten with a straw hat on, his school uniform pressed. There were other pictures of him surrounded by beautiful, grand mountains that were covered in trees as far as the eye could see. I went through the pictures memorizing every detail.

I wondered what it was like to have lived back then as I had heard that Taiwan was a poor country in the forties and fifties. I recognized Ah Goo from the family photo. Unlike the lady I met yesterday, this girl had a huge smile on her face and stood out as the only one who looked genuinely happy. Her parents sat in the middle looking serene but tired.

Behind her must have been her two older brothers. I remembered Mom mentioning Mary had four brothers, but only two of them were in Taiwan. The others must be their wives and kids. Then, there was the little boy who sat at his parents' feet, a slight smirk on his face like he knew no one could see him make a goofy face for a formal family photo.

His hair was distinctly lighter than the rest of the family, his eyes big and long like an American, and his nose stuck out a lot more. And yet, some resemblance to my mom was there. It was uncanny how similar they looked. I remembered photos of my mom around this age and how she'd had the same smirk on her face. I couldn't wait to show these to her. A shot of jealousy shot through me as I saw first-hand what I had been missing. This was my family. Family that I never knew. Then, a surge of happiness hit me at the memory of Mom standing up for me against Great Aunt Mary. Maybe this journey wouldn't be half bad because I was getting to know my family after all. Better late than never.

Underneath the photos was a little white notebook. It couldn't have been bigger than a postcard. The edges were covered in smudged fingerprints, as if touched by hands that used paint. Inside there were neat columns of what looked like titles, dates, monetary values, names, and addresses. It appeared as if it was a record of paintings sold. I scanned the list of street names and two popped out at me as I recognized them from riding on the subway these last couple of days. I put the notebook to the side. I would be taking it with me.

Next on the pile were drawings, beautiful sketches and chalk drawings of landscapes and people from Taiwan. Interspersed between these drawings were a kid's drawings. Ones you'd see of stick figures and multiple colors jumbled together with the word 'elephant' underneath it. So, art ran in the family. Mom would like that too. I spent a good twenty minutes absorbed in the artwork.

The next piece of paper had me confused. It was a US birth certificate for Harrison Lin. Interesting; he had the same last name as Mom. Born on November 12, 1947, the certificate looked original. Why wouldn't this be in his possession? Aren't original birth certificates something that you should always have with you? Maybe he never left Taiwan. A surge of hope had me thinking that it might not be too hard to find him.

Two envelopes with plum blossoms drawn on both of them were underneath the birth certificate. One couldn't be more than a couple of sheets of paper. The other was thick and heavy with nice cream paper and fancy print on the front. It looked like it had been opened before, but over the years the glue had sealed it back shut. I pried my fingers into the tiny spots holding the flap closed and pulled out a beautiful wedding invitation, hand painted with mountains in the back and skyscrapers in the front. Harrison was being married to a girl named Grace Chien. I wondered if Mary and her parents had attended.

Somehow this intimate piece of paper made him seem like a real person and I felt my breath catch. What was I doing? I gathered everything and slammed it back into the box. Closing the lid, I pushed myself away from the table. I couldn't do this. Not again. I knew all the emotions that it would wrought: the pain, the loss, the sadness.

The room was big enough for me to walk in circles and I did just that. I paced around the table, staring at the box that I knew would change my life again, and waited for something to ground me. Eventually, just the act of walking and being able to breathe normally again calmed my heart rate down. I started telling myself out loud that I could still walk away, even after looking through the rest of the box. I didn't have to say yes to anything. With that reaffirmed, I slowly settled myself back in the seat and rested my hand on the box.

What's the worst that could happen? Okay, maybe it was best not to answer that question right now.

I took a deep breath and opened the box again, this time taking everything out. I came across a journal at the bottom of the box. Could this be Harrison's journal? Deciding not to answer that question right now, I put it straight into my backpack.

I then looked at all the items in front of me before I sat back and closed my eyes, again wondering what was I getting myself into. Did I really need to know who my uncle was? I kept going in circles!

I looked at my watch and realized that I had been in here for quite a long time. Mom was waiting. I looked at the items again, my eyes alighting on the sepia photos. I knew that Mom would like to see the pictures so those also went into the backpack, followed by the little white notebook of paintings, and the two letters.

I then put everything else back nice and neat into the box and left the vault, wondering if Mom and Sebastian had bothered waiting for me. I found them quite content in the lobby, drinking boba milk tea.

"Where's mine?" I asked in way of greeting.

"You were in there for over an hour. We got thirsty and hungry and weren't sure when you'd be out," Sebastian said, sipping away at his drink like he had missed it his whole life. He was taking to this trip a lot better than I had thought.

"Honey, what did you find?" Mom said, tapping the seat next to her.

"Why don't I tell you on the way to get some boba milk tea for me?"

"Mmm, maybe I'll get a second one," Sebastian said while slurping the last drop of his drink.

"You do know we have this stuff in the States, right?" I teased him.

"Well, no one ever introduced me to milk tea in the States, so no," he said, now licking the straw and every square inch he could reach with his tongue. I couldn't help but laugh because he was far from the Sebastian that dressed well, behaved professionally, and was always in charge.

"Come on, let's go get you a second one," I said, hooking my arm through his.

CHAPTER 9

WE ENDED UP NOT TALKING ABOUT WHAT I'D found at the bank on the walk to the boba store because there were too many sidewalk vendors to distract us. There were stalls selling bracelets, hair ties, hats, cell phone covers, cups with Totoro on them, bowls with Hello Kitty on them—actually everything with Hello Kitty on them—cosmetics, clothes, you name it, the list went on. It's not that Mom didn't try to talk to me, but for some reason I was avoiding her questions. Sebastian was too absorbed in his surroundings to be curious. I hoped he'd ask me about my findings later on, or at least show some interest.

When we stopped out front of the shop, Mom said, "We're at the boba store now. Are you going to share with me what you found in the safe deposit box?"

"Yes, Mom. I'm just not sure how to start. There were so many things inside the box, and I'm questioning if we should be on this journey. I feel like we should discuss it all when we get back to the hotel."

"Why don't you start by listing the items like you have no emotional ties to them?"

"You really want to know now, don't you?"

"Is it that obvious?" Mom asked, not even breaking a smile.

"All right." I took a deep breath while we waited for our drinks. "There were a lot of drawings, some of them beautiful landscapes. You would love them. It looks like art runs in our family." I looked at Mom, but she was studying the menu without even glancing at me. "And there were photos of the family, and him of course. They're in my backpack, I can show you when we get back to the hotel." I waited for her to make a comment but still there was no response. I had the sudden feeling that she already knew all this. I quickly shoved it aside and continued, "There was also his US birth certificate. It looked like the original. Which made me question why he left his original birth certificate there? Don't we have to have the original with us at all times in case we need it? This makes me think that he's still here in Taiwan. There was also a small notebook of art items he had sold. I thought I could use the contacts listed in there to find people who might know him. What do you think?"

Mom shrugged.

What in the world? I continued hesitantly, "There was also a thin, unopened envelope and a wedding invitation."

I paused to see if Mom would ask me anything about that, but all she said was, "Is that it?"

"Yes . . . . You don't seem incredibly surprised. Is there something you're not telling me?"

"No, I'm just processing all this information. I'm in the same boat as you. I haven't thought about this brother of mine until you told me. To know that I had played with him once and didn't even remember it breaks my heart. I feel like I've been robbed of something. It's as if he's materializing into an actual person again." She looked up and caught my gaze as she continued, "I had stuffed that little boy so far back into my memory that I let myself think he was a figment of my imagination. What if he's still alive? Do I meet him? Would he even want to meet me? Did he ever know Mama was his mama and I was his sister? Should we even be looking into this? Would he be hurt if we found him and confronted him?"

"Mom, breathe."

At this point Sebastian put a hand on my mom's shoulder and one on my back.

"Are you okay?" he asked Mom.

"This is just a lot of information all at once today," Mom said.

"Oh, look. Here's our drinks," Sebastian said, changing the subject.

"Fantastic! Let's head back to the hotel," I said.

Now it was Mom's turn to avoid talking about what I had found. We walked back looking at all the items offered from the sidewalk vendors, each of us lost in our own thoughts.

CHAPTER 10

I sat next to Sebastian on the couch that night, thinking through all I'd learned today. The items I'd found in the safe deposit box were beside me. I had looked through the drawings, letters, and the book of addresses countless times already and was presently looking at the pictures again. I realized I'd never got a chance to show them to Mom. She had gone straight to her room and shut the door while we sat on the couch. Sebastian had fallen asleep watching American basketball on TV. Just seeing something familiar had made him relax, and when I'd massaged his head, he'd dozed off. The large L-shape couch was so comfortable that I wasn't sure if Sebastian would make it to bed tonight, and I admitted that I wouldn't mind staying here myself.

I had splurged on two of the largest suites they had, and when we checked-in they had thought we were newlyweds. We'd tried to correct them but I don't think the staff had believed us as there were fresh rose petals on our bed, and I swear they'd sprayed something in the air because it had smelled fragrant when we first walked in. It felt very luxurious in this room with Sebastian.

Looking down at him, my heart skipped a beat. I was the luckiest girl, here in Taiwan, with a man that I was falling in love with.

Aware that it was getting late, I refocused on the photos and sorted them based on the age of the boy. Rose's face looked back at me from the first photo; I couldn't take my eyes off of her. It felt like I had walked with her through life to a certain degree. My connection to my past was all based on those journals I'd read, and here I was, sitting on a couch in Taiwan with my Caucasian boyfriend, Taiwanese American Mom, and my insecure self, wondering if I should continue down this rabbit hole to find my other relatives. My heart was screaming yes, but my brain held onto that first picture for dear life, repeating over and over that I should just bring everything back to the bank and have a fun time in Taiwan with Sebastian.

Life was good right now. Why mess it up? As far as Mom and I knew, Harrison never came back into her life again. We didn't even know if he was still alive.

I had heard friends growing up with family secrets, but I never thought mine would be one of them.

"Anne, it's breakfast time. Anne, wake up. You said you wanted to get sao bing. The place closes soon."

At the sound of sao bing, I woke up with a start. I would never get this food back in the States. Part of me wondered if I could ship it to myself in Portland. Then it dawned on me that I could hire someone who could teach Cook how to make it, and I could have it at any time of the day, forever.

68

That made me begin to drift off again, but Sebastian wouldn't have it.

"Get up, sleepy head. I've been waiting two hours for you to wake up. The smell of greasy breakfast is calling and you're keeping me from it."

"Okay. Okay. I'm getting up."

I rolled off the couch and went to grab the coffee table when I realized all the items that had been on my lap last night weren't there anymore.

"I have them, Anne. Don't fret," said Mom, coming over with a cup of tea. "You looked like you could use more sleep, and all those items were going to fall or get squished so I took them to my room. I ended up finding something interesting in the journal from Portland."

"What is it?" Sebastian and I both asked at the same time.

"Take a look yourself." Mom handed me the journal and I noticed that she had taken off the ribbon. I paused. Noticing my reaction, Mom added, "And yes, someone had to pull the ribbon off. I thought it might as well be me."

The realization that I was going to see the inside of the journal made my hands start to shake. How could pieces of paper change my life so much? This one couldn't be more special than another one of Ah Po's journals.

"Look at the letter tucked into the front," Mom pushed.

I opened the journal and a letter fell out. I gasped. "This is a letter to me!"

"From whom?" Sebastian asked.

"It looks like Anthony's handwriting. I gotta start reading it."

"Not before we get breakfast," Sebastian said, pushing me toward the door.

"But I'm not even changed yet," I said, trying to head to my room. "And this letter won't take that long to read."

"Nope. You're fine in yesterday's clothes. I need food. You need food. Your mom needs food. It's time to go out before we miss the food. Plus, if I let you read that letter now, we'll never leave."

"That's harsh," I said.

"It's true," Mom and Sebastian said at the same time. And this time, both Mom and Sebastian pushed me out the door, but I didn't let go of the journal.

We walked to the first breakfast stand we found and I ordered almost half of the menu. I was going to gorge myself silly and then drool over the food pictures once I was back in the States.

We ventured to a neighboring park to devour the delicious food. Kids were running in all directions, climbing up ladders, crawling through tunnels, and swinging back and forth on swings and monkey bars. They were a good distraction from the noise in my head, but I couldn't stop thinking about the letter. What could Anthony possibly have to say to me that he hadn't said already? The whole time we were eating breakfast, I tried to keep up an appearance for the sake of Mom and Sebastian, but they saw straight through me.

"Anne, just read the letter from Anthony already. You look like you're going to bolt," Sebastian said.

"No, I don't," I said, avoiding eye contact.

"Sweetheart, you are a terrible liar. We both want to know what the letter says so please read it out loud," Mom said, snuggling so close I wanted to jump up and find a quiet place just to myself.

"A little room, please."

"Sorry, I just don't want to wait to find out what's in it until you've finished reading."

I took a deep breath, opened the letter, and began to read.

Anne,

I see you've found the journal. I'm sorry it was not with Rose's journals, but I wanted to make sure you read through her journals before you read this one. The thing about this journal is that it's not mine or Rose's.

Now, it was Sebastian's turn to exclaim. "What does he mean that this isn't his?"

"Well, I never actually opened the journal until now, so who would have known? Can we continue reading?" Thankfully, they both nodded.

This journal belonged to Andy. Yes, the same one that you met when you moved into the house.

"How would he know you moved in?" Mom exclaimed.

"Shhhh. We're never going to get through this. Remember, Sebastian was following me for years, so Anthony probably thought he knew me. I did end up moving into the house after all." At this, Sebastian's hands tightened around mine, and I glanced at him to see concern and happiness flash across his face.

"Let's keep reading," was all he said.

I hope you are enjoying my home, which is now your home, and remember what I said in the last letter about forgiving Andy. You will find his journey for making amends with your Ah Po in this journal.

There are also some notes in this journal, which will tell you my side of the story with Harrison. Yes, I know about Harrison. And knowing you, I would expect you're looking for him too. My tip: Mary knows all. There's been too many secrets in our lives, and these are not worth holding on to, no matter what others say. You and your mom have a right to know your family and I hope this will help you fill in some holes on your journey.

Much love,
Anthony

After rereading the beginning of the letter a few times, I finally looked at Mom. "This is Andy's journal." I could feel my heart speeding up. Reading Ah Po's journals was one thing. Reading Andy's would be something else. I actually knew Andy. He'd kept me strong since I'd moved into the house.

"Did you know about this?" I asked Sebastian.

"No," he said, combing his hands through his hair. "This is all news to me."

"Now I wish I could stay to help you find Harrison," Mom whispered.

"You still can, Mom."

"No, my agent called this morning and said the timeline for the paintings has been moved up, so I really have to go back to finish them."

"I understand, Mom. I'll keep you updated at every step," I said, giving her a hug.

Mom seemed distracted. She said, "I'm going to go for a walk." And sure enough, she got up and headed for a random path in the park. At the same time, Sebastian pulled me into his arms and I leaned back and nestled against him, breathing in his musky smell. He felt like comfort and home in a foreign land.

With his chin propped on my shoulder, and without another word, we started reading Andy's journal.

Monday, March 24, 1947

I need to tell someone, even if it's recorded in a journal.

I found a blank notebook someone left in the library. I hope it wasn't Lord Anthony's, but I don't care anymore. I feel so guilty for what I have done. Sir Anthony looks like he's been dragged through the dirt and left to fend for himself. He won't talk to anyone, he won't smile, and he has barely eaten a meal in days. Cook and I are very worried about him.

I wonder where Rose went because I know she did not go home. I was able to talk to her once through the door when Lord Wilkens had locked her in her room, and she said no when I asked if she would go back to her family.

What people don't know is that I love Rose too. She's so gentle and understanding. She never had a harsh word to say to anyone, even though many here say mean things about her behind her back. They still do. She's gone and all they can do is keep gossiping about her. As if she's not a human being, and not someone who contributed to this household. It makes me so mad. Cook is the only person I've been able to talk to. She loves Rose as well and is also very worried about her.

Tuesday, April 1, 1947

I can't find her. I've been asking my connections in town but no one has seen a Taiwanese girl of Rose's description. Although, I think they are just brushing me aside because they were initially happy to see me, but when I showed them a picture of Rose, they gave me odd looks. I knew what they were thinking. Why was I so interested in a Taiwanese girl? They said they didn't recognize her, but I think they just couldn't tell her apart from the other Asian girls in town. I don't know how they couldn't. Rose is more beautiful than any other girl I've seen. She also has a kind heart. If I could only find her.

Cook has made a meal for her every day, and I find some excuse to leave the house for an hour. I wander around town hoping I'll bump into her or somebody will point me in the right direction. I know, April Fool's Day to me! But I'm going to keep trying.

Friday, April 4, 1947

I think I got a break! Someone saw a woman like Rose at Becker's Bakery. It was at the end of my hour so I couldn't pursue the lead, but I'm going to check it out tomorrow. Cook has already said she's going to add in a few slices of carrot cake because she knows that's Rose's favorite. I'm going to have to start doing something when I go out though, and not come back sweaty with a package of food still in my hands. Betsy was on my case the last few days. Laughing that I must have found a girl and was sneaking out to see her. If they only knew how true that was, even if it's not for the reasons they think.

If my family didn't depend on me keeping this job, I would be out looking for a new one right now. But Lord Wilkens pays better than many around here, and I was lucky to have gotten it. It's part of my guilt. I understand Rose in more ways than she thinks. We might have different color skin and be treated differently, but inside, we hold the same values about our families. I miss her so much.

Saturday, April 5, 1947

I found her! She looks so sad.

I had found Becker's Bakery with no problem. It was early in the morning and there was a line at the till. I saw Rose behind the counter packing people's orders. How I wish I could have gone to her right then and there, but I didn't dare show my face in case I startled her.

I am so relieved she is somewhere safe. At least, it looks safe. I was able to sneak around the back and caught the owner, Josephine. She reminds me of Cook: plump, colorful, and vibrant. Except Josephine could be our mother. What made it even better was that she said Rose was living with her upstairs. Knowing Rose has a place to live and is earning money makes me happy.

I didn't tell Josephine where I came from, just that I was an old friend of Rose's, and that I wanted to see if she was okay. Josephine tried to get me to come in, but I made her promise to not let Rose know I was there. I think Rose would have broken down in tears and I can't stand to see her cry anymore. She deserves better. Josephine said she'd give Rose the meal Cook had made.

Tuesday, April 8, 1947

Okay! Who am I kidding? I love her. I want to be the one taking care of her. I'm so mad at Anthony for ruining everything. He deserves to be miserable. I'm going to tell Rose tomorrow that I'm quitting my job with the Wilkens and I'm coming to be with her.

Wednesday, April 9, 1947

I am kidding myself. I'm not the one she loves. Anthony is the one she loves, and Anthony has been nothing but kind to me. He's started seeking me out, which is a bit scary. I know he's going to take over the family business when Lord Wilkens steps down. Rumor is that it's going to be sooner rather than later because Lord Wilkens hasn't been doing well health-wise. So, if Anthony is seeking me out, I should try to befriend him so that he'll keep me on.

But I hate doing that. It's deceiving. I don't know what to do.

Friday, April 11, 1947

I received a letter from Mother today. She works at a department store selling clothes and says Father had an accident at work at the shipyard. He's okay but he broke his arm. This means that he's not working for the time being, which in turn means that my brother and I will be taking the brunt of the financial obligations. I need this job . . .

Monday, April 21, 1947

Cook has come up with the best plan! She told Lady Mary that she would like to learn different kinds of cuisine. To do this, she will need a day off from family cooking to practice the other recipes she is coming up with. So, once a week, I am to go and pick up an order of food from a restaurant in town. The plan is that this food would randomly be sourced from Josephine's bakery, but only Cook and I know that. And now I have an excuse to go out once a week to check on Rose and no one will be the wiser. How great is this?

Friday, June 27, 1947

Something must have happened earlier this week. The girls are different. I can tell that Josephine is on edge, and Rose has the look of someone who has steeled herself for a fight. She is still too skinny. I was able to stand behind some customers while she was busy and I caught a gleam in her eyes as she was looking at people directly, instead of down at the baked goods or cash register. There's still a cloud around her but she seems stronger. I still don't dare let her see me. That would be both our jobs if Lord Anthony saw us. I couldn't imagine what he would do to Rose if he knew she was still around.

Anthony, on the other hand, looks more dejected than he has in the past. I hadn't thought that possible, but he hasn't eaten in the last two days except for maybe a piece of bread and butter. It's like he's built himself a prison inside his father's house. There are rumors that he and Sally are getting married next week. I wish I could tell him about Rose. That she's doing well. But I know Anthony would run straight to the bakery, and then Rose's life would be worse off.

Tuesday, July 1, 1947

This can't be true. I'm seeing things. How did I not notice this earlier?

Rose has become happier and happier over the last month. There was a week there where she looked like she'd been crushed again, but it went away as fast as it came. I continue to visit her once a week and watch from a distance. There is a set of regular customers that come in the morning, and I know whom I can hide behind due to their height. I only stay inside for a glimpse of her before I leave and watch her from across the street.

Everything has been going so smoothly since Cook came up with the scheme. I've also been given more responsibility around the house. Hopefully this means that I'm financially secure. Mother is happy that the money I'm sending back is enough to help the family. But what I saw today could ruin me, especially since Anthony started confiding in me. I have no idea why, except that he knew I was close to Rose, too, and that I liked her.

If he only knew. I've had to start hiding this journal. I hate not being able to tell him about her, but what am I supposed to say? I love her, too, and I feel your pain? No, that wouldn't do. I would get thrown out of this house faster than I could get to my room to pack. So, I just sit and listen to him. He usually catches me in the garden when I'm doing

77

my rounds, making sure all the little tasks around the house are being taken care of. He knows he can't be caught talking about Rose. I bet he hasn't thought about me and my position here—that I'm dispensable if we're caught.

Cook has told me to tell him that I'm not interested in listening, but I can't do that. In a way, it's a relief to know there's someone else in the household who cares as much for Rose as I do.

But, back to the surprise! I went to pick up the food today as I don't go to the bakery directly—I'm not stupid. Tony always meets me halfway. We went to school together and he was my best friend . . . at least, he used to be. In any case, I knew I could trust him with my secret. And usually, it's a quick exchange between us: food, money, a quick hi, and we're done. But today, Tony was chatty. He kept going on and on about a girl he was infatuated with, but after today, he had changed his mind. My curiosity was piqued, so I kept asking him questions until he mentioned that the girl wasn't white. Somehow, I knew this wasn't where I wanted the conversation to turn, so I started walking away but he wouldn't stop. Long story short, he had a crush on Rose. My Rose! And the reason she couldn't be his girl anymore was because she was "definitely pregnant." I didn't know if I should punch him for the fact that he liked my girl, or that he could assume that she was pregnant. There was no way Rose could be pregnant.

So, of course, I had to go and see for myself. Not caring that the food would get cold, I'd made my way to Josephine's bakery. Hiding behind other people, I'd craned my neck to see through the window. Rose was in front, as usual. But when she came out from behind the counter, I almost dropped the food all over the sidewalk because there was a distinct bump around her middle that had not been there before.

This couldn't be. Was the baby Anthony's? Did anyone else know? I only took comfort in the thought that if Lord Wilkens knew then Rose would not be in the city right now. What am I going to do? I don't like keeping secrets.

Tuesday, July 15, 1947

I've kept my mouth shut and I'm going to keep it that way. Over the last thirty days, I've been visiting Rose once a week. She doesn't know I'm there. There's been too much going on, and she is better off starting her life over than having me interfere. Besides, she looks much happier. There's been a shift, though. Josephine is on guard, and I think she saw me when I stopped by today.

Wednesday, July 23, 1947

Yes, Josephine definitely saw me last week because she was waiting for me when I showed up today. She had me meet her around back. To my horror, she told me that she knew everything. How Rose had worked at the Wilkens's residence as a seamstress. How she'd fallen in love with Anthony, and that someone had told Anthony's father about their relationship. (Which had been me! Thank goodness she didn't know that little detail.) Then, Josephine added that Rose had been kicked out with nowhere to go.

I couldn't believe that Rose had told her everything! Josephine told me to never come back, but I told her I only had Rose's best intentions in mind and that I never wanted to hurt her. I also told Josephine that I, too, worked for the Wilkens. I made it clear I wasn't a Wilkens though. I'm not sure that was any better but she seemed to calm down a little.

She said she'd be watching out for me, but she wouldn't mind me ordering food from her still. Then I told her of my and Cook's scheme. The food I ordered fed the Wilkens family, but it allowed me to come out once a week to check on Rose. I explained that I cared about Rose and wanted to know she was safe.

Josephine seemed to soften a bit at that, but reprimanded me for coming so close to Rose when I knew someone could be following me. Truthfully, I hadn't even thought of that, but since she'd mentioned it, I felt awful. I left with my tail between my legs. I'm just as bad as Anthony, putting Rose in danger.

I was about to go on to the next entry when I noticed some notes on the side. On a closer look, I saw that this was the first of Anthony's notes that he had added to the journal.

Dear Anne,

Please understand that Andy didn't think I knew what he was doing, but I had someone follow him a few weeks after Rose had gone. I knew he and Rose were close, but I did not know he loved her and my heart breaks knowing that he, too, could not be with her in this world of ours.

Once I'd verified what he was doing, I followed him once and saw her. Rose looked radiant. Sad, but radiant. There was no denying that she remains the most beautiful girl I have ever known. I started confiding in Andy soon after that day I'd followed him. I'm sad to read that I made him feel uncomfortable, but knowing he cared for Rose made it bearable to be around him. It was difficult but I never went back to the bakery—I knew my father was keeping tabs on me.

I looked up from the journal to utter silence. Mom had returned, and both she and Sebastian had contemplative looks, as though they were digesting what they had just heard.

Sebastian was the first to break the silence. "This was not what I expected. Andy loved your Ah Po?"

"I knew he cared for her, but . . ." I drifted off.

"This is not going to be an easy search," Sebastian said.

I just nodded.

The silence stretched.

Mom suddenly stood. "Let's go for a walk. I found a nice pond over there." She grabbed our things and walked away without looking, knowing we'd follow.

CHAPTER 11

"SO, WHERE ARE WE GOING TO EXPLORE TODAY?" Sebastian asked while devouring breakfast the next morning.

"Slow down my eating monster," I laughed. "You're going to get sick and then you won't be able to go anywhere."

"I can't. There's just so many different foods to try, and I know that I won't be able to get this when I go back home."

"Well, we could stay longer."

"Nah, I belong in the States."

I tried again. "I didn't mean permanently but maybe a little longer?"

"How much longer?"

"Just a couple more weeks. I want to find my uncle, and even you said yesterday that this is going to take a bit of time. I'd love for you to help me, and then we might also have time to do a road trip around the island and some other touristy things."

Sebastian slowed down in his eating, and I held my breath, waiting for an answer.

"I only said it wasn't going to be easy. You think this search is going to take a bit of time?"

"Yeah, only because we've hit so many roadblocks."

"We've only hit one roadblock. Your great aunt won't tell you about your uncle, but she did give you the key to the safe deposit box. Didn't you find a lot of stuff in there that was his? The birth certificate—use that. Look up his name, and voila, you'll have found him."

"I do know his name, but what if it takes longer than our trip to track him down? Would you be willing to stay on with me?"

"I don't know. I have work to get back to. This is just a vacation, Anne. We're supposed to be having fun."

"What are you two love birds talking about?" Mom asked, coming to the table with a tray of tea.

"Oh, it's nothing. We were discussing what we should do with the day," I said.

"Anne thinks looking for your brother will take longer than we think. I'm of the mindset that we should enjoy our time here, and if we find him, we find him. There's no need to find someone who clearly doesn't want to be found."

I gave him a glare. "Sebastian, you know how I feel about keeping family secrets."

"I know. I know. Finding out about your Ah Po was a huge discovery and has made your lives a lot better."

"No need to be so sarcastic."

"Sorry, I just really want to go and see the sights with you. I don't want to be stuck in a room poring over long-lost pictures and journals."

"It won't be forever."

"Okay, why don't we go to a museum today?" Mom interjected, having sat there with her head on a swivel watching us. "And afterward, Anne can start on finding her uncle again. You can join us, too, if you want." She then gave him such a long stare that he went back to eating and didn't utter another word.

My nerves were bristling. I'd thought Sebastian would be eager to help me. After all, we were together and he flew here to support me, didn't he? He knew we were coming to Taiwan to search for my uncle. Why was he being so stubborn about it? We were here for enough time to explore and find my uncle.

We visited the Chiang Kai-Shek Memorial Hall. When the taxi dropped us off at the entrance, the wind that blew through the plaza had me wrapping my arms around myself.

I had seen pictures of it and it did not disappoint. The sight was breathtaking. It reminded me of Washington Mall but with Chinese architecture. To my left and right were massive auditoriums decorated in Chinese Deco. They had red columns and bright orange roofs. The buildings were long and framed a large plaza that led to a pagoda at the end. From where we were standing the pagoda looked tiny, but I knew from pictures that it was massive. If not for Taipei 101, and the other skyscrapers in the background, you would have never known this oasis was in the middle of Taipei City.

The entrance to this whole place looked like a Roman waterway. Five big arches topped with blue Chinese Deco roofs welcomed you into the plaza. I could also see secret gardens tucked into the sides. There were people walking with determination, families having a quiet lunch, students reading their books, and tourists posing with the pagoda in their hand or jumping in the air.

We got to the flagpole in the middle of the plaza and gawked at the stairs in the distance that led up to the pagoda.

"I think I will let you two young ones attempt the stairs. I'll wait at the bottom," Mom said, rubbing her legs.

"I did read that there's a museum on the ground floor.

Hopefully there's elevators? You should really come up to see the monument," I said.

"We will see," Mom said.

"Well, I for one will race you to the top," Sebastian said with a gleam in his eyes.

"You're on."

We left Mom to walk the rest of the way while we ran and took the stairs two at a time all the way to the top.

"Ha! I won!" I yelled, pumping two arms into the air and doing my best Rocky impersonation. Everyone turned to stare. Some laughed but some gave me disapproving looks. I guess people didn't yell out loud here. Sebastian came up right behind me, clasped me in his arms, gave me a big smooch on the lips, and then used my shirt to wipe the sweat off his face.

"Stop that!" I laughed, trying to get out of his arms. "There are other people here."

"So what?"

"We're not in the States, and that's ticklish," I said, almost falling to the ground. There were definitely people glaring at us now, and some were foreigners from other countries as well.

We ended up sitting on the top steps, looking back at where we had just come. The view was amazing. I would say it rivaled Taipei 101 because you could see the details across the plaza and above the tree line to the surrounding city. The orange rooftops of the concert and theater halls stood out like spotlights, pointing their way toward the arches. There were trees, buildings of various sizes, and people and cars were milling about. I could have sat there for the rest of the day with Sebastian by my side.

I put my head on his shoulders while he wrapped an arm around me.

"It's something special, this trip," he said.

85

"It is."

"I want to do more of this stuff with you. I know how much finding your uncle means to you and I don't want to take that away, but I want to explore and have fun too. I want to see what you do when you're traveling, and I want to help you with that blog of yours."

"That's quite a lot of wants," I said, giving him a smile.

"You know what I mean."

"I know and we still can. No one is taking the adventure away." I sat up and turned to look at him. "I'm here, and I need to take advantage of the fact that I am here to find him. He's my mom's brother. She's never had a sibling. Would it not be awesome for her to have a sibling after all these years?"

"I don't know. I don't have any siblings and I've turned out fine, and don't give me that raised eyebrow look."

"Well, I've always wanted a sibling. Someone who can relate to me. I bet Mom would have liked someone to commiserate with about her mom. Sometimes it's lonely being an only child."

"Yeah, I guess so. Look, I'll help you. I know I don't show it, but I am curious about who this person is."

"Aw thanks, Sebastian!" I gave him a huge hug.

"Am I interrupting something?" Mom asked, coming up behind us.

"Mom! You made it."

"Well, don't act so surprised. I'm not completely useless. You two sure got a lot of attention."

"Yeah, it was fun though. How did you get up?"

"Just like you said: museum, elevator, voila. And wow, the view up here is spectacular."

"Yeah, I love watching the people walk around. I like to wonder where they are going."

"Wow!" said Sebastian.

We turned to see what he was looking at and found that on the inside of the pagoda was a huge statue of Chiang Kai-Shek, sitting in front of us. It reminded me so much of the Lincoln Memorial. I felt like I should kneel or something and simply take in his awesomeness. Right then the changing of the guards started and we watched, mesmerized.

I'll be the first to say that I am more American than Taiwanese in a lot of things, but definitely more Westernized. I felt a bit guilty because I had always associated the changing of the guards with London, but right here in front of me were soldiers manning a statue they respected and being very professional about exchanging weapons and stations. I made a note to myself that I should travel around Asia more often in the future.

I admitted to myself that I'd been scared to come. I didn't grow up with a lot of Asian people and being around them made me nervous. I felt like a fraud. But the people here had been super kind and generous, and we were eating like kings given the food was so cheap here. There were restaurants and numerous street stands; you could eat to your heart's content and still not touch the plethora of food choices on offer.

I wondered if there were old temples or anything else around that were from a bygone era. There was so much to research and include in my blog as well as things I wanted to find out for myself. I had a yearning passion to learn where I came from. Who were my ancestors? And how did my uncle fit into my family's past?

"Earth to Anne. Hello?" Sebastian said, knocking his knuckles on my head.

"Hey, stop that."

"We've been calling your name a few times. You looked like you had gone to a new dimension."

"Very funny. I was thinking about all the things I still had to learn about Asia."

"You and your thinking. Can't you just relax and enjoy where you are?"

"Anne has never been like that and it'd be futile for you to try to change her," Mom said, "but I do agree, we should enjoy this place a bit more. There's an exhibit downstairs. Come on, Anne, let's go."

"All right," I sighed. I guess looking for my uncle could wait a bit more.

Mom hooked my arm and turned me toward the elevator.

Sebastian came and hooked my other arm. "I could do with a cold drink," he said.

The downstairs was magnificent. There was a 3D model of the entire plaza with the theaters and the Memorial Hall. You could see the gardens off to the sides, the arches at the entrance, and tiny little people milling around, going about their business. In the back, there was a self-guided tour of Chiang Kai-Shek of when he arrived in Taiwan. I had read a little bit about him, but it was still impressive to see pictures and artifacts up close, including a life-size replica of the man himself sitting at his desk. It was a little creepy, but I learned more about Taiwanese history there than I had ever learned in my lifetime.

I could have spent the whole day in the museum reading every placard, every sign, but Mom was flying out tonight, so we went back to Din Tai Fung for one last hurrah before she had to leave.

CHAPTER 12

T ODAY WAS THE DAY OF THE WEDDING. A FTER dinner last night, Sebastian had made us go shopping at Taipei 101 to buy proper wedding attire. Thankfully, Mom had time to come with us before heading to the airport. She explained to him that this wedding would not be glittery and fancy, and that I could probably pass with a simple but still presentable dress, while he could wear a suit instead of a tuxedo. However, I did buy a jacket that was worth more than what I had made in a month about four months ago. It was practical though, and I knew I would wear it again for non-wedding events.

"You're already dressed?" Sebastian asked, coming into the bedroom after catching up with some work emails.

"There's not much to it. Put on the dress. Put on the jacket. Brush my hair. And eventually, put on my shoes."

He just stood there and shook his head. "You're like no other woman I have ever met."

"That makes me happy because I don't want to be like those other women you've been with."

Sebastian took a bit longer to get ready, but eventually we were in a car and on our way to Mary's house. Mom had explained to me that in Taiwanese culture the male's side of the family comes to the female's side of the family to "pick her up" and take her to live with the male side. So, today's celebration was only the engagement party. It was all so foreign and I just hoped we weren't late.

We both stood out like a sore thumb. As we entered, every eye turned to us and the conversations all stopped at once. An older woman came up and asked if she could help us. When I mentioned I was Mary's great-niece from America, it was like everyone's defensive walls came down and we suddenly had hands on us, pulling us inside. I could hear someone introducing us to everyone we passed and next thing we knew, we were seated in the living room next to Mary. She took my hand and gave it a gentle pat but made no mention of the conversation we'd had the last time we met.

"Mary, can you tell us what is happening here?" Sebastian asked.

"Everyone here is part of the groom's family. I am seated because I am old, and you two are with me because you are foreigners. So, we gave you the best seats in the house. My family is all behind that curtain with the bride."

"Why is she hidden?"

"She needs to be introduced and pay her respects to the groom's family before she is accepted into their family."

"Uh huh . . ." Sebastian turned to look at me and I just shrugged. I didn't know any more than he did.

Over the next thirty minutes we watched as the bride came out, served tea, gave out red envelopes, and was then in turn offered lots of presents from the groom's family, including what looked like gold bracelets and necklaces. It was so interesting to see the detail that went into every movement, and all the motions that the families went through because of tradition and respect. I felt Sebastian's hands cover mine and when I turned to look at him, I could tell he was just as moved by everything as I was. Maybe it was because we were watching the engagement, but his thumb deliberately traced my ring finger. No, it was probably where his thumb had naturally landed. All the same, I liked the feeling of his fingers rubbing over mine.

After the ceremony had come to an end we got up to leave.

"Mary, thank you so much for having us over. That was wonderful. I had never seen anything like it before," Sebastian said.

"Oh, we're not done yet. You're going to ride with Ah Yi, and she'll take you to the banquet hall."

"Of course, how could I forget! Even in our tradition we must eat afterward. Let's go!" Sebastian said.

I had not seen him this excited since he'd came back from the night market. I loved seeing him this way, and I didn't know why, but I started giggling.

"Come on giggle mcgee, let's go eat with your family," he encouraged.

Now, I really liked the sound of that. Because this was my family.

Mary hadn't been kidding when she said that we'd eat at a banquet hall. We had thought the meal would just be for the people who'd been at her house, and even then, there had been about thirty people there. But the sight before us was something else. I couldn't even count all the round tables that were stuffed into the room. There were hundreds of people here, pouring in and from the side, and I saw the staff rolling out more tables to set up in the hallway.

"Is this all of your family?" Sebastian asked.

"I don't think so . . . but I really couldn't tell you."

When we got closer to the entrance, I noticed a long table with a white tablecloth. Behind it was a lady with what looked like a ledger book. People were lined up and handing over red envelopes.

"Oh! I almost forgot. Mom gave me this beautiful red envelope and said she already put some money inside it. It's their wedding present. Mom asked Mary how much to put in from us. It's in my purse, hang on. Ah, here it is."

"How much is in it?" Sebastian said, a bit distracted.

"Wow! It's a thousand US dollars!"

"What? I mean, I know you're rich, but a thousand dollars for a wedding?"

I shrugged. "I'm just going to go with it."

I had enough money that I could give out a thousand dollars without blinking an eye. Well, my eyes were blinking, but my brain was trying to catch up. We were the next in line and that's when I realized why Sebastian had seemed distracted. The lady behind the table was opening the red envelopes and counting all the money right in front of everyone! Then she was recording the amount in the ledger.

I didn't have to look at Sebastian to know that it was taking all his willpower to not let his jaw drop open. I took his hand and squeezed. I needed his support as much as he needed mine. My mind started running through the thought that maybe a thousand dollars wasn't enough. What if others were giving more? I should have asked about the traditions here so I didn't mess up. But it was too late to change anything now because it was our turn.

"Welcome," the lady said warmly. She took our envelope,

opened it, and I watched as all the cash was taken out and counted. Her eyes seemed to grow big as it dawned on her how much money there was. "This is very generous of you." She wrote it down in the ledger and we were showed to the side to write a note for the happy couple.

"Well, that was anticlimactic," Sebastian said, eyes still glued to the lady counting the money.

"Sure was and there's probably more surprises inside."

"Anne, I've been looking for you," Mary said, sneaking up on us. "I want you to meet your family. These are Ming-Yue's brothers and all my grandchildren and great-grandchildren. I don't know where her sister is."

The littlest one had run up to Mary and lifted his arms. Mary swooped down and cuddled him while giving him lots of kisses. Part of my heart hurt a bit from knowing that I never got to know that feeling or the love of my own grandmother, but I quickly pushed it to the side. There was no place for sadness on this day.

"How many people are here?" I asked.

"About seven hundred," Mary said, not missing a beat.

"Seven hundred?" Sebastian said, spinning his head around to stare at Mary.

"Yes, family members, coworkers, and people who we have known our whole life. There are also some politicians here and the local theater group I used to work with."

"And you had to invite them all?" Sebastian asked, running his hand through his hair. His other hand had tightened around mine. He seemed more nervous than usual.

"Yes, this is a celebration," Mary said, giving him a look that said, "What did you think it was?"

Unlike the rest of the immediate family who had to sit in the hallway, we were shown to the front where we could sit next to Mary. I felt guilty for taking up a spot from someone who was closer to the happy couple, but Mary shushed me and starting ladling food onto my plate. Sebastian had seen the feast on the table and was already helping himself. There were abalone slices drizzled with mayonnaise, fried shrimp balls with pineapples, fried lobsters, bamboo with mushrooms and fungus soup, crab over sticky rice, shrimp, rack of lamb, whole steamed fish, seafood smorgasbord soup, and four different kinds of dessert. Sebastian looked the happiest he'd ever been. We gorged and it was wonderful.

By the time the bride and groom got to our table we were happy to stand up. There were probably ten other people with them, keeping them on pace, but what stood out the most was the guy who came straight up to Sebastian and shook his hand. Then he started talking in flawless English about how he had gotten a degree at Yale and lived in America for ten years before moving back. I had to hold back my laugh at the look on Sebastian's face. He was polite and said the right things, but I could tell he was super uncomfortable and not sure about what had just happened.

Slowly, people started progressing to the exit. While I was picking a piece of candy out of the basket the bride was holding, someone tapped me on the shoulder.

"Are you Anne? Uncle Charlie's granddaughter?"

"Yes. You are?"

"I'm Ming-Yue's oldest sister. Mama mentioned that you are looking for Harrison."

"Yes!" I hadn't meant to yell so loudly. Everyone had turned to look at us, so I walked her over to the side where we could discretely talk. "Did you know Harrison? Anything you could share with me would be fantastic."

"Mama doesn't want me sharing anything."

Ugh! Why wouldn't anyone share something straight with me?

"But I think it only fair that you be warned," she continued. "I grew up with Harrison. I think what you are doing is unnecessary and will only bring you pain in the long run."

"Oh!"

But before I could ask if she could tell me more, she volunteered, "Harrison was not a nice person. He always found ways to get me in trouble with Mama. He liked to play pranks on me. He also tried it with my brothers, but they would find ways to get him back so he stopped after a couple of times. It was always me thereafter that he targeted. You and your guy should go home and leave my family alone."

I stared at her and said, "I'm your family too."

She actually shook her hand at me as she said, "I'm just giving you a warning." And with that, she left. Just like that.

I was shocked. I was not only getting push-back from the Wilkens, but also from the Lin family to butt out of the family secrets. A stubbornness settled deeper inside me. Who was she to tell me what to do?

Just then, Sebastian returned from the restroom. "You look like you've just fought with someone."

I didn't deny it. "It's time for us to leave. Now." I grabbed his hand and hightailed it out of there, not even bothering to say goodbye to Mary or the bride and groom.

Back at the hotel, Sebastian rubbed my back by the side of the pool. We were the only ones there, thank goodness, because I really didn't like wearing a bikini in public. Sebastian had come back from his tour with Ming-Yue at the night market and bought me a bikini. When I told him it was early April and still a bit cold outside, he said the hotel had an indoor pool that was heated and I would be just fine. In other words, he wasn't going to take no for an answer. He said he knew I didn't bring a bathing suit and he planned on relaxing by the pool with me. He was so proud of himself when it fit perfectly that he gave me the biggest smile that I couldn't say no to. I did, however, wrap myself up in a bathrobe before heading to the pool, then begrudgingly took it off. Though, I had to say I felt sexy and Sebastian was pretty good to look at too.

"Why so tense?" Sebastian asked, kneading his hands down my back.

"I'm just wondering about my uncle and wondering where he is. Why do people want to keep him hidden?"

"Sometimes a secret grows bigger from when it first started out as things are blown out of proportion. I think you're reading too much into this. Your uncle is probably retired, sitting in his glorious mansion, and relaxing by his pool. Just like you should be doing now." He pushed a little harder into my muscles and then murmured, "I swear every knot I get out of your back comes right back when I move on to the next spot."

"I never noticed them until you started kneading them."

"Well, someone had to. You're going to be stiff when you get older, and I need you nimble for a while still." He planted a kiss on each of my shoulders before trailing up my neck.

"Stop it, Sebastian," I said, swatting his face away. "People will see."

"What people?" he asked, waving his hand at the empty room. "Anne, I had a wonderful time with you today. I want to continue that tomorrow. It'll be Sunday and you can think of it as a no workday. Look, this is me talking and I'm a workaholic. I'll admit to that. Come with me on an adventure and I can take that worry line away from your lovely forehead."

"My forehead?" I couldn't stop laughing. That was the most unsexy thing he could have said. I turned around to look at Sebastian. He had the sweetest smile, and I could tell that I was his whole world. I felt so special and I knew I'd do anything to make him happy at that moment.

"Okay, where do you want to take me?" I asked.

"You're going to come?"

"Yes. Don't sound so surprised. I can be flexible when need be."

"All right. Be ready tomorrow, bright and early."

CHAPTER 13

THE TOP OF A HIGH HILL—THAT'S WHERE Sebastian took me. This added more to my worry lines rather than decreasing them. "Why are we here?"

"You'll see."

"You still won't tell me?" We had hopped into a car service Sebastian had booked and driven an hour to Yilan, which was on the east coast. We were meeting up with someone that Ming-Yue knew, and she had suggested this activity to Sebastian. Apparently it was something both of us had to do while in Taiwan.

"No, just relax. You'll find out soon enough," Sebastian said.

"Are you taking me to a secret hideaway?" I pushed.

"No, but now that you mention it . . ."

"I was just joking!" Next thing I knew, I was pulled into his arms and receiving the sweetest kiss.

He broke away to say, "Just relax. Trust me. It's going to be fun."

"Okay, but I am a bit nervous."

We walked for five more minutes and I couldn't believe

what I saw. In front of me was an open area with a bamboo clump at the end. A big kite-like contraption lay in front of us. It was easily thirty feet or longer. I felt my heart race. He wasn't going to have us do what I thought he was, was he? "Sebastian, we're not going to . . .?"

"Yes, we are," he said with a huge grin on his face.

"No way!"

"Yes way. You are going to let your hair down and go parasailing with me today. Just you and me in the air. Well, maybe not together. We'll each have our own instructor, but I'll be flying right next to you."

I didn't know what to say. I was scared of heights. It's the one thing I didn't take exception to. Sebastian knew that. Then, it dawned on me.

"You booked this knowing I'm scared of heights!" I said, glaring at him.

"I sure did. You would never have said yes otherwise, and parasailing is not scary. It's like you're floating in the air. You'll love it."

"Sebastian . . ."

"Come on, you go to different countries all the time and experience new surroundings and new people. You can handle this."

"But the height . . ." I murmured.

Then, we couldn't talk anymore because the instructors were coming toward us. They had helmets on and straps galore. Did those things really protect you from plunging to your death?

"Very few people actually die from having adventures," Sebastian whispered in my ear while gently pushing me forward.

"I love adventures. Just not ones that require me to drop from unfathomable heights."

The next thing I knew I was being strapped in and

attached to my instructor, his front to my back. He explained that I had to run as fast as I could, that it wouldn't seem like I was doing much, but we needed the momentum to get us going into the air.

"I'm right behind you, Anne! Woohoo!" Sebastian cried.

How did I let him talk me into this? Sure enough, the first time we tried to get going we didn't go fast enough and therefore couldn't get enough lift. We ran right into the bamboo grove. Stick after stick smacked me in the face, arms, and legs. I was so embarrassed, but I also got an adrenaline rush and I wasn't going to back down now. We repositioned ourselves and this time I pumped my arms and legs as fast as I could during the run-up. All of a sudden, the ground disappeared from under me. I was flying! It was the most incredible feeling—the sensation of feeling weightless, soaring through the air, then floating while you drifted down like a feather.

I could hear Sebastian behind me, whooping for joy. We were doing big slow swooshes back and forth, heading for the beach below. Occasionally, I would spot Sebastian, and he would blow a kiss to me. We landed gently on the beach and no one could wipe the smile off of my face.

"Looks like someone enjoyed herself," Sebastian said, sauntering over to me after we'd stripped off the gear.

"Let's do it again," I said, which brought out a huge laugh from him. It really had been amazing and not scary at all. I'd felt like I was on a cloud slowly drifting down to the beach, then softly deposited on the sand. "Seriously, let's do it again."

"Well, I only paid them the once and it looks like they're packing up. Let's do it another time. Instead, I was told of a restaurant we should try if you're up for eating?"

"Okay, I'll concede to that," I said, slipping my hand into his. His large hand enveloped mine and I felt safe. He seemed extra happy today and that made me glad to have come on this adventure with him.

Sebastian had been by my side since the bombing, tending to my every need. At one point, I'd had to ask him to back off and let me do some stuff, but it had been really nice to have someone besides my mom caring about me.

A sudden thought came to me. "Sebastian, can we stop at a place after we eat?"

"Of course. Where would that be?" he said. However, I could tell that he had gotten distracted by something.

"It might be near here," I replied. "I need to check, but it's one of the addresses in the book of sold paintings that I found in the vault. I remember one of them was in Yilan."

"Let's go eat first," he replied.

"Are you sure this is the place?" Sebastian asked.

"It's the correct address if that's what you're asking," I said, but even I wasn't so sure.

After lunch we had headed to the address in the little white book. Staring back at us was a single storey house shaped liked a horseshoe. The main entrance was laid out in the middle of the grounds and the house looked quiet. We had driven into the mountains and there was not a sound around us. Not even a cricket. I could feel my heart rate start to slow down. Every thought seemed to seep out of me the longer we stood here. One look at Sebastian showed he felt the same way. There was something in the air that just made us want to stop.

I took Sebastian's hand and led him to the house. There was no doorbell to be found so I called out to see if anyone was home. Silence. The peace was settling and by some unspoken agreement, Sebastian and I went and sat on the bench that was propped against the side of the house. We were both in our own worlds but I couldn't imagine being here without Sebastian. I was glad we were sharing this experience.

There was something about quietness. The more you stayed quiet, the more you started noticing little things you had never noticed before—like the wind blowing through the screen door, the hinges giving an imperceptible squeak, or the rustling of leaves as the wind blew through, even your own heartbeat. I had never realized mine beat so fast.

"Who are you?" A loud, sharp voice in Mandarin snapped us out of our daydream, and we were on our feet in the next breath, Sebastian pushing me behind him, my heart beating even faster.

In front of us was an old lady with short white hair and sun-kissed skin. She wore a straw hat with a wide brim, the strap dangling below her chin, a long button-down shirt that had seen better days, comfortable pants, and sandals. Distinct wrinkles covered her hands and face, but there was a tautness to her that made me think she still worked in the fields every day. Her shoulders were a little bit stooped and her arm was carrying a wicker basket filled with greens.

Sebastian nudged me to answer, and the realization that he wouldn't be able to answer for us shook me out of my daze.

"Po Po, ni hao, I'm Hong-Mei, and this is my boyfriend, Sebastian. I got your address out of this book," I said, pulling the little white notebook out of my pocket.

At the sight of the notebook the old lady almost dropped her basket of food. Before either of us could help her, she had already caught it and was walking toward the house, gesturing for us to follow.

My curiosity was piqued. I looked at Sebastian, who shrugged, and we followed her through the screen door.

The inside was simple like the outside, neat and orderly. The lady told us to sit before she disappeared. So we sat and waited. I could hear noises in the kitchen and was about to get up to see if I could help when she charged through the door with a tray of fruit and tea.

"How do you know Fei-Hong?" she said with full authority.

"Who?" She was very direct, even for me.

"What is she asking?" Sebastian whispered in my ear.

"She's asking how we know Fei-Hong," I whispered back.

"Who's that?"

"Your guess is as good as mine."

The lady never took her eyes off of us during this little exchange.

"I'm sorry, we're here because we're looking for a man named Harrison. He would be about sixty-four now. I didn't bring a picture with me today as I wasn't expecting to come here." I was starting to feel awkward sitting here, with her staring at us like she was analyzing everything about us.

After what seemed like forever, she finally said, "Give me that book."

"Sure." What harm would it do?

We watched as she rubbed her hand over the front before opening the notebook carefully as if it was going to fall apart in her hands. I was surprised to see tears glistening in her eyes. I got so worried I went and sat by her.

When she spoke, it was not with the authority that she had held earlier. "This was Fei-Hong's. I gave it to him."

"Who is Fei-Hong?"

"He was the 'lost boy.' Only thirteen years old when my husband found him, starving on the road. He would not tell us where he came from, but I knew he was not from around here."

"Why do you say that?" I asked.

"What is she saying?" Sebastian asked. I didn't want to break her thought, so I just waved him off.

"He did not look Taiwanese."

Could it be? I willed myself to stay quiet, but my hands tightened around my purse.

"He had brown hair and green eyes. Have you seen a Taiwanese person with green eyes?" she asked, sitting a bit straighter and looking me in the eyes. A bit of her spunk was back, and I felt a touch of relief knowing that she was going to be okay. "He wanted to stay and help me with my vegetables. I let him for six months. Did not ask any questions. During that time, I noticed he liked to draw, so I brought him to the city and made him pick out art supplies. He was very scared going into the city. I do not know why. He wanted to leave as soon as he could. He never went back with me again and made me buy supplies for him if he ran out. Let me show you something."

She motioned for us to stay seated while she got up and walked into another room. I used the time she was gone to update Sebastian, who had been impatiently waiting for me to translate.

When she returned, she was holding two canvases. Not big. Maybe a couple of feet by three feet. They were framed on the front and unfinished on the back. Sebastian and I were both wowed by the first one when she turned it around. The man had talent. It was a picture of the house we were in but with a younger version of the lady in front of us.

When she turned the second one around, we gasped. It was the same scene as the first one but in so much more detail. Every crack in the house, every angle of the woman, the different hues of the house, the surrounding greenery. Everything popped in this picture, and I touched it to make sure that what I was seeing was really paint and not a print.

"It's beautiful," I said.

"Yes, he had a lot of talent. I told him he had to do more, and I began taking them to the city to sell to my customers. He started believing he could paint and be a part of the world again. On the day he left, he gave me this one as a gift," she said, holding up the first painting. This second one came in the mail many years later. You see his signature here?" she asked, pointing to the bottom right-hand corner.

"That's a plum blossom!" Sebastian said before I could utter a word.

"What did he say?" she asked.

"He said it's a mei hua," I translated.

"Yes. Yes. He insisted on using that as his signature. Never his actual name. I tried to make him change it. Why would he use such a common flower instead of his beautiful name? I could never figure it out."

Sebastian and I exchanged a look but kept silent. If the lady didn't know, there was no need to share. It might crumple her, and she looked to be in her eighties. But why would Harrison be using a plum blossom? Did he know about Rose and Anthony?

"I gave him this book to record his first sale. He put us as his first one even though he would never accept any money from us. I never saw him again after he left except for an occasional letter. Let me see if I can find them."

She disappeared again and came back shortly with a box. "You may take them. I am old and it will be nice for me to know that they are with someone who cares about him too."

I could see Sebastian sucking in his breath at the sight of more things to read, but inside I was jumping for joy. They would hold more details to discover. Coming here today was quite the find. I couldn't help but think that it was meant to be.

We spent the rest of the afternoon following Po Po around the property and seeing the extent of her farm. It was on the side of a mountain, and at times we had to cross a plank that was not secured in any fashion to get to a patch of farmland. Sebastian and I had a blast. We declined her offer to stay for dinner and headed back to the city.

This day had been the best, for both of us. Sebastian and I had gone out and had fun, and I had also found out more information about my uncle. There was nothing to worry about. I could balance our relationship and my mission just fine.

That night, when Sebastian went to bed, I made myself comfortable on the sofa and opened the journal.

Tuesday, August 12, 1947

She's met someone. A Taiwanese boy. My heart is breaking. I thought I knew better, but something inside me must have been holding out hope. I can't let Rose go, but I have to. She's moving on and deserves better, and I'll keep doing what I can to help her.

Friday, September 26, 1947

What is going on? Do I have to lose her again? First, she is forced to leave here, then she finds someone else to love, and now she's physically leaving the city?

I broke my promise to Josephine and made her tell me what was going on. Thankfully, Josephine, being the polite woman she is, did not tell me to leave immediately. She told me Rose was getting married to Charlie. She, herself, had reunited with an old beau, someone named David. She also said that she and David were going to move with Charlie and Rose to Astoria by the end of the month. She had decided to keep the bakery open a little bit longer during the transition, but they would no longer be in Portland anymore.

This was not what I wanted to hear. I had gotten used to seeing Rose from time to time, and even though I couldn't be with her, I liked to know and see that she was doing okay. Which, given Josephine's news, I guess she is. I hate admitting that, because without my help, it's clear that Rose is going to be fine.

Monday, September 29, 1947

I made Josephine give me their new address because I want to send a wedding gift to Rose. I don't know what that will be yet.

Thursday, October 16, 1947

Cook once again came to the rescue. She had plates that Lady Mary was discarding, and hence, had said Cook could have them. Apparently, they were out of fashion and she was getting new ones. How I wish I had that kind of money to just throw away perfectly good items whenever I wanted. But that's not the point right now. Cook said that I could have the plates as a wedding gift to Rose from us both. They came with utensils and matching cups and saucers. I had been racking my brain on what to get them since most of my money was going to my family. I knew Taiwanese people liked to give each other money in red envelopes, and I had one of those with some money I had saved in there, but I didn't want to just give Rose money. It was too impersonal, but the plates, they would be a fantastic gift.

Saturday, November 1, 1947

I received a note from Josephine today. She said my gift was very thoughtful and that she will pass it along to Rose—without telling Rose who it was from. She told me that Rose and Charlie are doing wonderfully, and that Rose is due any day now. It's good to know she is happy.

Saturday, November 22, 1947

Rose has a son! She has a son! Who looks like Anthony! At least that's what Josephine's letter said. With green eyes, brown hair, and skin that was pale. I don't know if I should be excited for her or scared that he looks so much like his father. Hopefully no one ever makes the connection. I have the first week of December off, so I think I might go to Astoria . . . . No one would need to know. It's not that far away. Only a couple of hours.

Saturday, December 6, 1947

I have to say that the resemblance between the boy and Anthony is uncanny. I meant to only stroll by the bakery and catch a glimpse of them. I know, stupid idea, but instead, I saw Josephine, who was not happy to see me. She gave me a big lecturing, but in the end she let me meet Harrison.

She had sent Rose and Charlie away for the day for some time off together while she looked after Harrison. I could tell she was smitten. I was, too, to tell you the truth. I couldn't get over how similar the boy was to Anthony. My heart broke a bit knowing that he would never know his father or any of his family on that side. I wonder if Astoria is far enough away to allow them to live a life without interference from Portland? The fact that Anthony still doesn't know he has a son baffles me.

Monday, January 26, 1948

Oh no! Why did I think going to Astoria was a good idea? Josephine took pity on me. She has been keeping me updated on Rose and Harrison, but her last letter was very disturbing. She said someone had come asking about Harrison. Asking if his father is Caucasian and if he's from Port-land. Thank goodness Josephine is stubborn. She stood her ground, claiming that Charlie was his father and that the man should leave. Clearly, Harrison is mixed, but the guy must have bought it because Josephine said he hasn't been back. I never put my return address on my letters, so the only thing I can think of is that someone followed me to Astoria.

How could I be so stupid?

Saturday, February 21, 1948

Last week was Valentine's Day and Josephine said someone broke into the bakery. Rose, Charlie, Josephine, and David had gone out for dinner while a neighbor had taken care of Harrison. Thank goodness for that because the person who had broken in didn't take anything. They seemed to have gone straight to the baby room and thrown all the sheets from the crib on the floor. Sheets from the other rooms had been tossed off the beds, too, almost as if they'd thought the baby would be hiding. I am horrified that someone would be after Harrison, because once again, it's my fault.

Saturday, March 13, 1948

They're leaving! Rose is leaving the States! This last note from Josephine has hurt me more than the rest. Josephine said that someone tried to kidnap Harrison. Apparently they beat up Charlie when he was out on a walk with Harrison, and then tried to take the baby. Thank goodness there were a couple of people around who saved Harrison from being taken. But because of the incident, Rose and Charlie are moving to Taiwan!

This means that I won't be able to see Rose again. I won't get to see Harrison grow up. How did what started as a fantastic job opportunity with the Wilkens turn into this? I'm heartbroken.

I took the day off and wandered down a hiking trail. I had no idea where I actually went, I just went to a place I've gone many times before and started walking. The guilt just keeps piling on.

Saturday, March 27, 1948

I got another letter from Josephine. She said Rose and Charlie have changed their mind. They are now staying in Astoria, but Harrison will be going to Taiwan. I thought that was ludicrous. Why would Rose be separated from her son? But I realized Rose was a lot less selfish than the rest of us. She had resumed sending money to her parents again, both of whom were still working in the garment factory. Rose knew that she could make more money in the States and moving to Taiwan would not be financially smart. However, the baby was going to live with Charlie's parents. He would still be with family. Rose thought that by sending him to Taiwan, Harrison would be harder for Anthony or his family to track down.

All because I couldn't keep my mouth shut. Apparently Harrison is going to stay with Charlie's family in Hong Kong first and then they'll find a way to get him into Taiwan. Rose must be devastated. He's only five months old. He won't remember them. What have I done?

There was another note from Anthony in the side of the notebook. It read:

This is where Andy's story ends and Mary's picks up. Mary is very closed off, but I know she means well, and after all these years I can only believe that she wants to let go of this burden. I hope she shares her story with you.

I was bawling and the tears were flowing freely down my face, so much so that I couldn't read anymore. I now understood what Andy had been carrying this whole time, and how he could be smiling when he passed away. A great burden had indeed been lifted. From what I had found in Taiwan so far, Harrison had gotten to Taiwan and had made a life here. But why had he left?

CHAPTER 14

"Did you stay up all night?"

I looked up to see Sebastian looming over me. I felt stiff and could barely move my neck.

"What?" It was all I could manage.

"You fell asleep on the floor, Anne," Sebastian said, lending me a hand to get up. "How many letters are there?"

I looked down to see the opened envelopes scattered all around the spot where I had been sleeping.

"Oh . . . um . . . a hundred?"

"A hundred?" Sebastian exclaimed.

"But I haven't read any of them yet. I just looked at the addresses." Why was I defending myself?

"Addresses! Of course, you can go to the return address and find your uncle there—mystery solved."

"It's not that easy. The return addresses are all from different places. It looks like he didn't stay in one place for very long."

"Then, please tell me you're not planning to read through every single one of them?"

I turned to look at him, wondering if he was serious. "Of course I am. Why wouldn't I?"

"Because it'll take you days and I won't see you during that time."

"And what about all that time you were working in Portland and I didn't see you for weeks?"

"Really? That's where this is going? I couldn't . . ." Sebastian let out a loud groan and punched the air behind him. "You know I can't tell you what I've been working on. You know I would spend time with you if I could."

"What could be so important that you can't share it with me? Huh?"

"You wouldn't understand," Sebastian groaned again.

Now, I was really on fire. This was the same argument we'd had at home. To have it here where he was supposed to be supporting me made it even more infuriating.

Before I could say another word, Sebastian held up his hands in surrender. "Look, I don't want to fight. You know I support you. I had a lot of fun with you yesterday and was hoping we could do more of the same while here." He took a deep breath, this time changing the subject. "Tell me about what you read in the journal last night."

"How did you know . . .?"

"The journal is open and you drooled on it," he said, pointing to the wet blob on the last entry I had read. "And looks like you looked at the other journal too. The one from the safe deposit box."

I blushed, my anger sweeping away to be replaced by embarrassment. "You want to hear about what I read?"

"Yes, I want to hear. I do love you, Anne. I'm annoyed but it doesn't mean that I don't care."

"It's nice to hear you say that." Letting loose a breath, I said, "Yes, the other journal is Mary's but I've only glanced at it. Andy's journal was interesting. I just learned that

Harrison went to live with Charlie's family, even though he was only five months old. By himself! What mom lets their son go live somewhere else? I'm dreading to read the journal I found in the safe deposit box. There are so many secrets. What if something bad happened to him and that's why Aunt Mary doesn't want us to find out more about him? What if it's all because she's protecting us?"

"Whoa," Sebastian said, laughing. "You're working yourself up for nothing. Like I said before, he's probably living a perfectly nice life and you and Aunt Mary are worrying for nothing." He paused to make sure I was listening. "Anne, I'm here for you. I just really want to have some fun times with you while we're here." By this time his arms were around me and I loved the feel of his chest at my back. His musky scent relaxed me even more and I realized how ridiculous I was being by picking fights with him.

"I thought we could go check out the Gong Guan neighborhood. I heard it's a happening place," Sebastian continued. I could hear the happiness in his voice and I found myself getting annoyed at him again because it was such a quick change of subject. My reasonable side told me to stay quiet, that I should be glad that he was happy and there was nothing to read into.

Sebastian must have taken my silence as consent because he then said, "I'll let Ah Yi know we're going and maybe she'll meet us there. We could talk about the road trip we want to do. She seemed interested in taking us."

Pushing aside my angst, I forced a lightness to my tone. "That sounds fantastic, Sebastian."

Sebastian appeared to have gotten his spirit back at the thought that we were going to go exploring whereas, I, on the other hand, was still a bit annoyed.

We met up with Ming-Yue at Gong Guan, and sure enough the place was hopping. There was just as many people here as there had been near Taipei 101, but in a different way. Here, it wasn't just businessmen or tourists, but there were also tons of students everywhere. The subway dumped us right in front of National Taiwan University, otherwise known as NTU, and Ming-Yue met us at the entrance.

"How has your stay been?" she asked.

"It's been good. We're really happy to be out and about again," Sebastian said, a little too cheerily for my liking.

"That's good to hear. I'm sorry for the way my mama has been." And that was all Ming-Yue said. It suddenly dawned on me that she would know my uncle. I don't know how I had missed that. I was about to ask her about him when bells started chiming.

"Those are the bells from NTU," Ming-Yue said. "They signal the time and the change between classes."

"It's nice to hear that some things are universal," Sebastian said, putting an arm around me and dropping a kiss on the top of my head. I leaned toward him, holding his hand, and we walked onto campus. For a second, I thought I was at Stanford. I'd never attended Stanford, but I knew that Stanford University had a long walkway lined with palm trees, and here I was on the opposite side of the world looking down a long walkway also lined with palm trees. It was like Sebastian had said—some things were universal. I instantly felt at home.

Sebastian and I strolled down the walkway in silence, soaking everything in around us. On either side of us were super old buildings that must have been here when the school was built.

"NTU was founded in 1928 when Taiwan was still under Japanese rule. The building in front of us is the main library,"

Ming-Yue said. My heart rate started racing and Sebastian laughed next to me.

"You just said the one word that makes Anne the happiest person alive," he said.

Ming-Yue raised a brow. "What is that?"

"Library. We should go have a look because I know you won't be able to focus on anything else until you've seen it," Sebastian said, squeezing my hand.

The library was old but modernized and filled with books in Chinese. I felt disappointed. The library was one of the original buildings on campus. Due to its facade, I had held this glorified image of a charming old library with vaulted ceilings, gilded banisters, and old wooden shelves that reached so high that you had to use a ladder to reach the books. But this was not the case. It looked like any other library that I would have walked into in the States. I realized that the grand libraries I had been to, or seen pictures of, were all in Europe, and I reminded myself that I needed to focus my travels on Asia in the future.

Sebastian must have noticed my disappointment because he started steering me out of the library and I didn't pull back. Once outside, I reset my emotions and told myself to enjoy our time out. I was so on edge with what I wanted to do. Part of me wanted to be with Sebastian and explore, have fun, and enjoy our trip. The information I would gather would be awesome for my blog. But the other part of me just wanted to hunker down and research everything I could until I found my uncle.

"Are you doing okay, Anne?" Ming-Yue asked.

"I'm fine, just disappointed," I said. I told her my feelings about the library.

"The library was renovated in the nineties, so that might be part of the reason," Ming-Yue offered.

"Well, I'm glad we aren't in there because that could have

been hours lost," Sebastian said, shooting me a smirk. "I think we should go grab something to eat. You haven't eaten anything this morning."

"Food is a good idea," I said to him. I turned back to Ming-Yue to add, "I just have a lot on my mind and I would actually like to go back into the library to read some of Mary's journal."

"Ah Yi, can I talk to Anne, privately?" Sebastian asked.

"Of course. I will walk ahead and scout out food choices."

As Ming-Yue walked on ahead, Sebastian pulled me back and we watched in silence as the students rushed back and forth across campus. I wished I was back in university. Life was so much simpler. The only thing to worry about were classes and when we were going to meet up with friends for food or a movie. And Brian . . . he would have liked being here. I immediately felt guilty thinking about him when Sebastian was walking right next to me.

"You can't stop thinking about your uncle, can you?"

"No. I try but I can't let it go." *I hope he hasn't noticed how warm my face is.*

"I'm really not trying to make your life miserable by dragging you around when you don't want to."

"I know that, Sebastian. I know. I'm sorry, I've been so grumpy. I just . . ." I trailed off, not knowing what to add.

"We should compromise. Instead of doing both—searching for your uncle and exploring—let's each do one thing at a time. After all, we're grown adults. We don't have to do everything together all the time and we can share our experience with one another each night. That doesn't mean I don't want to spend time with you here, but maybe it'll give you some time to research your uncle while I go explore things for us to do later. What do you think?"

It felt like a huge burden had been lifted from my shoulders and I could breathe again. "Sebastian, I would love that. But what will you do?"

"I was going to ask Ah Yi if she could show me around. Plus, maybe she can teach me some Mandarin too," he said with a smirk.

I didn't know how much I had missed that smirk. "You are amazing, you know that?" I said, stopping in the middle of the road to give him a kiss.

"Yeah, I know," he said.

We walked a bit faster after that. I felt like there was a bounce in my step now that we had sorted through the tension between us. We caught up to Ming-Yue, only to realize that we were now at the back of the campus, and right in front of us was none other than Starbucks.

"Oh, I have to go and get a coffee," Sebastian said, pulling me along past Ming-Yue.

"It's like you haven't had the chance to get coffee until now," I said, laughing.

"This is familiar, though. It'll be extra good because it's Starbucks."

I felt so lighthearted now that I couldn't help but laugh. When we entered Starbucks, I saw Sebastian relax. This was a place he could relate to. Somewhere he could let his guard down. We walked up to the counter and as he was about to order, I felt some tension return in his arm.

"It's all in Chinese," he murmured.

"Well . . ."

"Don't say it."

I watched as he took deep breaths, calming himself down. We looked at the menu and I wasn't sure if they had the same drinks that we were used to. There was only one way to find out.

"Could I have a Caramel Frappuccino?" I asked, mixing both Mandarin and English.

"What size?" the cashier asked in Mandarin.

Well, that was easy. "Tall."

Sebastian ordered his own drink, and the lady replied in perfect English. I felt him relax again. This is where I should have taken him earlier in the week.

Drinks in hand, the three of us walked down the accompanying ally. It looked like a road but narrower. Lined on both sides were restaurants and fresh fruit groceries. These weren't restaurants like Olive Garden or Chipotle, these were one-room holes about the size of a one or two-car garage. A typical one would have a sign over the door letting you know its name, a garage door size opening to walk through, a small kitchen in the front where you watched them cook and ordered your food, and five or six tables in the back. Also, they only focused on one type of food and not just Taiwanese, American, Italian, Greek, etc., but dumplings only, a handful of breakfast items, marinated pork with buns, tapioca drinks, or fruit drinks. Every single restaurant had their own specialty. Then there were the Western restaurants. Owned and cooked by Taiwanese people, but decorated like a Western restaurant. These ones had colorful signage on the outside, and everything on the inside matched the marketing theme of the cuisine.

Sebastian was so excited to see non-Taiwanese food that we ended up at a Mediterranean restaurant. There were four tables inside and they served me one of the best gyros wrap I'd ever had. I felt guilty that I was surprised; I had gotten stuck in one type of thinking. Of course, anyone could learn to cook any cuisine if they put their mind to it. It was a good lesson to learn.

Halfway through lunch, Sebastian said, "Ah Yi, would you be willing to show me around? Anne and I were talking about giving her some time to research Harrison more while I scout out places for us to visit."

"I'd be glad to. Anne, when did you want to do your research?" she asked in Mandarin.

"I was hoping that I could do that now, after lunch. I could hang out in NTU and read more of the journals."

"And I'd like to see more of the area we're in," Sebastian said. "Are you familiar with this area, Ah Yi? I'd like to walk around here a little more and learn what's what."

"Yes, we can do that," she said.

"Great, then we have a plan," I said, feeling happier than I had this morning.

"I'm glad to see you happy again. I don't like seeing you down," Sebastian said, giving me a hug.

"Thanks. I really mean it," I replied, leaning in for a kiss.

All of a sudden, Sebastian jolted back. "Oh yes, I almost forgot. The road trip. Ah Yi, you had mentioned that you'd be willing to take us on a road trip. Could we still take you up on that?"

"Yes. Yes. I want to take you and Anne to see the east coast. It is very beautiful."

"That would be fantastic. What do you think, Anne?"

"I'd love that too," I said, and I meant it. I was going to be able to find my uncle and go on a road trip. It was going to be a win win. I couldn't wait to get started.

"We can talk more about the road trip later," Ming-Yue said. "Why don't we let Anne go and study?"

"Yes, let's do that. I'm ready to go and explore too," Sebastian said, already standing up.

"All right, we have a plan. Let's go."

With that, we went back to the library. From there, Sebastian and Ming-Yue continued down the long walkway, back to the campus entrance while I entered the library, itching to read the next part in the journal.

CHAPTER 15

I FOUND A QUIET NOOK IN THE CORNER. I PULLED out Mary's journal from my bag and looked at the cover for a bit. It was a paper notebook, only about half a centimeter thick, a typical-sized school or work notebook. There was nothing special about it. I could probably go into a store right now and purchase one. Actually, that wasn't a bad idea. I'd been wanting to stock up on some of these notebooks. They were thin, spread flat, and would be awesome to travel with. I made a note to stop by the school store and purchase a couple of notebooks for myself.

I found neat handwriting covering the pages, every word in its place. Not one word was crossed out, and there wasn't any white-out as far as I could see. The few times I'd tried to keep a journal, I had crossed out so many thoughts that you couldn't decipher what was kept and what was not.

I was itching to hear more of Mary's side of the story. I wondered what had happened. What had made her not want to tell us where Harrison was? I hoped he wasn't dead already. That would be devastating after all this searching.

Left alone in the quiet room, I finally opened the journal and started reading.

37年4月7日 (Wednesday, April 7, 1948)

Rose and Charlie are here! I am so excited! Just out of the blue too. Well, at least for me. My parents didn't seem to be too surprised. I was so excited to see her and Charlie. Charlie teased me about hugging him. It was an American custom he never picked up, and I in turn gave him the biggest hug. Rose, of course, gave me one right back. It was so good to see both of them after these last six months. And they brought Harrison with them. He is the cutest! He won't let me hold him yet, but I'll win him over. It doesn't help that Rose won't let him go most of the time either, but I'll win her over too.

37年4月23日 (Friday, April 23, 1948)

This isn't happening! What are my parents thinking? We've had the best times with Rose and Charlie here, but it all turned bad on Wednesday. Rose and Charlie returned home tonight, but they left Harrison behind! That's right— they brought their five-month-old baby and left him here! Ah! There it is again: The sound of a crying baby echoing in every corner in this two-bedroom place. I am already under a pile of pillows on my bed and I can still hear him. I love Rose, but this is a bit much, isn't it? What had happened for her to send her five-month-old son all the way to Hong Kong so that his grandparents could take care of him?

Mama, Baba, Charlie, and Rose had come to an agreement that it was for the best that Harrison would never know who his real parents were. Here in our family, he would be son number five. I missed Charlie, so at first, I told myself that this would be like having a mini-Charlie around. I would have another brother to play with. But the incessant crying—it's torture. My parents are exhausted and so am I. I'm supposed to be enjoying life, not babysitting, because who's watching him when my parents are working? Me. Me. Me. But as much as I want to be mad at Harrison, I can't stay mad at him. He's so cute and cuddly at times—when he's not crying. He's curious about everything. His eyes follow every movement on the street, be it a vehicle, a person, or an animal. We stand on the side of the road just staring at all the cars that are going by. We go on walks for hours. One of his favorite things to do is hang out in front of our convenience store. And there, I can at least sit inside and watch him.

Being the sixth kid in the family, my parents don't really watch over him all that much. It's me that's worried for his safety. The crying at night is torture though, and no amount of shushing, rocking, or singing will calm him down. It's terrifying to hear in the middle of the night. Thank goodness none of the neighbors have said anything, though I'm sure they are talking amongst themselves about how inappropriate it is that my parents would have another kid at such an old age. Very irresponsible of them. I've been asked more than a few times where this kid came from, or if he's mine, but we just hand Harrison over and have him cuddle in their arms and change the subject. It's hard to stop the questions though, because he looks so different. He doesn't look like a Taiwanese person at all, and he has the most beautiful green eyes I've ever seen. Not that I've seen many green eyes, but they remind me of the blue eyes I saw on all the students in the States. His hair is an obvious light brown, which in itself sets him apart since we all have black hair. And when his hair is in the sun, there are streaks of yellow and red in it. It's the oddest thing and I can't help but stare at it and touch it.

I don't know how he's going to get through life here,

looking so different. Our neighbors are opinionated and the students at school will be too. I feel sorry for him. Harrison should be home with his own mama and baba. Nothing should be so terrible that he needs to be separated from them. I disagree with this whole arrangement, but I'll help him however I can. I do love him. He is my nephew after all.

37年5月18日 (Tuesday, May 18, 1948)

This isn't going to work—saying he's Mama and Baba's fifth son. He just looks too different. His skin also burns a lot easier too. I have to make sure that he's in long sleeves and pants when we leave the house. And wearing a hat. The neighbors are talking more as well.

37年6月4日 (Friday, June 4, 1948)

I might have a way to make this okay. But I don't like it.

37年6月5日 (Saturday, June 5, 1948)

I'll tell you my plan first. I can be Harrison's Mama. Mama and Baba are too busy and too old to be his parents, and the store is suffering because they are so tired. I think we should move back to Taiwan and say he's my son from a white boyfriend. Second Oldest Brother can help with the store. Yeah, I don't like this idea at all.

37年6月6日 (Sunday, June 6, 1948)

Mama and Baba need a break. They should be in Taiwan where they can see their family. Harrison needs a mama. I should be the one who sacrifices my life. I've put Mama and Baba through enough in America. Trying to fit in and be American almost ruined my family.

37年6月7日 (Monday, June 7, 1948)

I did it. I told Mama and Baba my plan. They were

surprised, but I've really grown up since living in America. They didn't want me to say he's my son, something about me being too young, but after many hours, I persuaded them to agree to my plan. They couldn't think of another explanation for having Harrison with us. Plus, it's not like I have anyone else to hang out with, and Harrison is already attached to me. We're moving back to Taiwan.

37年6月11日 (Friday, June 11, 1948)

It's the dragon boat festival. As it's our last big holiday in Hong Kong, we took Harrison to see a dragon boat race. I think he's traumatized for life. I can't help laughing though. Mama and Baba thought he'd love it. According to them, all of their kids loved going to see the dragon boats. The cheering, the drums, and the artistry of the boats is magical. Nothing compares. But all of that seemed to scare Harrison, and we ended up having to leave early.

37年8月1日 (Sunday, August 1, 1948)

We've been back in Taiwan for two weeks now. I don't think I've stopped moving since we made the decision to move back here. I'm either working, packing, doing schoolwork, or taking care of Harrison. I had to write today in my journal though, because he called me Mama today! He called me Mama. I almost cried. This little boy has lost his parents, his whole life, and he calls me Mama! How I'm deserving of this title, I don't know, but he clearly must not remember his real mama. I spend most of the day with him. He also calls Mama and Baba, Ah Po and Ah Gung. I can't help but love him.

We went to the beach today. Harrison loved it. Xi Shin Twan is my second favorite place in the whole world and Taroko is my favorite. Maybe I'll take Harrison there, too, when he's older. He would love it. Today, we picked up rocks and threw them in the water. He was fascinated as only a child can be by all the different shapes, colors, and shades; especially of how the rocks changed colors when they were wet versus when they were dry. Little details that I had stopped thinking about a long time ago and now just took for granted. If only we could hang on to more of this innocence.

We played tag with the waves, him giggling the whole time. I could listen to him laugh all day long. The pure joy that comes out of him. I want to protect Harrison from the people who make comments about him—the ones who come over to visit Mama and Baba and talk about his light hair and his other differences as if it was a disease. I can't bear seeing and hearing him treated differently. I remember how that felt when we lived in America—to feel like an outsider. I will protect him no matter what.

37年11月1日 (Monday, November 1, 1948)

The boy can eat! If we didn't own our own convenience store, I don't know how we'd feed him. He's almost one and we've started to let him eat rice. He's eaten two bowls of rice, some lamb, steamed egg, and more rice today. He loves mashed up apples and bananas. He calls me Mama all the time now. I haven't the heart to correct him. He needs someone to be his mama. I hear people talking to my parents and whispering when I walk by. The rumor going around is that I'm the mama, and Harrison has a white baba; that I got in trouble, and my parents had to bring me home. None of us are doing anything to correct the rumor. No one would believe us anyway. They would think we were just trying to hide the truth.

37年12月14日 (Tuesday, December 14, 1948)

How does a little one so small run so fast? Harrison went from standing to waddling to walking in one month! I almost lost him in the market today. The old ladies love him. They're always trying to entice him with treats. It's all I can do to make sure he doesn't eat everything. Sometimes I don't even know what they give him.

The market is my favorite place to go. We attend regularly as Baba has a stall there. The smell of fresh meat is enticing. Unlike in America, the open markets are more common here. I can imagine my friends in America would not like what they saw here. It might be considered unsanitary in their view. Or maybe they'd be intrigued. I hope it is the latter.

Harrison and I like walking through the market every day. I help Baba set up in the morning before I go to school. Harrison helps, too, by placing everything I've done in a different pile. As a result, I have to do everything twice. It gets frustrating, but the older ladies in the other stalls play with him and I think they enjoy his company.

We have buckets of fish and rows of fresh vegetables. Sometimes Baba will have sweets too. Fresh pulled taffy and buns with red bean in them—whatever friend he has met recently who happens to have a surplus. They'll give them to Baba to sell. It really takes a community to survive. I appreciate this more and more every day. I have evening classes now. No more going out with friends. Not that I have any. Plus, between Baba's shop, taking care of Harrison, and trying to finish school, I'm done at the end of the day. I just want to crawl into bed and disappear from the world.

The next entry was five years later. I took a break and wondered what it would be like to raise a child. Mary, who hadn't even finished high school was basically taking care of a one-year-old. I don't know if I could have done it. There would be no freedom to go out and have fun, although, I had to admit that I didn't really do that to begin with. But all the extra time I read, traveled, did whatever I wanted—it would have been out the window.

My mind wandered to Sebastian. Did he want kids? Would I want to have kids with him? I think he'd be horrified if he knew I was asking those questions.

Swallowing, I turned back to the journal.

42年8月10日 (Monday, August 10, 1953)

Mama and Baba say Harrison has to go to school. He's five and needs to be with kids his own age. His whole world has just been us to this point. He has spent each day at the store with Mama and Baba until I get out of school. Now that I think about it, I have no idea how I got any of my homework done these past four and a half years. Good thing I wasn't big on hanging out with other people. Though, I might have stunted him in the social area. Maybe it's my fault he's so quiet. I should have taken him out more and made friends with local kids his age. Then maybe he would have been more accepted.

Round and round my mind goes. What I could have done, what I shouldn't have done, how mad at Rose and Charlie I am for dumping Harrison at our doorstep—at my doorstep. Of course, then I feel guilty for feeling like that because I love Rose and Charlie. I wish they were close by. Why couldn't they just live here? Why stay in America?

I don't know how Harrison will do in school. Ever since I finished high school two years ago, I've been trying to get my teaching certificate so I can be an English teacher. I've also been tutoring on the side and working at our store. You would think I'd be glad he is going to school, because now I'll have time to focus on my own work and maybe even go to college. But I'm scared for him. How will the other kids treat him?

42年9月11日 (Friday, September 11, 1953)

Harrison has had two weeks of school and it's gone better than I thought, though I still hold him at least once a week while he cries himself to sleep. He's upset because he looks so different from everyone else.

Harrison came home after his first day of school with a sad face, one I'd never seen before. I took him out for shaved ice, and we got all his favorite toppings: red beans, green beans, mochi, lots of syrup, and grass jelly. He was quiet the whole time we walked around the park. Then he told me what had happened at school. He was assigned to the back of the classroom amongst the other boys. The teacher had separated the girls and the boys onto either side of the room, and he had realized that he was without his family for the first time.

I was nervous for him. To say I was more nervous might have been an understatement, and I could tell he was trying not to cry. It made me realize that he was still so small. I picked him up and put him on my lap and just held him until he finished crying. Then he told me the kids would come up to him and call him names when the teachers weren't around. They would touch his hair when he was walking around outside, and he said it made him feel uncomfortable. He didn't know why they were doing it. At this, he looked at me with his big, round American eyes, and at the time I didn't know what to say. How was I to explain to a five-year-old that they were doing that because he looked different? That they were ganging up against the one person who didn't look like them? He made them uncomfortable because he was not part of their known world, and he was struggling to show them that he was just like them. How was I to explain all of that to him? I couldn't, because I hadn't known how to deal with it myself when I lived in America. So, I just held him until he stopped crying.

Mama made his favorite dinner of lamb with green onions that night, but he never smiled that day. It broke my heart. The second week was a little better. Not by much, but we were getting used to the new routine. His teacher wasn't horrible, but she didn't see what the other kids did to Harrison, and he was too nervous to tell her.

42年9月16日 (Wednesday, September 16, 1953)

Having lived in the US, and been the one who was different, I get very upset when people make fun of Harrison. Mama and Baba say I have to let it go, it's just how life is and people here don't know any better. But they can learn! They could keep their mouth shut. Keep their comments to themselves. But that's not how the people are here. They like to gossip. They like to point out what's different. I admit, most are not being mean, but I still can't help thinking that they shouldn't say such things to begin with, or they should just show some love to Harrison. After all, that's all he wants: to be loved and accepted. Isn't that what anyone wants? I just don't understand people.

42年9月25日 (Friday, September 25, 1953)

An angel arrived this week. Mei-Jing was new to the area and it was her first time in school too. I could tell something had changed when Harrison came home today, smiling. We hadn't seen that sweet smile in a long time. She was in his class. He said she didn't see his brown hair, green eyes, or pale skin, but would play with him and sit next to him at circle time. At such a young age, maybe she didn't see the difference? I wonder if she feels some sort of bond with him?

42年10月2日 (Friday, October 2, 1953)

Mei-Jing is an angel. Mama and Baba think I'm crazy, but I know she is. She is the sweetest kid I have ever known, and

I know a lot of them now. She stands up for Harrison when someone tries to pick on him. I asked her today why she is attached to Harrison. She said she used to be teased. Her baba told her she needed to stand up for herself, and so he taught her how to punch. That gave me an idea. Harrison could learn Kung Fu. Second Oldest Brother worked at a Kung Fu studio. This is only a thought, but maybe I could start taking Kung Fu classes too? Harrison and I could both join. Because after what happened in America, I want to learn too.

42年10月3日 (Saturday, October 3, 1953)

Mama and Baba like my idea, but Baba said he could only afford to send Harrison to Kung Fu classes, and only because it was out of necessity. But someone has to escort him there and back so I could learn something from the side. Plus, someone has to practice with Harrison. Second Oldest Brother worked it out so that Harrison would have private lessons with one of the younger Sifus, Zhang Liang-Chun, twice a week until he was older and could defend himself. In exchange, Liang-Chun's family would get a discount at our store.

42年10月30日 (Friday, October 30, 1953)

Harrison is fighting us on learning Kung Fu. He doesn't like it when Liang-Chun comes at him. I don't blame him. Liang-Chun is hard on him, and if I didn't know Liang-Chun, I would think he didn't like Harrison because of how different he looks. But I know Liang-Chun. He is the cutest boy I know. We went to elementary school together before we were separated into all girl and all boy schools. I remember having a crush on him. He came to my defense once when one of our classmates was being mean. He lives nearby and his baba is a doctor. That in itself makes all the girls want him as his family has a lot of money, whereas the rest of us are sometimes living day to day.

We never really talked, but we knew of each other. Whenever I see him, he's always with a group of girls. Being his girlfriend has always been a daydream of mine, but a small store owner's daughter, and one that was known as the 'teacher's pet' (another term I picked up in America), was not a match for a boy who was handsome, came from a well-to-do family, was popular in school with the students and the teachers, and is a really good Kung Fu teacher.

42年12月18日 (Friday, December 18, 1953)

Harrison is getting better at Kung Fu, and Liang-Chun is really making him work for his next belt. He's not getting teased as much anymore, and Mei-Jing is still sticking next to his side. Mei-Jing wanted an English name like Harrison so I gave her the name Grace. I think it fits her very well. Life is getting a little better for us all.

42年12月28日 (Monday, December 28, 1953)

Liang-Chun asked me out! Okay, he asked Harrison if he wanted to get a rice roll after practice but he invited me too. The three of us went to the shop around the corner and picked up some fresh rice rolls with ground meat in the middle. They were so delicious, but we could have eaten stinky tofu and I still would have loved it.

He's funny. Harrison has really taken to him and I can tell he looks up to Liang-Chun.

While we were eating the rice rolls, Liang-Chun said he'd like to take Harrison to Taipei for a competition. He said that Harrison is only six and will be the smallest one there, but Liang-Chun says he's a natural. I'm nervous for him. Liang-Chun says it's just to let him see others fight, that he's not really going to compete, but he's set up an unofficial event within the actual event for Harrison to compete against another kid who's six. There's not a lot of people here who do Kung Fu, and this will let him see who he could become if he keeps practicing. I think it's good just to get Harrison out into a different environment for a bit, but I'm still nervous. He is only just starting to adjust. And I'll admit here, but nowhere else, that I'm a little nervous to be traveling with Liang-Chun too. We'll be sitting in the same train all the way to Taipei . . . we'll be in the same train!

"Anne?"

I answered absentmindedly without looking up, "Oh hi. Did you have a good time exploring?" As I asked the question, I was pulling myself up out of the chair while simultaneously leaning down to pick up my bag. When Sebastian didn't answer, I looked up and saw someone I didn't think I'd ever see again: Brian. He was standing there, looking as handsome as ever.

For a moment I just stared, wondering if all my thoughts about him had manifested his presence. In that one movement of grabbing my bag, I missed it completely and my body began to tip over.

"Whoa, are you okay?" he asked, coming to my rescue before I could slam into the floor.

The feel of his hands on my arm sent sparks all the way to my chest, and I cursed myself for still having feelings for him. I straightened up and shook my arm so that he let go of it.

"You okay?" he asked again.

"Yes, thank you for saving me," I said, trying to gather my composure.

"It's funny to bump into you, Anne, and here of all places. It's good to see you." I could feel myself blushing under his gaze and cursed myself again. I have a boyfriend, Brian dumped me, I reminded myself.

"Funny, isn't it?" I tried to say but it came out as more of a half laugh.

"What brings you here? You finally making your Asia trip? Going to other countries?"

"How do you know about that?"

"I read your blogs."

"You do?" I asked, a bit shocked that he would read my work.

"Yeah, they're rather good. I actually took your advice on how to pack and travel light."

"You did?" I was gob smacked. He'd been following my blog. I felt flattered and guilty all at the same time. Would things have worked out if I had been a bit different? Was he looking to get back together again? I have a boyfriend! And I love him! What in the world was I thinking? But I couldn't get the thoughts out of my head. They rooted me to the floor and rendered me speechless.

"Well, it was nice to see you," Brian said while he made to walk away.

"Wait." Why didn't I just let him walk away? I pushed the thought aside as I asked hurriedly, "What are you doing in Taiwan? You'd never shown interest in coming here before. I mean, I know you came with your family growing up, but you seemed like you were happy to let it go." Wow, I couldn't stop rambling.

"You haven't changed," he laughed.

What was that supposed to mean?

As if he'd read my mind, he rushed out, "In a good way. In a good way. You just always start rambling when you get nervous."

"I'm not nervous," I said, trying to muster up all my strength.

"You forget I know you."

"Right . . ."

He gave me a slight smile. "I'm here for my job. Apparently, knowing how to speak Mandarin and read Chinese comes in handy when your boss needs someone to travel to Taiwan and China to meet customers. As a result, I got a huge salary bump and a promotion. Plus, all the perks with traveling: miles, hotel points, and seeing sights on the company dime. Our customers take us out to dinners, tourist locations, etc. It's been great. And all because I know Chinese. We're here for National Taiwan University at present, and I was taking a break by walking around campus. I thought I'd wander around the library and that's when I saw you."

"Wow, you've really moved up." I had no idea what to say. He'd done really well for himself. Here I was, blogging on my site, traveling, rich as can be, and completely a mess when it came to my family.

"Brian! Oh, I'm so glad I found you. Shelly has found a great place for dinner, and the perfect place to go party afterwards . . ." The girl rushing toward us suddenly came to a stop as she saw me standing with Brian. "Oh, hi."

She had on so much makeup, and black wavy hair that ran down to her waist with what looked like clip-ons. She wore a t-shirt of no significance, shorts that I swore her butt was going to pop right out of, and very sensible tennis shoes. So, this was the type he was hanging out with now? And he had the good notion to blush during this interlude. That made me happy.

Brian cleared his throat. "Chi-Chi, this is Anne. Anne, this is Chi-Chi. We just met last night. She and her friend are showing me around." I didn't think he could get any redder, but he did.

"Hi Chi-Chi," was all I could say, because I was trying to hold in the laugh that wanted to explode.

"Man, there you are. Chi-Chi found you." From behind

the shelf stepped out a six-foot white guy with dirty blond hair, blue eyes, blue button-down shirt, business slacks, and brown leather shoes. Your average businessman. "Hey, I'm Joe. I work with Brian. Are y'all friends? You want to come out with us? Shelly found us a great party and we're going to crash it. Well, Shelly said she got us an invite. But man, there's going to be some hot girls there!" He held up his hand to get a high five from Brian. At this point, I couldn't help but let out a small laugh. I had to or else the big one would come right out. Brian was such a shade of red, and I could tell he just wanted to get out of here.

"Great to see you, Anne. We're going to head out now," he said.

"Have fun tonight," I said while Brian ushered them all out. He turned back once, and I could have sworn there was sadness in his eyes. But what did I care? He wasn't my problem anymore.

CHAPTER 16

"THAT WAS QUITE A LOT YOU LEARNED TODAY," Sebastian said with a mouth full of noodles. We had met up at a beef noodle soup place in Gong Guan. Ming-Yue had returned home after bringing us a gift of boba milk tea with black sugar. It was so good that I made a note to get one every day we were in Taiwan. The black sugar just made it taste that much better.

I had updated Sebastian on what I had learned from Mary's journal, leaving out the part about Brian showing up unexpectedly.

"I don't know if I could have done what Mary did, even if it was a child of one of my siblings," I said.

"I don't know. I'd like to think I would. Kids are precious, especially if they're family," Sebastian said.

I'd never heard Sebastian say anything so sweet about kids. For a moment I contemplated asking him if he wanted children, but I didn't have the guts. I was glad when Sebastian changed the subject.

"Oh, I want to tell you what I found today."

Sebastian told me that they had walked through the

streets of Gong Guan and its neighborhoods. There were multiple universities near NTU, and one of them called Xi Da, had really grabbed his attention. He'd met others that looked like him and he was so excited. I couldn't help wondering if that meant he might now know how I felt in the States, but I didn't have time to ask him before he started talking about the class he'd just signed up for. He had met a few Fulbright students while touring Xi Da, and they had raved about the language courses there. He figured that since we'd decided we would be staying a bit longer, he'd go ahead and enroll himself into a beginner Chinese class. I had all sorts of feelings about this. First, I was happy that he was glad we were staying longer. Second, I wondered how he could enroll in a structured course without consulting me first? Third, why would he have to consult me to begin with? Fourth, I wished I could have been on the tour with him. And on and on my mind went.

I really needed to focus on what he was saying—there was something about class starting next week, and he thought we should spend tomorrow going down the east coast. Then before I knew it, there was silence.

"Earth to Anne. Earth to Anne."

"Oh, sorry . . . I just have so much on my mind. What was it you were saying?"

"Do you want to go on our road trip tomorrow? It's during the week, so crowds should be smaller at the tourist locations. If it's too much . . ." He looked like a schoolboy waiting for his prize. Was I that hard to get?

"Yes. Yes. Let's go on the road trip tomorrow."

"Great! I'll let Ah Yi know. She thought we could drive to Taroko National Park."

"That would be fantastic!" Taroko was somewhere I had always wanted to go, and one of the places Mom said Ah Po loved most. "But Sebastian, can I ask one thing?"

"Of course. You know you can always ask me anything," he said, looking at his phone, probably sending a text message to Ming-Yue already.

"I'd like to bring Mary's journal and the white notebook," I said. "If we go to Hualien, I'd like to visit a couple of families who Harrison sold paintings to."

"Sure, that sounds great." Then his head popped up and he looked at me funny. "Wait, you're going to go up to people's doors and ask them if they knew your uncle?"

"Yeah, what's wrong with that? We did it in Yilan, and we got wonderful information."

"Yeah, I'd chalk that up to dumb luck. I don't think you're going to have a lot of people as nice as that lady was. She could have thrown us out."

"I have to start somewhere. Mary's journals are good and all, but they don't tell me where he went or what happened to him. I really want to know if he's still in Taiwan. Or even alive."

"Wait, you're saying you're not even sure he's alive? Wouldn't Mary have known and shared that with you?"

"I don't think she knows," I said.

"How could she not? From what you said, she loved him like her own child."

"I think she lost touch with him after he left home."

"Well, if you think it'll help, I'm all for helping."

"Yeah?"

"Don't sound so surprised." Sebastian reached across the table and took my hand. "I don't know how many times I have to tell you that I'm here for you."

"I know. I'm just unsure of why I'm conducting this search. I can't help it. I've never had any interest in learning more about my family, but ever since Ah Po's journals, I can't stop wanting to find out more . . . even though every new discovery scares me."

Sebastian pulled his chair around so that he was sitting next to me, and gave me a passionate kiss right in the middle of the restaurant. My cheeks instantly turned red, but I didn't care. I was so happy to have him here, and to hear him say that he was here for me.

I brought my thoughts back to our road trip and felt myself getting excited about finally seeing Taroko National Park.

As if he'd read my mind, Sebastian said, "I looked into a hotel in Taroko and they have a fantastic one where we can stay."

"Yeah?" I was really getting excited at the prospect of staying there.

"Should I go ahead and book the rooms? Ah Yi will need her own room too."

"Well, how much are they?"

"You don't have to worry about that now," he said, smiling.

"Oh . . . right. I still forget sometimes, but now I'm curious."

"They're about $420 a night."

"What?" At my outburst, the whole restaurant seemed to go silent, and all heads had turned to stare at me.

"Like I said, you don't have to worry about that now," Sebastian repeated.

"Yeah, but still." My heart raced just thinking about paying $800 for one night in a hotel. It must be something out of this world!

"If you don't want to stay there, Anne, there are other options."

"No. No. It sounds lovely. I just need to get used to being able to get whatever I like. It's still such a foreign concept, and I feel guilty having this much money when there are so many who don't."

"Well, maybe we could start a foundation for someone you want to help?"

"That's a fantastic idea!" This time I really did smile, and Sebastian relaxed just a bit more.

"There's the smile I love," he said.

I couldn't help but beam at him. "I'm so glad I have you here with me."

"My pleasure. I want to help you however I can, but I also know you can't keep your head buried in your family affairs all the time. You have to come up for air."

"Easier said than done."

"Why don't we start with tonight? One of the Fulbright students invited us to a party. I wasn't sure you were up for it, so I didn't bring it up, but it'd be a good distraction."

"That sounds like a grand plan."

"Really?"

"Yes," I laughed. "I'm not a total curmudgeon."

The party wasn't far away. I could hear techno music pouring out of the doors before we had even crossed the street. There was loud music, people dancing—some a little too close for my comfort—and a fancy bar off to one side that was crowded with people. There were people everywhere. This really wasn't my scene and I wanted to turn around, but Sebastian was so excited. Yet, I didn't feel as nervous as I would have been if we were in the States. Something about being abroad made me let down my guard and try new things, and loud, gyrating masses of people mixed with music was one of those new things.

"Are you okay? I know this isn't usually your scene," Sebastian yelled into my ear. He pressed one hand against my lower back, and I was glad he was next to me.

"I'm doing good. Let's get a drink."

Sebastian steered me toward the bar and as we got closer, I could see the whole bar was made of glass or what looked like glass. You could see right through to the other side, and I realized that this was the other half of the club. Behind the bartender waiting to serve us were other bartenders and people dancing around. It was mesmerizing. This club was huge. How many people could this place hold? How could people be so close to each other for such a long time? Weren't they sweaty?

"It's a mirror," a familiar voice said.

Oh . . . of course it was. How could I have been so stupid? I looked over to my right, to where Sebastian had been, and realized that he was talking to another foreigner to his right. Then who had just told me it was a mirror? I looked to my left and sucked in a breath.

"Funny to bump into you here. Last I remember, you weren't big on these kinds of parties," Brian said, looking quite comfortable in these surroundings.

"I'm not. What are you doing here?"

"This was the party Chi-Chi had invited us to."

"Where are you friends?" I managed to say. It took all my concentration to make my mouth work. Was I still hung up on Brian? With Sebastian right next to me!

"I don't know and I don't really care. We didn't really get off on the right footing earlier. How have you been?"

"I'm here with my boyfriend," I said, reaching out for Sebastian, but my hand grabbed empty air. *Where did he go? Was he coming back?*

"Oh, I figured you were with him. You wouldn't have let him touch you like that if he wasn't your boyfriend."

I knew I had gone red all over. I needed to leave before things got worse. Brian was too close, and of all places, why was he here? And what were these feelings that were bubbling up inside of me?

"Look, I'm not here to make your life miserable. I was stupid to have dumped you. I'm—"

"It's too loud here," I shouted, cutting him off. I waved to tell him goodbye and turned to head toward the entrance. Sebastian could take care of himself; I needed to get out of here.

I started pushing through the crowd but almost got turned back into the mix of people and if it wasn't for a strong arm pulling me out at the last minute, I would have been carried into the epicenter.

"I'll walk you out," Brian said into my ear. He was still as strong as ever. I could feel my mind start to wander again and willed myself to focus on the door as he steered me toward it. I could see it, and I was going to walk through it and keep going until I got back to the hotel.

We reached the door and I almost sprinted outside, I was so happy to be out of there, but my happiness was short-lived as Brian remained at my side.

"Where's your boyfriend?" he asked.

"I'm sure he's still in there searching for me because I left so abruptly."

"I can go back in and find him."

"No, that's unnecessary."

Brian was about to protest when I saw Sebastian exit the same door. I couldn't run toward him fast enough.

"There you are," Sebastian exclaimed. "You gave me quite a scare. I left you at the bar and went to grab some pamphlets from the guy I had met earlier, and then when I came back you were gone."

"I know. It became too much for me in there. It's just not my scene."

"Why don't we go get some shaved ice, then? That's

never a bad thing," Sebastian said while holding me close to him and brushing my hair. *I could stay here forever.*

"Hi, I'm Brian."

Shoot, Brian! He was still here.

"Hi, I'm Sebastian. This is Anne."

"I know."

"You two know each other?"

"Yeah, we're—" I started to say, but thankfully Brian finished for me.

"We're old friends from college. Went through engineering classes together. I escorted her out."

"Well, what are the odds? All the way from the other side of the world even." And before I knew it, Sebastian had invited him to have shaved ice with us, and that was that. I couldn't help groaning inside. Why was this happening?

CHAPTER 17

"YOU COULD HAVE TOLD ME OR GIVEN ME A SIGNAL that he was your ex," Sebastian said, storming into our room. "I feel like a complete fool."

"I tried but I couldn't get one word in between you two."

Much to my horror, Sebastian and Brian had hit it off instantly. They might not have looked the same, grown up in the same culture, or ever met each other before, but you would have never known. I was so horrified by the bromance playing out in front of me that I couldn't get my mouth to utter the words "Brian was my boyfriend during college," for which I was now paying the price.

What made it worse was that I knew that Brian had enjoyed being out with us. He even gave me a kiss on the cheek before leaving. And that wasn't even the worst of it. Chi-Chi was there too. Yes, that's right, I had to talk to her the whole time the boys were bonding. It wasn't until Sebastian and I were alone in our taxi that he thought to ask me why I'd never mentioned Brian before because we seemed to know each other well. And now, here Sebastian and I were: in the hotel room with Sebastian incredibly angry with me after I'd told him the truth.

"And I actually like the guy!" Sebastian exclaimed.

"Yeah, he's very likable," I mumbled.

"What did you say?"

"Nothing. I'm sorry I didn't tell you who Brian was. I was just so shocked that you two hit it off so well. Still, I should have told you."

"There's nothing to be done about it now," Sebastian said, running his hands through his hair. "Being able to be outside and talk English to someone else that wasn't you—that was amazing. My brain could actually focus."

"You're telling me. I know I'm fluent in Mandarin, but when I talk in English with you, it's like my brain goes to sleep and I can operate on autopilot."

"I didn't know that."

"Yeah, I only just noticed it these last couple of days. On a lighter note, do you want to talk about the road trip? Anywhere you want to go in particular?" Anything to keep the subject from going back to Brian.

"Yes." At this, Sebastian came and took me in his arms and gave me a twirl. He always started dancing with me when he was at his happiest. "I want to drive down the east coast and enjoy the view. It's supposed to be beautiful. I know Ah Yi will be with us, but she won't share a room with us. It'll be nice to have some quality time together for a few days."

"I like the sound of that. I have missed just hanging out with you."

"But you're still going to bring the journal and notebook, aren't you?"

"Yeah . . . if that's okay?"

"I think you would sulk the whole trip if I didn't say yes," he said, laughing.

Maybe it was good for him to talk to someone American, even if it was Brian. It was nice to see him so happy.

CHAPTER 18

"Ah Yi is going to come pick us up in twenty minutes," Sebastian said.

"I'm glad we have her to show us around."

"Yeah, but it's kinda cramping my style."

"We'll get alone time, don't worry," I said, giving him a peck on the lips.

"Also, we're only going for a few days. What is all this stuff?"

"My essentials. You didn't say anything when we packed for Taiwan."

"Because we were coming for two weeks."

"Well, it's all the stuff I need to survive the next three days. I see you're going to wear the same pants every single day."

"It's efficient and it means that I can carry your stuff instead."

"Fair enough," I laughed.

By the time we— I mean I—finished packing, Ming-Yue arrived. We went downstairs and I almost turned around when I saw that Mary was standing by the car, looking her regal self.

"Ah Yi, why is Ah Goo here?" I whispered to Ming-Yue when she came to help us with our bags.

"She said she wanted to talk to you before we left. I told her we didn't have a lot of time, but she insisted."

"Right . . ." *Was she going to tell me about my uncle? Talk to me about her journal?* "Ah Goo, ni hao."

"Hello Anne. Would you mind coming with me to the cafe on the corner? Sebastian can stay here."

I looked at Sebastian, and his face reflected what I was feeling. *What was this all about?* I followed Mary into the cafe, and we sat in the corner, me staring at her while she looked out the window, seemingly oblivious as to why we were here. I was starting to think that maybe she had changed her mind about talking to me.

"I assume you've been reading my journals?" she finally said.

"Yes, I don't understand though—"

Mary held up a hand, cutting me off. "In time you will. I cannot tell you where your uncle is because I do not know myself. He left us when he was thirteen and moved around so much that I could never find him."

"Why are you telling me this now?"

"Because something your mama said has been rolling around in my head."

"What did she say?"

Mary turned to look at me. "She told me that we were all young once and we have all made mistakes. Then she said that she hoped I wouldn't make the same mistakes she did and keep family secrets from you."

"That would be—"

Again, Mary held up her hand, cutting me off. "I still think

I did the right thing, keeping Rose's secret I mean. It was the right thing to do at the time, but it's been long enough. You already know so much. Our family has been disconnected for so long, and I do wish to get to know you better."

I could see tears forming in her eyes. "I'm trying to understand. I want to understand, Ah Goo."

"I know you do. Ming-Yue has told me what a beautiful person you are. I believe her. Now, I understand that you have a road trip to go on so we should move on."

I felt a surge of anxiety at her words. She was finally opening up and I wanted to know more. I pushed, "Is there not more you could share?"

She shook her head. "That's it for now. Just keep reading." And with that, the conversation was done. She walked me back to the car, and gave me and Ming-Yue a hug before she left in a yellow taxi.

"That was the strangest conversation," I said to her daughter.

"Mama can be like that. She means well. She's allowed me to share what I know with you, that's if you're interested?"

"Yes!"

Sebastian sighed. "We can't get away from this, can we?"

Leaving Taipei City was not an easy feat, but the scenery was one we had gotten used to: tall buildings, old buildings, cars and buses going every which way, and most of all, there were mopeds everywhere. We'd get to a stop sign, and there would be a hundred mopeds—in front of us, on the side, and behind us. Prior to driving, we had been taking the subway everywhere, and I couldn't imagine crossing the street at these busy intersections.

Eventually, we got on the highway and the suburbs flew by. These weren't cookie cutter, single family homes and big shopping centers. These were cookie cutter sky rises, bespectacled with metal balconies that were adorned with clothes flapping in the wind. Hardly any vegetation was around but concrete was everywhere. Everything was old looking, too, with a layer of dust on it. Maybe it was just the air here, island country and all, but I'd been in modern buildings where things looked new.

I turned my focus back into the car and noticed that Sebastian had fallen asleep. I took the opportunity to question my aunt. "Ah Yi, can you tell me about my uncle?"

"I can share with you what I know. I don't know much though. I'm the youngest of my sister and brothers and I never met your uncle. He was gone before I was born. This is probably why Mama is okay with me sharing," Ming-Yue laughed. "My oldest sister lived with him the longest and they did not get along. I remember that much."

"Yes, I met her at the engagement party. She did not mince words when she said he was not a nice guy."

"Yes, my sister is stubborn. Just like Mama. I am trying to persuade Mama to call or at least write to her. She's so stubborn though. I'm sure you've noticed."

"Honestly, anything you can tell me would be great. Anything at all."

"A package was delivered once from outside of Taiwan. We never got international mail. I was about eight at the time. I'd almost forgotten about that now, but when you came, I started remembering," Ming-Yue trailed off.

Was that all she knew?

"I'm not sure if it's related now that I am thinking about it. But I left for a friend's place, and when I came back, I found Mama crying in her room. She was holding a painting in her hand. I remember being confused. Mama never showed emotions. She was strict with us about keeping our composure. To see her fall apart was something I couldn't let go of. I needed to know what had upset her. So, that night I snuck into her room and went through her closet. She always hid our presents in the back of the closet, and I found the painting with no problem." Again, she trailed off. I was going bonkers waiting to hear what this thing was.

"Are we talking about Harrison?" Sebastian asked, suddenly awake.

I gave a quick nod and turned my attention back to Ming-Yue. "What was it you found?"

"Oh, this is probably nothing. It's all old memories."

Ahhhh, would anyone tell me anything straightforward?

"We'd really like to know what you found even if it's unrelated," Sebastian spoke up.

"Yes. Yes. Sorry. Old memories. It was a beautiful painting of Mama and Baba."

"Did it have a name on it?" I was sitting forward in my seat now, gripping the driver's headrest.

"No. That was what was so weird. I was only eight, but whenever Mama did paintings with me, she always made me sign it. This one only had a plum blossom in the bottom right corner."

"A plum blossom?" Sebastian turned to give me a knowing look. Neither one of us had figured out why he would use this flower.

"Was there something significant to it?" I asked.

"Not the blossom specifically, but it reminded me of a couple of letters that we had received. Or my mama had received."

"What were they?"

"I don't know. I remember bringing them to Mama. She was really upset when she saw them. They had hand-drawn plum blossoms in the corner of the envelope. I don't think

Mama ever opened them. I found them in her desk, tucked under some paper when I went to look for some stamps one time."

"What is it?" Sebastian asked me. I turned to look at him but no words came out of my mouth. *It must be that letter and wedding invitation I found in the safe! Now I'd have to wait till we got back to Taipei to find out what was in the letter!*

"I'm sorry, that's all I know," Ming-Yue continued. "I was too young to put anything together. Mama never talked about Harrison. The stories I would hear were how he stole things from Da Jie, and got her in trouble. But my brothers would later tell me that Da Jie was just jealous of him because Mama loved him so much."

"It's okay. What you've shared is relevant. I found two envelopes in the safe in Taipei that had plum blossoms on them. One was a wedding invitation and the other was unopened. I still need to read the letter."

"Oh, I would like to see them if it's okay."

"Yes, that would be fine."

"Do you want to turn back now? I know how important this is to you," Ming-Yue asked, already slowing down to turn around.

I felt Sebastian tense and his hand slipped from mine. It was enough for me to reply, "No, we've been looking forward to this trip. I want to keep going. There's time to read the letters when I get back."

Sebastian relaxed just as quickly as he'd tensed, and I willed myself to enjoy this trip, to not think about my uncle for the time being. Easier said than done.

The view outside was a good distraction. I couldn't help but compare what I saw with what I remembered on my road trip across the States. We'd seen ranches and farmhouses next to the highway. Here, concrete buildings that somewhat matched the ones we saw in the city popped up here and there down dirt roads. Clothes waved in the air on every balcony. People with straw hats were bending down and picking rice out of the ground, knee deep in muddy water. And everything was so green. It made me think of home, and I felt calmer the further into the greenery we went.

Then, the view become even grander. The ocean suddenly opened up to our left. I'd been to the beach, but this was something else. The vastness of the water made me feel small and insignificant. The sight of it reminded me that we were on an island surrounded by water. Sebastian must have felt the same because he slid over and both of us stared out of the window. No one said a word for a good hour.

"We're getting close to Toroko," Ming-Yue said. "You see the big rock out there?"

"The massive one you can't miss?" I asked.

"Yes, it's known as Guishan Island. Turtle Island in English. My brothers and I used to make up stories when we drove this road. It was always a comforting sight when we drove past Turtle Island because we knew we were getting closer to a simpler pace."

"It's so calming here. I feel like I've let everything go."

"Yes, I love coming down here, away from the city."

"Away from all the stress and nonsense of city living," Sebastian murmured.

"I never knew you didn't like living in the city," I said, taking a good look at him.

"I love living in the city, but in the last year I've started rethinking what I want."

"The whole Wilkens debacle messed you up, too, huh?"

"I wouldn't say messed me up, but it has got me thinking about what's important," he said, putting an arm around me. I hadn't felt more connected to Sebastian than I did in that moment. I let myself relax against him.

My thoughts drifted, and after a while I found myself

thinking about Brian. Why of all times had I bumped into him? It must mean something. I believed in fate and this was really bugging me. Probably more than it should have.

I looked over at Sebastian and wondered how things would be different if it had been Brian who'd come with me on this trip. I knew without thinking on it too much that we would have eaten our way across Taiwan. Brian could easily talk to everyone here, which would have made everyone comfortable . . . and he would have been comfortable too.

Sebastian wouldn't admit it, but I knew he still thought about Isabella. How could he not with their long history? I couldn't say I wasn't jealous from time to time, but I never mentioned it.

"What are you thinking about?" Sebastian suddenly asked.

"Oh, nothing. Just wondering about those letters."

"Well, Ah Yi just said we're almost at Taroko. We could do a couple of stops before heading to the hotel. What do you think?"

"I definitely want to see whatever sights she has in mind! This trip has been on my bucket list forever. I saw pictures of Mom there with her feet in the water, sitting on boulders the size of our house. Yes. Yes. Let's go."

"I'm glad you are so excited," Ming-Yue said from behind the wheel.

We watched as the mountains got closer. Farmland continued to dot the side of the road, but those majestic peaks were amazing. I'm not a mountain climber and have no interest in being one, so maybe these weren't the highest peaks around but they sure were impressive. It prompted me to open my notebook and start taking notes.

Since coming here, my job had been pushed to the back of my mind, but last night I had lay in bed thinking that maybe this trip would provide the necessary inspiration to write my next blog. Taroko, Hualien, the ocean—road trips always brought out the best stories.

Before we knew it, we were outside a big red arch that was decorated in ancient designs. I'd only ever seen anything like it in a Chinese movie at the royal family's palace. It felt like the mountains themselves were inviting you through their own royal entrance. The instant we went under the arch, we were on a two-lane road with a barricade, which was a necessary safety precaution preventing us from driving off the road and into the ravine.

White, gray, and every hue in-between glistened off the surrounding walls. We had been transported into a different world. The only other place I could compare it to was Yosemite National Park. Many have tried to capture the grandness of the mountains, how high they are, how massive they are, but nothing compares to seeing them in person, standing at the foot of them and looking up until you didn't think that you could look any higher. It took my breath away to say the least.

Sebastian and I were silent as we drove toward our desti-nation, both amazed by what we were seeing. It wasn't until the car pulled into the parking lot and the trees blocked my view that I realized it was time to get out.

Outside, the air took me by surprise. I grew up in Astoria, a nature focused community. We had trees galore compared to other west coast cities. But this—this air was fresh, crisp, unpolluted.

"Earth to Anne," Sebastian said, coming up behind me.

"Do you smell it?" I asked with my eyes closed.

"Smell what? It doesn't smell like anything."

"Exactly."

"You've gone crazy," Sebastian said, laughing.

"No, it's so clean here. I could sit out here forever."

"Well, let's go in and see if we can get some water. Ah Yi

had to run to the bathroom. She said there's a museum on the other side."

"Oh, a museum? Let's go."

We walked across the parking lot with a crisscross cement design and grass growing up in-between the concrete to a path that led to a big building. There was a little eatery there and sure enough, we found a small museum dedicated to the indigenous people who lived here. I was sucked in to the first tapestry hanging on the wall. Sebastian walked through the whole building, reading some of the signs. Thank goodness they were in English, too, but he quickly grew bored with the history.

"I'll wait for you outside," he said.

"Okay," I mumbled, too enthralled by what I was seeing. I vaguely remembered him planting a kiss on my cheek before heading out.

I felt like such a fool. Looking at these tapestries, I knew that even with all my travels, I was still naive to the enormity of the human race. Growing up in the States, we learned all about the Native Americans and the beauty of their work. We'd seen pictures of the clothes they wore, the textiles they made. But here, I was on the other side of the world looking at items that looked familiar—blankets hand woven with vibrant colors and a variety of designs, a people who lived off the land, making handmade pottery, jewelry, and clothes. I should have visited ages ago. My guilt for exploring Western culture but ignoring Eastern culture was a new feeling for me. I told myself that at least I was here now, and the more I explored, the more I wanted to learn.

"Anne?"

I turned to see Ming-Yue beckoning me over.

"Is it time to go?"

"Yes, we still have far to drive before we get to the hotel."

We walked in silence back to the car. Sebastian was

looking at the mountains with his hands in his pockets, as handsome as ever. I wanted to stop and enjoy this moment. Finding my uncle wasn't the be all, end all. Maybe I should let it rest for this trip.

"You seem relaxed here," I said, coming up behind him and giving him a hug.

"I am."

We stood like that and breathed in the fresh air. I wished I could have bottled this moment up so I could bring it home with me. Ming-Yue had gone ahead to the car. She was so patient with us. Letting us do our thing.

"You think we'll ever make it to Hualien?"

"We can always go down to Hualien another time," he murmured.

"That means if we stay longer, right?" I asked him with a raised eyebrow.

"Anne, you know when it's all said and done, I will stay with you as long as you need me to," he answered, turning around and enveloping me in his arms.

Oh, how I wish we could have stayed just like that with not a care in the world. But Ming-Yue was waiting so we eventually walked back to the car.

We drove further inland and as we did, the mountains appeared to be never-ending. Eventually we came across luscious trees. The view became interspersed with little waterfalls before being closed off by walls of granite. Beautiful was too simple a word to describe the views here. Mesmerizing might work. Grand—that worked even better. Yes, it was grand just like a big gala when the woman walks in, dressed not in frills, but in a simple black silk dress with a diamond necklace, and her hair done in a bun at the nape of her neck with little tendrils floating here and there, framing her face. She held her head high and walked in like she knew where she was going and who she was going to meet. She was confident. And in this way, I could feel the confidence emanating off the marble walls. How grand those mountains stood as we minions looked upon them.

"We're here," Ming-Yue said.

"You've been daydreaming a lot since we started this trip," Sebastian said, giving me a side grin.

"I was writing my blog about this place. It's so serene. Oh, that's a good word."

"Let's get inside," Sebastian said, grabbing our bag and laughing at me while he walked toward the hotel.

I didn't follow him straight away. Instead, I stood there by the vehicle and took a look around. I couldn't believe how we came to be so lucky. How many people got to come here? The hotel looked very modern and new, and I later found out that it was not new but had gone through many transformations in its lifetime. Behind me was what seemed like a little market, and I could smell food from where I was standing. My stomach started gurgling but it couldn't distract me from what had taken my attention—the view on my left.

I walked toward the sidewalk that led to a metal bridge and saw that on the other side there was yet another bridge, this one enormous, and that it crossed a gorge. The path then led to what looked like stairs. It looked intriguing and I made a note to go there in the morning. The gorge was enormous, a river with boulders the size of a two storey house. It was amazing to see.

Sebastian, almost to the hotel, turned around and called out to me, "Anne, come on in. We have all day tomorrow to explore this place. I got some food delivered to our room."

He knew food was the only thing that could distract me. "Coming." But I took one last look around before I went inside. Just dazzling. That's a good word too.

CHAPTER 19

WE SLEPT LIKE LOGS. IT WAS THE BEST SLEEP I'D had in a while, and I usually slept well in the mansion. When I awoke, Sebastian was still slumbering next to me. My stomach was growling though, so I decided to find some food and let him rest. Before I left the room, I grabbed Mary's journal just in case I had some time to read it.

Downstairs, I found a restaurant that charged an exorbitant amount for breakfast, but I couldn't deny the food was delicious. They had a Western omelet with mushrooms and spinach. I had two pieces of toast and some freshly squeezed orange juice. On a full stomach, I started walking the grounds. I didn't get very far though. There were benches in the parking lot, and though it wasn't very romantic, the view was spectacular. I also felt guilty at the thought of crossing the bridge to explore without Sebastian. So, I settled myself in under the trees on a brown park bench and opened the journal.

43年1月23日 (Saturday, January 23, 1954)

The trip up to Taipei was wonderful! I sat with Harrison near the back and answered his questions about everything he saw. His face was glued to the window for the whole trip, and we watched as the mountains faded away and the air became less clear. Part of me was excited, glad to be going someplace outside of Hualien. I loved it there and it would always be my home, but my time in America and Hong Kong had opened my eyes to possibilities—going into new environments, reinventing myself and starting over. It sparked a joy that until this moment, I didn't realize I needed.

Liang-Chun came and sat next to me near the end of the trip. He handed me some water and I almost dropped it when his hand touched mine. I could have sworn he blushed a little, but I was too busy trying to keep myself from shaking. Maybe he desired to travel too. Harrison loved him and was soon talking to Liang-Chun as if they were the only two in the train.

We stayed with Oldest Brother who owns a bookstore in Taipei. His wife and I got along well, but I could tell she was very curious about Harrison and that made me uncomfortable. I don't like people acting abnormal around him. Their kids had already graduated from college, but they took out some old toys for him and he seemed to like them. It made me sad seeing him so used to people acting weird around him.

43年1月24日 (Sunday, January 24, 1954)

Liang-Chun sent me away this morning because he wanted Harrison to focus during his morning practice. So I went for a walk and found myself walking in a circle around the studio, not willing to venture far. I went into a jewelry store across the street just to have a look, but I immediately found a piece I had to get. It would be a present to Harrison when he finished this weekend: a light pink, glass blown plum blossom. It looked just like the flowers Rose used to draw. It was Rose's favorite flower, and something that would tie his mama to him without them even knowing.

It cost a month of my salary to buy the item, but it was too pretty not to get. When I got back to the studio, Harrison was sitting on the side watching the older boys practice. He looked so small. I went and sat down next to him. He crawled into my lap and we sat there together just watching . . . well, me watching Liang-Chun most of the time.

Later that day, Harrison did so good! He beat the other six-year-old without a problem. True, the six-year-old had some penalties, but Harrison stood his ground. There were a lot of people watching, and it was very noisy, but he didn't run. He did what he had practiced and finished his round. It was more than Liang-Chun and I had hoped for. We were so proud of him!

After everyone had left, we took him out for some shaved ice. I was so happy. I was with two of my favorite people and the three of us had laughed and enjoyed each other's company. We could have been a family and no one would have known. I wished I could have held onto that moment, and made Harrison's world that happy for the rest of his life.

We did a quick trip to the zoo and saw the famous Lin Wang, an elephant they say served in the war. I hadn't seen Harrison so happy before. That evening, we took the train back to Hualien. Everyone was quiet but not a bad quiet. There was a peace in the air. Liang-Chun sat next to me while Harrison sat on my lap. He wanted to snuggle and I was all for it. He held the plum blossom in his hand the whole ride home. And halfway through the ride, Liang-Chun put his hand on mine. I didn't move and we rode like that through the dark all the way home. My heart soared and I ended up falling asleep with my head on Liang-Chun's shoulder.

"Did you find anything new in there?" Ming-Yue asked, coming up behind me.

"Yes, but nothing to show where Uncle would be."

"I wish I could be of more help."

"It's okay. You've already made us feel so welcome. I am so thankful to you for bringing us here."

"It is very calming here," she agreed. "You should cross the Pudu Bridge, go up to the top, and read the rest of your journal there. It is very peaceful and it is early. There will not be a lot of people up there."

"I would love that, but I'm waiting for Sebastian."

"I can let him know that you are there. He can catch up later when he wakes up. You should take advantage of the quietness before others wake up."

"That would be great. Thank you, Ah Yi."

"It's the least I can do. I wish Mama would be straightforward with you."

"Well, the more I read about her, the more I can understand why she isn't. I think she's too shy to tell me her history. This was the best way she could think of."

"Very true. Now, you should go. Go on," Ming-Yue said, putting her hands on my shoulders and giving me a gentle push. I left her standing under the trees staring up at the mountains.

My heart was pounding, I was so excited to cross the bridge. I walked across the car bridge and then looked at the pedestrian bridge that must have been a hundred yards long. I started walking across it and had to stop every ten feet. I willed myself to look down; I couldn't believe how high I was. Thank goodness the bridge was steady because I could feel my heart dropping to my feet. I noticed my hands were gripping the sides and turning a faint red, but I couldn't peel my eyes away from the drop. I'd never seen so much marble before in my life. Maybe on the walls of a bank, or in an old library, but that was it. Here, it was everywhere given the gorge and all the mountains were made of marble.

By the time I had gotten to the other side, I noticed there were a few people starting to come across the bridge, too, and when I looked back at the hotel, I saw people starting to trickle out of the building and head in this direction. That spurred me to keep going; I was going to hold onto this peacefulness for as long as I could.

At the end of the bridge was another one of those old red gates. Stairs led up to a long path that wound up the hill. When I got to the top, I stopped in my tracks and stared at a big Buddhist temple that had one of the largest Guan Ying statues I'd ever seen. She stood there on the platform, surrounded by tall mountains that could cover the whole sky. Luscious green trees coated every inch. A pagoda sat at the top of one of the mountain peaks, and another sat behind me in the trees. The quietness enveloped me like a soft blanket, and I went to find a quiet place to sit before the masses descended on this oasis.

I found a spot at the end of the platform about half a mile away, breathed in the clear mountain air, and opened up the journal to continue on.

43年1月29日 (Friday, January 29, 1954)

This week has been what the Americans call glorious. I have been in heaven. Harrison is so happy because he got a medal. He's been wearing it around the house whenever he can. I bet he would even wear it into the bathtub and in bed if we let him. Well, given he brings it to bed with him, I guess he is sleeping with it. It's so hard to say no to him.

School seems to have gotten better. He wore the medal to school one day and everyone ooed and aahed over it until the teacher made him put it away. I was surprised the teacher didn't take it away, but there were no incidents all week. The kids seem to have a new respect for him.

My kung fu is improving too. I have been meeting with Liang-Chun after school for half an hour whenever the two of us can find time. He brings a snack for us, usually stinky tofu or a sticky rice roll, and we sit and eat for a bit before starting practice.

It started off as nothing more than just practice. He showed me how to defend myself against attackers, then how to kick and punch anyone I didn't want near me. I was very grateful, and even though I secretly have a crush on him, I didn't make any moves toward him . . . until yesterday! We sat and ate like usual, but this time he sat a little bit closer and I did too. He brought me a taffy treat, freshly made by a neighbor who made it in front of his house. He told me about his older brothers and I told him about mine. We shared about what scared us the most, and I told him about my time in America. He thought it was fascinating, and we talked about our dreams to travel abroad, meet new people, and how we'd get off Taiwan and away from all this political madness. Practice was all but forgotten.

43年2月3日 (Wednesday, February 3, 1954)

Today is Lunar New Year! Kung Fu is closed, the shop is closed, the house is clean, and everyone is happy. Mei-Jing's family joined us for dinner, and Liang-Chun gave me a red envelope with a note inside it telling me that he wanted to see me more. Life is great right now.

44年2月14日 (Monday, February 14, 1955)

I haven't written in you for a whole year! I am loving life. I've almost got my teaching certificate. Harrison is growing so tall. He's made another friend. Liang-Chun has been inviting me out, just the two of us. Life is so good right now.

"Hey, sorry to bother your sanctuary," Sebastian said, settling down next to me.

"Oh, hi."

"'Oh, hi.' That's the best you can do? I book this gorgeous place for us to stay and 'Oh, hi' is all you can give me?"

"Sorry. I was engrossed in the journal. You want to read the rest with me?"

"I was only kidding and that would be lovely. It's nice up here."

I snuggled right into his arms. "I know, really tranquil, isn't it? I wish we could stay up here longer."

"Well, we can."

"We can? They have room for tonight?" I asked, turning to look at him.

"I booked for two nights thinking you might like it and want to stay."

"Oh, I love you," I said, giving Sebastian a big kiss on the mouth. He held me tight for quite a while and I buried my head into his chest.

"You love me, huh?" he asked, tilting my face up so that he could see me.

"I do," I whispered, and I could feel the huge grin on my face.

When his lips touched mine, I felt shivers skipping down my back. I never wanted him to let me go.

"I've missed our time like this," he said, holding me back so that I got a good look at his face. He really did love me. I could see it in his eyes.

"I know, me too. We should make more time for each other."

"We should. We don't even have kids yet, and I feel like we're too busy with our own things." *Why had I mentioned kids?*

"Kids huh?" he chuckled, letting me go but keeping one of his arms around me.

"Well, I do want them. Do you?" *I might as well find out now since I brought it up.*

"Of course I do," he said, and I swear my heart grew three-fold.

"It makes me so happy to hear you say that." I could tell he was getting uncomfortable as there was a slow creep of red crawling up his neck, so I changed the subject. "Speaking of children, do you want to hear what Mary and Harrison have been doing?"

"Yes, read away."

44年5月10日 (Tuesday, May 10, 1955)

Liang-Chun asked me to marry him today! But then he told me the most horrible news. I don't know what to do. I see myself as Harrison's real mom. It was my plan from the very beginning. But I had hoped the gossip about me being with a white man would slowly go away. And for a long time now, I haven't heard anything and had thought people stopped caring about it, that everyone had accepted us. But I was just oblivious. Apparently, everyone else still talks about it! As far as Harrison knows, I am his mother so I can't say anything differently. But Liang-Chun's parents will not let him be with me! They think I have been a bad girl, and therefore a bad influence on Liang-Chun. I am a disgraceful girl! Liang-Chun said he will not give up on me, but I don't know what he can do. His family is influential here in Hualien.

"Why is it that when I finally get to catch up to what you've been reading, it becomes so morbid?" Sebastian asked.

"Bad timing, I guess? Shall I continue?"

"Yes. Yes. It just baffles me."

"I'm sure it couldn't be all bad," I said, but I had a sinking feeling it would be.

44年7月5日 (Tuesday, July 5, 1955)

Liang-Chun's parents are not changing their mind. They will disown him if he marries me. I am heartbroken. He has chosen me but he can't have me. I am garbage as far as his parents are concerned. He can have any girl here and he'll be snatched up soon. My heart is broken.

44年7月11日 (Monday, July 11, 1955)

I've tried to not cry in front of Harrison, but he has noticed. He comes and snuggles with me in the morning. He hasn't done that in a long time. I need to get myself together. He doesn't understand why he has a different Sifu at class now, or why we haven't seen Liang-Chun in a while. He's hurting more than me because he doesn't understand.

44年7月12日 (Tuesday, July 12, 1955)

Harrison thinks he did something wrong. My heart is breaking even more. He doesn't deserve this.

"I think that's enough for now," Sebastian said, closing the journal on my hand.

"Hey! I was reading that."

"We're here on vacation. You're already starting to cry. Come, let's go walk around and explore. We could go into the temple and pray."

"Pray? When have either of us ever done that?" I laughed.

"Don't mock. I've heard it can be quite healing."

"All right, let's give it a go."

I tucked the journal under my arms and we walked over to the temple. At first, we just stood there in front of it and soaked it all in. There was a monk standing to the side with what looked like three statues of Buddha sitting in the front. The middle one was the largest. There were neat rows of kneeling stools in front of us, clearly for use if we wanted to go and pray. There was also lots of gold. Or maybe it just looked like gold. I realized that even though I was Buddhist, I didn't know a single thing about the religion. I felt guilty standing there wondering what I should do.

The monk started walking toward us and before I could back away, Sebastian was asking him questions about what we could do. Thank goodness he seemed to know what Sebastian was asking because I was too embarrassed to help translate. He told us to press our hands together at our chest and give a bow. Just to show our respect. That was easy enough, and I sighed with relief that that was all we had to do. It was so simple. I would have to tell Mom that when I saw her next.

For the rest of the morning, Sebastian and I sat out in the open and enjoyed our view. We talked like we had just met. About our goals, wishes, dreams, jobs, friends, parents, and family. We even ventured into the territory of our future. For lunch, we wandered back to the hotel to eat, but right after we'd headed back up the hill and sat on the patio. It was so serene up here. I had even ventured back to the temple a couple of times to pay my respects. On one visit, I prayed that my relationship with Sebastian would last. We were different enough that it still baffled me that we were even together. But here we were, together on the other side of the world in a remote location in a beautiful national park. How could life get any better?

CHAPTER 20

WE STAYED AN EXTRA NIGHT AND WENT BACK TO Taipei on the third day. I would say both of us were the most relaxed we'd been in a while. Life was good. It was awesome, actually, and I wouldn't change a thing. Sebastian would give me little kisses here and there, just because, and we held hands the whole way back to Taipei. During the journey, we talked about expanding his clientele internationally so that he could travel with me. We'd be nomads living around the world with Portland as our home base. I'd never been happier.

We got to the hotel and I went straight up to our room. Sebastian said he had to go and get something and would meet me back upstairs. After about thirty minutes of waiting, I called him, only to be delivered to voicemail. What could he be doing? I had imagined us coming up together, unpacking, then planning a leisurely stroll through Taipei to find something else to explore. Maybe eat lots of food. That was the one thing I missed—being able to step out of the hotel and pick whatever cuisine we felt like. And all of it being really affordable, because even with all this money, I still couldn't stop thinking about the cost of things.

While unpacking, I came across the white notebook. I laughed when I saw it, thinking we really did have a blast over the last couple of days because I hadn't even thought about the addresses I had marked off. I couldn't wait to share this with Sebastian.

My stomach was grumbling and I was starting to get a bit worried about him, so I went downstairs only to find Sebastian slumped in one of the armchairs in the lobby.

"Hey you. What's with the long face?" I asked, playfully sitting on his lap. He moved me off to sit next to him without even raising his head to acknowledge me. "Really, what's wrong, Sebastian?"

"I'd rather not say at the moment."

"Did something happen? Is someone hurt?"

"No. No. Could you do me a favor and grab a pearl milk tea for me? And for you, too, of course."

"Yeah. . . sure. . ."

I left him there and took the long way to the drink stand, got the drinks, and then took a different long walk back, thinking that that should be enough time for Sebastian to brood.

"Sebastian, I—" I froze as I saw the person next to him and demanded, "What are you doing here?"

"Anne—" Sebastian started to say.

"No, I'm not talking to you. I'm talking to *her*," I said, pointing at the blonde-haired woman sitting across from Sebastian. Her whole physique shouted rich and put together. Her whole demeanor exuded confidence, and I could tell she thought that she had the upper hand. *What in the world was she doing here in Taiwan of all places? Goodness, did Sebastian know she was coming? She's the one we suspected was responsible for the bomb in my car! He better not have known she was coming.*

"Before you get all in a tizzy, Sebastian has been trying to persuade me not to come. But no one tells me what to do, isn't that right, dear?" Isabella said.

"What?" I almost screamed. If it wasn't for the fact that we were in the lobby with others milling around us, I would have yelled at the top of my lungs.

"Anne, technically I still work for the Wilkens's family until I can get all my work transferred to someone else at the firm," Sebastian said, emphasizing his words while looking at Isabella.

"Yes, but . . ."

"Come on, Sebastian, just let her know what we've been working on," Isabella said with a slight grin on her face.

How I wished I could go over and wipe that smile off her face. "Yeah Sebastian, what have you two been working on?"

"We"—Sebastian pointed at Isabella and himself—"are not working on anything. I am working with Jack."

"Jack, he's involved?" He was the only sibling of Anthony's who wasn't indifferent or disgusted by me. I never thought Jack would be against me. But he *is* part of the Wilkens family.

"Anne, it's not what you think. Jack is not against you," Sebastian said, suddenly appearing in front of me.

How did he know what I was thinking? I didn't even see him get out of his chair. The room was starting to sway. I had thought the Wilkens were finally going to leave me alone.

"Anne, are you okay?"

"Looks like she's going to fall. Hmmm, I don't think I've ever seen anyone faint before."

"Isabella—not helping," Sebastian seethed.

"Well, I'm sure this will help. Dear Great Uncle Jack is actually on your side. I have no idea why he likes you and hates my grandmother," Isabella said.

"That's a bit harsh, don't you think?" Sebastian said.

"No, he said it to my grandmother's face the last time we all got together."

Sebastian and I could only stare at her. Had I started this hatred between the siblings? No, what was I thinking? It'd been in the works for decades. My appearance in their lives probably didn't help the situation though. *Sigh*. Would all of this never end?

"Anne dear, I do want to let you know how sorry I am that you went through that bombing and were in the hospital. I sent some flowers. Did you get them?" She said all this with a neutral expression on her face.

It didn't matter. I still thought it had been her and her mom who had done it. "No, I did not. Isabella, why are you here?" I asked, finally getting a grip on myself. I had done nothing wrong and there wasn't anything they could do to hurt me. I had to stand up for myself.

"The family would like to ask you if you'd be willing to sell us the Hawaii house? And there is a small rumor that you have a house here as well."

I'd forgotten about the Taiwan house. My whole focus had been on my uncle. I couldn't believe I hadn't thought to go and see it. I owned it after all. This inheritance was taking some getting used to.

"What makes you think I want to sell them?" I asked her.

"I know people, Anne. I just do. You don't seem like the kind of person that hangs on to possessions. I don't think you even know what to do with the house you live in. We are ready to give you a hefty sum. Sebastian has even drawn up all the papers."

I turned a shocked gaze on him. "You have, have you?"

"I dictated it and someone at my firm drafted up the paperwork," he admitted slowly. "Anne, I need you to know that I'm not for this."

"Sebastian, that's not what you said on the phone,"

Isabella said, putting a hand on his arm. I was glad to see Sebastian swatted it away.

"Isabella . . ."

"Shall I tell her?"

"Isabella, please do," I said before Sebastian could answer. "It seems Sebastian can't be up front with me."

"You said this would be good for Anne, because she has enough stress as it is. That if having less property would get us off her back, you could help unburden the stress. Does that about sum it up?"

"Yes," Sebastian moaned, his head buried in his hands with his elbows on his knees. "Except I was supposed to be the one to tell her."

"You were taking too long. Shall I tell her the other part?"

"Yippee, there's more," I mumbled.

"No, I'll tell her," Sebastian said with a growl. "Geraldine found her father's letter. It was mentioned in his will, but no one knew where the letter was. It said he wished for the house to be donated to charity if none of the family wanted it. Geraldine interprets that to mean it should never have left the family and that Anthony had no right to give the house away. Therefore, it nulls everything in Anthony's will. Anne, I think this is insane. Anthony had full right to do with the house as he wished because it was his. This is why I haven't been around as much. I've been fighting this, and Jack is on our side."

A small part of me knew that Sebastian was on my side and had been doing all he could, but my body was frozen and I couldn't say anything. How could something all the way back to Lord Wilkens still be haunting me now? I thought we had put this all to rest.

"So, Anne, you see, it would be a lot easier if you would just sell the house back to us. There's no need to go through any more legal matters. Like I said, I can read people, and you're not the type to hold onto possessions."

Having Isabella here, and Sebastian knowing about all of this without telling me was too much for me. I felt like everything we had done together in the last few days had just been wiped away by the smirk on Isabella's face.

"Well, aren't you two quite the pair," I finally said. "And Isabella, I'm never going to sell my houses to any of your family."

"Anne, no wait—" Sebastian started.

"Don't talk to me."

I turned and walked away. What was with Isabella? What had made her the way she was? And why was she directing all her anger at me?

CHAPTER 21

I walked to Chiang Kai-Shek memorial, thinking back on that day when we first visited. Everything was so much more carefree then. Mom was still here, and I had only just started reading Andy's journal . . . and I hadn't fallen even more in love with Sebastian.

I kept rubbing my chest, hoping the more I rubbed, the more the hurt would go away. But it just made things worse. It felt like the rubbing made the hurt spread from my heart to the rest of my chest. I didn't have a destination in mind. I wandered all over the grounds, went to the stores across the street, ate some noodles, and walked around some more. At some point, I decided that I should get my bearings and start heading back to the hotel. But then my feet would find a new path to go on and I'd take it.

I hadn't hurt this bad since Brian and I had broken up. *I wonder if he's still here?* Why would I think that? But Sebastian had been talking to Isabella and not told me, and who knows how long they'd been talking for? I was so confused. Our road trip was now forgotten.

Did I want to sell these houses to the Wilkens? I hated to

admit it, but Isabella was right. I didn't need all these houses and I didn't like holding on to things. It was a waste to just let them sit there, empty, and no doubt Isabella knew better than me about how to manage multiple homes. But she'd hurt me. In my mind, there wasn't a single doubt that she tried to have me killed. That bomb hadn't just gone off by itself.

"Are you okay?"

At first, I didn't know who had asked me. But when I looked up from where I was sitting, I found a five-year-old boy standing in front of me, hands in his pockets. His big eyes were looking right at me as he waited for my answer.

"I'm okay. I just have a lot on my mind."

"You were walking back and forth. Mama and Baba were worried about you."

"That's very sweet of them. Walking helps me think. Let's get you back to your mama and baba."

"They're talking. They won't notice me for a little bit."

"You shouldn't do that. What if you got kidnapped?"

"I'm safe here."

His level of confidence at such a young age baffled me. "How do you know you can trust me?"

"I just do. You seem like a nice person. I'll go pick some flowers for you."

"Flowers?" But he was already gone.

I figured he had run off, gotten distracted as kids did, but not more than five minutes later he was back by my side with a handful of picked flowers.

"Mama got mad at me because I'm not supposed to pick flowers here, but they're already picked so here you go."

"That's very kind of you," was all I had time to say before he ran off again. I saw him run to his parents who waved at me.

It hit me then: Total strangers let their boy run up to me,

and all he had wanted to do was give me flowers because he knew that I was sad. I sat there and cried. People walking by probably thought I was crazy, but I didn't care. All the feelings I'd been bottling inside came flooding out of me. I didn't ask for this life. I had been quite happy with the way things were going before Lord Anthony had left me his fortune in his will. Money just caused trouble. Here I was on the other side of the world, chasing a family member I never knew we had, with a boyfriend who couldn't get away from his ex-girlfriend. It was a ridiculous situation.

After a while, when I had let my emotions have their time, my rational thoughts began to push through. I realized I never gave Sebastian a chance to respond, and I had let Isabella get to me. I called him, hoping he would answer.

"You never let me explain," Sebastian said after the first ring.

"I know and I'm sorry."

"Where are you? I'll come meet you."

"No."

"Anne . . ."

"I know you love me. And I love you. I know there's a good explanation for Isabella being here, but I can't be near you while you're still their lawyer. While you're still finishing up your duty to them."

"I understand," he said.

He sounded so dejected. I wanted to run over and tell him I would be waiting for him. "Sebastian . . ."

"You don't need to explain. I love you, Anne. Go find your uncle. I'll take care of what's going on here."

"Thanks Sebastian."

"I love you, Anne."

"I love you too," I said, but he had already hung up.

I stayed where I was until the sun started to set. The hotel was off limits now. It would be too weird for me to go back there. I couldn't go and find Mary either as I wasn't ready to confront her again. But this house that I owned in Taipei—maybe it was time for me to go pay it a visit.

This couldn't be right. This place was tiny. How could a Wilkens own this? Maybe it was unassuming from the outside and ostentatious on the inside? That would be about right. But this was Anthony we were talking about. Maybe it had wood carvings all throughout too? Okay, I shouldn't make fun of the guy. I *am* looking for his son after all . . . who might be a crazy person for all I knew.

I rechecked the address I had in my hand. The taxi driver was adamant that this was the correct address.

It was a condo complex. Probably about twenty stories tall. Big U shape with everything—and I mean everything—in concrete and tile. It was brown and tan in color, with a big black gate. It seemed in pretty good shape for a complex that Anthony had bought in the fifties. The people who owned the other buildings must have enough money to keep it well maintained. And you couldn't say that for a lot of the other older complexes that I'd seen around Taipei.

I buzzed the intercom and said that I needed to get into a unit in the building. A security guard met me when I walked in.

"Who are you here to see?" he asked in Mandarin.

"No one."

"I can't let you stay then."

"No. No. I own one of the units. I inherited it actually." I hoped that I'd translated the word 'inheritance' correctly in Mandarin.

"Which unit is it? I have never seen you before."

"Unit 2078."

"You are the owner?"

"Yes. Why?"

"Nothing. That unit has been vacant for a long time. A cleaner comes once a year, but recently he has been coming every two weeks."

"A cleaner? Someone is actually taking care of it?"

"Yes. Do you know why?"

I could tell he was fishing for information and I started to feel uncomfortable. "I don't, but I'd like to go up now."

"You have the key?"

"Yes, yes I do." Thank goodness Sebastian had insisted that I bring all the information about the condo, even though at the time I'd had no interest in visiting it. I was guessing that Anthony bought the condo to get close to Harrison. It couldn't be Rose, because Rose was in Astoria. She'd also had her own family. I wondered if Anthony and Harrison had ever met. Why else had he kept this house all this time?

I took the stairs, thinking that it would prolong the inevitable. What was I going to find in there? But by the fifth floor I was tired; I was really out of shape. The elevator dinged and when it opened, I got on. It started moving back down and I let it. At some point it stopped and an older gentleman came on. I didn't think anything of it until I saw the bucket he was pushing with a mop and broom. He was dressed in slacks and a button-down shirt, a far cry from a cleaner. I was so mesmerized that I didn't realize he had pressed the button for the twentieth floor until the door opened. Somehow, I knew he was going to my unit. Don't ask me why. Weirder things have happened before that I trusted my instinct on this one.

The guy got out. I followed him. He looked at me. I didn't blame him. And yet, he didn't say anything or stop. He just kept going, and I kept following him.

"You have the key?"

"Um . . . yes." How did he know I would have the key?

"Open it then."

"Oh, okay." I dug through my purse until I found the key ring. A blossom, of course, was at the end of the key ring. I put it into the door and sure enough it opened. We both walked in. The place was immaculate and I loved it from first sight.

"I just need to grab my vacuum and I will be out of your way."

"Oh, you're not in my way. Did you know I was coming?"

"I did not know when you were coming, but I did know you were coming at some point."

"How?"

"I received a letter earlier this year that said you were the new owner. It requested that I get the house ready for you. I was to come once every two weeks to make sure it stayed clean."

"But how did you know it was me? You didn't seem surprised at all."

"The letter had a picture too."

"That would do it," I said under my breath. "Do you remember who it was from?"

"It started with an S and was long. My English is good. That's why Anthony hired me, but I have not talked to someone in English in a long time. I cannot remember the name."

"Oh, that's okay." I was pretty sure it was Sebastian. A part of me tightened up at the thought of him. I wished he were here to share this with me. He would have been so happy and supportive, but I had pushed him away. And then there was Isabella. I did not want her here—ever.

"You said Anthony hired you?"

"Yes."

We both stood there for a while waiting for the other to

speak, until I asked, "Can you tell me anything about Anthony?"

"Yes."

There was a pause and I thought I'd have to persuade him for more details, but I didn't have to wait long before he said, "Anthony was a kind man. Odd, but maybe because he wasn't Taiwanese. His chopstick skills were funny to watch, but he never let anyone stop him from learning and perfecting the technique. He was better at using chopsticks than I was by the last time I saw him. Do you know how he is?"

"He passed away last year."

He only nodded. "I always thought he wouldn't come back. But I had hope. I would have liked to have seen him again. I never knew why he required me to continue to clean the condo."

"Did he ever have guests?"

"No guests. Always alone."

"Oh . . ."

"Do you think he came here to see someone?" he asked.

I didn't know this guy well enough so I thought I'd err on the side of caution. "I don't know."

"How did you inherit the house?"

"It's a long story. Do you mind if I just explore a bit?"

"Yes. Yes. I'm leaving. Let me grab the vacuum."

I watched as he wound up the cord, pushed the vacuum across the living room, opened the door, pushed it out into the hallway, and closed the door inch by inch. He really wanted to know more but I was tired of answering questions. I needed time to process this new place and figure out my next steps.

I did a slow three-sixty in the living room. The room was only about fifteen by twenty feet. A small four by six foot dining area was next to it. Behind the dining area was a bathroom that could only fit one person at a time but had an enclosed glass shower. I went back to the living room and faced away from the entrance. There were two sets of stairs, one went down and the other up from this floor. The bedrooms must be upstairs, and was that the kitchen below?

I ventured down and sure enough, I was greeted with a galley kitchen with tiles everywhere and stainless steel counters. I opened up the cabinets to find they held the bare necessities but had the prerequisite butcher's knife. I wondered if Anthony had done his own cooking here or if he'd hired a cook. I wondered if that cook was as talented as Cook at the mansion. Something told me he or she might have been if Anthony was involved. But maybe he had cooked his own meals—or did what we did, which was eat out every day. But then, why stock up the kitchen?

I left the puzzle behind and went up the stairs. There were two bedrooms, one on either side of the staircase. Both were simple and quite small compared to the rooms in the mansion. They were both about the same size as the living room, with a queen bed in each, and there were built-in closets and a desk in each room too. Other than that, the place was quite bare, but everything was clean and made up.

It still astounded me that all of this was mine—I didn't need to ask permission to live here or use anything.

I thought about the cleaner. Even he knew Anthony better than I ever would. And given his age now, he must have been quite young when he was initially hired. I couldn't believe he was still around.

I decided to treat myself to a night out at Gong Guan Night Market and ate my fill of gua bao and pearl milk tea. With a full belly, I went home and put myself to bed after having a good long cry.

CHAPTER 22

THE NEXT MORNING, I WAS WALKING THROUGH THE lobby when the security guard surprised me. All of a sudden, he was right in front of me.

"You're Anne."

Not so much a question as it was a statement. I felt trapped and started looking for an escape route.

"Um . . ."

"I called Mary and she verified who you were. Told me to share what I know about Anthony with you."

Well, this changed things a bit.

"There was a boy who once came to visit Anthony," he continued.

My heart lept. "You saw the boy? Who was he? What did he look like?"

"He had green eyes, just like Anthony. I think they were father and son. The boy looked white and Taiwanese. It was a very odd combination but he was handsome and they looked similar. He was probably in junior high at the time. Did you know them both?"

"Not really. Did you ever talk to the boy? Did Anthony ever talk to you about why he was here?"

"Yes, but who are you? Mary would only give me your name."

He knew something. I could feel my heartrate increase at the knowledge that he knew something else. Unlike the cleaner, I threw caution to the wind. It didn't matter that the security guard creeped me out a little. I told him an abridged version of who I was, only mentioning Ah Po as someone Anthony knew and befriended, and that Anthony had given me a clue to finding a long-lost uncle. To say the guy was shocked was an understatement. I couldn't help it though. I needed to know more and any clues I could get would be helpful.

"You should come in," he said, motioning me into his office.

The place was immaculate and it was obvious that he ran a tight ship. I watched as he grabbed a notepad and a pen. He seemed to be in a rush all of a sudden.

"Here's my baba's address."

"Your baba is still alive?"

"Yes." He gave me a look as if wondering why I would think his baba had died. And then I remembered that Anthony had died young compared to most old people these days. I felt ashamed at the thought.

"Sorry, I jumped to a conclusion."

"Baba was the security guard here when Anthony bought the place. Baba learned the love of independence from Anthony. So much so that he wouldn't move in with us when he got older. It is quite frustrating as I don't like him living by himself, but Anthony had given him enough money to live comfortably for the rest of his life, so he's determined to stay in his house till he dies. He at least let us hire a nurse to make sure someone's there if he falls."

"Does he fall often?"

"More than normal in the last two years."

"Do you think he'd mind if I went over to ask questions?"

"No. I think he would enjoy the company."

"Could you tell me a little bit more of what you know?"

"I met the boy. He came looking for Anthony. I do not know what they talked about or what they did because they went straight to the condo. I'd never seen anyone like him before, so I remember him well. But Baba was working here then. I was only dropping lunch off for him, so I didn't stay. I don't know if the boy ever came back.

"Baba would talk about Anthony a lot. He seemed to idolize him. But he never mentioned the boy except once. He said Anthony was extremely sad and very much wanted his family. I know Anthony came back one more time, just once when I had started working here. He was a nice man. All the neighbors liked him, at least the ones I talked to. Everyone thought he was . . . what is that word you use? Exotic? Girls wanted to get to know him better. He didn't give them any notice though. He was polite but he never went out. My baba will know more. He loved the man."

"Thank you for sharing."

"I hope you find your uncle. I've always been curious about what happened to him. I never saw him again and Anthony never talked about him, but I saw once that Anthony was carrying a picture of him in his wallet. He was giving me his card access when the photo fell out. I recognized the boy. He must be a Ah Gung now. Do you know anything else?"

"Only that Mary is looking for him too." I wasn't sure how much more I should share with him. "What else can you tell me?"

I waited till I thought I was going to burst. He seemed deep in thought and I didn't want him to stop sharing, but this silence was driving me crazy.

"Mary's the one who's been managing the cleaning service here."

"Why?" I exclaimed. Why would Mary have anything to do with this place?

"She came to visit once while Anthony was here. I remember because Anthony never had visitors. When he did, everyone knew. News travels fast here. I'm sure all the neighbors know about you coming today already."

"Great," I mumbled.

"What was that?"

"Nothing. Please keep going."

"Mary comes by about once every six months. I don't know what she does here, but she asks me to keep an eye on the place: make sure no one breaks in, make sure the cleaner has access to it, you know. Ah, the cleaner— have you talked to him?"

"Yes, but he didn't share anything useful."

"He's interesting. Anthony was the only person who was ever nice to him. He was cleaning here before Anthony bought the place, and everyone here made fun of him. He doesn't talk a lot. Keeps to himself. Mumbles to himself sometimes. We all think he's strange and not right in the head, but he was loyal to Anthony. He's also honest. We've never had any issues with him going into people's homes when cleaning. Nothing stolen."

"That's good . . . Ah, I think I need to go now. Thank you for the address. Do you think it's okay if I stop by your baba's house now?"

"Yes, he's always home."

"Thank you for the information."

"I'll let you know if I think of anything else. It's been such a long time."

The security guard's baba was not that far away, only a short ten minute subway ride. The building blended into everything that surrounded it: brown, brick, and only two stories tall. The whole complex looked like it had been there for decades if not for over a century.

I rang the button and a female voice came over the intercom. "Hello?"

"I'm looking for Mr. Lu. His son who works as a security guard at my condo complex asked me to come here." I should have learned his name.

"Come up," was all I heard before a buzzer went off.

"Thank you," I said, but she had already hung up.

I walked through a tiny courtyard, big enough to fit a car and maybe a motorcycle, and up the stairs. After that one time in the elevator in Mary's complex, I avoided small elevators. Unit 222 looked like it could have been an apartment door in the States. It was made of metal and looked worn. I knocked on the door, hoping I wasn't intruding. I didn't have to wait long before a nurse about my age opened the door.

"Hi, I'm Anne."

"I'm Sophie. I only use that name here and during English class. No one really calls me that although Mr. Lu insists that everyone has English names. I don't know why. I think it's odd."

"Is he here?"

"Yes, he's out on the balcony people watching. It's his favorite thing to do. He says he used to do that when he worked as a security guard. It creeps me out, so I just leave him on the balcony and clean up the place while he's out there."

I had to admit that creeped me out, too, but I guess as a security guard there wasn't much else you could do.

"Thank you. Is it okay if I go out to see him?"

"Of course. He might be sleeping."

"Okay."

I walked to the balcony and saw an older gentleman dressed in slacks and a button-down shirt, sitting in a wheelchair gazing off at what I could only assume was his imagination as he didn't seem to be looking at any one person or thing.

"Hi," I said while tiptoeing up to him. I didn't want to startle him.

His head slowly turned toward me and for a second, I thought this visit would be a waste of time. There was no way this man looked coherent or even capable of remembering someone from so long ago. No matter what his son said about him loving Anthony.

"You are Anne."

"I am," I said, startled.

"You are wondering how I know."

"Yes . . ." I looked back inside wondering how the nurse had been so quick to announce my presence before I had arrived. But that was impossible. I had come straight out. Why was I even arguing with myself?

"Mary was here this week. She told me about you. Showed me a picture. You're very pretty for an American girl."

"Um . . . thank you," was all I could muster after the shock of hearing that Mary had been here. Mary and Mr. Lu knew each other? What else was Mary holding out on me?

"Come. Sit. I see you have a lot of questions. Mary said she couldn't share anything with you. I think the old lady is holding onto the past too tight, but that is her decision. Me, I'm less so. I like to share my stories so that others will remember them for me. I'm not getting any younger. Someone needs to know them or the stories will get lost."

"Do you have something you want to tell me?"

"Is that not what I was saying?"

"Yes . . ." I think I'll just sit here and be quiet.

"You're here to ask about Harrison."

"Yes." One word answers seemed safe.

"I cannot tell you much about Harrison, but I can tell you about Anthony."

"That would be great." *Anything would be good.*

"Anthony was a gentleman. He was the best I ever met, nice to everyone, and always thinking of others."

Uh, maybe this guy was a bit biased . . .

"When he first arrived to look at the condo, he looked sad. Like a big burden was upon him. He dressed very nicely. Always in a suit. Always well dressed. Nothing was out of place. Over time, he told me about his life in America. He didn't want to go back. He wanted to stay here but he couldn't. He had a family in America."

And they didn't know he was here. Thank goodness they never found out. I can only imagine what crazy schemes they would have come up with to get ahold of this property and Harrison.

"What a great man he was. He ran a big company, had a big house, could provide for everyone, and live a really good life."

Money. It's always the money.

"A boy came to visit him once. He seemed to be the same age as my son. He looked like Anthony, but had Taiwanese features too. Now, you see more children who are mixed, but not then. I don't have anything against them but why go mixing up culture? It only causes trouble. Anthony is a good man. He didn't need all this trouble. The boy was whiter looking than Taiwanese, and he stood out. I knew he couldn't have had a good life here. I could tell there was nothing good that could have come from Anthony meeting with him, or for either of them for that matter. They should have left everyone to their own lives."

"But they were baba and son."

"Ah, so they *were* baba and son."

"You just said . . ."

"I only guessed. They looked alike but I didn't know. Anthony was very quiet about the details."

Sheesh, I needed to keep my mouth shut more.

"He looked even more worn out after the boy left. He came back one more time, but after that he didn't visit again. That's when Mary started showing up. She was even more quiet about the details. Never saying more than she needed to. Nice enough but very secret. Are you the same?"

"I . . ."

"No need to answer. I'm old. I miss him. He was so interesting to talk to. I've never met anyone like him again. I always wondered what happened to him. Do you know?"

"He lived a good life with his family. Ran a good business. He passed away last year."

"Oh." I thought I saw a tear rolling down his cheek, but I didn't want to do anything to offend him. The guy really liked Anthony. Almost worshipped him. Not for the first time, I wished I had met Anthony in person. It would have been nice to know the man who literally changed my life.

"I think I'll leave now. Thank you for sharing so much with me."

"Wait, there's something you should have." He pressed a button and the nurse came in. There was something in the back of his closet that he needed to get. Very important. Must give it to me before I left.

What could he possibly have that I must have? But then again, Mary was in contact with him. Maybe his story was just as entwined with the rest of us. Was he a secret relative I didn't know about? Please no. I couldn't learn about another new family member at this time.

She came back ten minutes later holding a rectangular box.

"This painting arrived at the condo one day, addressed to Anthony. I've been holding on to it all these years, hoping he would come back and I could give it to him in person."

Mr. Lu handed me the box and I took it with greedy hands. Finally, something tangible from someone who was willing to talk. I opened up the box and saw a beautiful portrait of Anthony and Harrison. The amount of detail that was in the painting took my breath away.

"Thank you for this. It means a lot."

"No need to say thank you. I'm glad to see it go to someone who will take care of it. I need to rest now. I'm not young anymore."

"Thank you. I mean, I'll go now. It was really good to talk to you."

"Oh, one more thing. There is a letter in the back of the painting."

I turned the painting around and sure enough, there was a yellowed envelope tucked into the canvas.

"You notice the flower in the corner?" Mr. Lu continued.

I looked down to see Harrison's plum blossom in the bottom corner of the painting. Once again, there was no signature.

"I never found a signature on the painting so I don't know what it means."

"I think I do," I said, smiling.

"Good. Good. I'm glad someone does. Let me know if you find the boy."

"I will."

I felt a rush in me that I hadn't felt since I'd arrived in Taiwan. The painting wasn't a clue to help me find Harrison, but it was something tangible. And then there was the letter. I couldn't wait to get back to my place and read it.

I'll never get tired of eating here. The last piece of fried chicken went into my mouth, followed by a big gulp of boba milk tea. I'd be surprised if I hadn't gained ten pounds by the time I left Taiwan. I lay on the sofa thinking about the last week. We had come here to find my uncle and have a vacation. I missed Sebastian. I wondered what he was doing. It made me upset that Isabella was in the picture again. Why couldn't her family just leave mine alone? And why was Mary helping Anthony all these years? I thought she hated him.

It was at that moment that I remembered the letter. I rummaged in my purse until I found it. It had yellowed with age, and the glue gave with the slightest touch. I pulled out a thin piece of paper with neat block handwriting.

Anthony,

Harrison will not send this to you, but I know he wants you to have it. He spent weeks painting this, and I know he is conflicted about his feelings for you. Maybe this painting will allow you to reach out to him again.

Grace

He was still with Grace! Renewed energy surged through me. I went to grab the white notebook. I remembered there was one more address in Taipei that I had circled—something to tackle in the morning. All of this was spurring my curiosity and I decided to read some more of Mary's journal. If it was a tearjerker then I could eat and sleep on it for the rest of the day.

44年7月31日 (Sunday, July 31, 1955)

Mama pulled a miracle today. She told me that she was tired of seeing me so sad and useless. So, she went to Liang-

Chun's grandmother who she knew well because she has been coming to our store for a long time. She didn't tell me what they talked about, but his grandmother gave me her blessing! She's going to let us get married! I couldn't believe Mama had done that. I'm so happy.

44年8月6日 (Saturday, August 6, 1955)

His parents are saying they won't help us financially in any way, but Baba said that is not a concern. Liang-Chun has come to visit, and we are both very happy. We will figure out how to survive without his parents' help.

44年11月18日 (Friday, November 18, 1955)

We are married! It was a small wedding in our living room. We had my two older brothers with their family, Mama, Baba, Harrison, and one of Liang-Chun's brothers in attendance. We went to a restaurant to eat because it was a special day. Then we were in our bedroom in the back of Mama and Baba's store, the happiest couple.

45年6月4日 (Monday, June 4, 1956)

We are so happy. Harrison loves having Liang-Chun around all the time. He has started calling him Baba, which makes us all smile. Our baby will be coming soon too. Harrison likes to poke me in the stomach to make the baby move. He is doing well in school, and I'm happy with our lives.

45年8月7日 (Tuesday, August 7, 1956)

Chi-Yue was born today. She is perfect. Forty-three centimeters, more than two and a half kilograms, and cries so much. But we love her and I cannot wait for Harrison to meet her.

45年10月5日 (Friday, October 5, 1956)

Harrison put the baby outside in the cold today! He says she doesn't belong here, and he was waiting for the mail person to come and pick her up. He had found my mail supplies and stuck a stamp to her forehead. My poor Harrison. I have not been giving him a lot of time. Liang-Chun is tired too. Chi-Yue is keeping us up all night. Harrison is complaining he's not able to sleep because of her crying. I'm so tired. No more writing for a while.

46年4月6日 (Saturday, April 6, 1957)

I got a letter from Rose! She is coming in July! Harrison won't know who she is and she wants to keep it that way. She's coming to introduce her daughter to her family. Her daughter, Josephine, is eight! Only one year younger then Harrison. I didn't even know she'd had another child. I'm an Aunt! I cannot wait to meet her and for her to meet Chi-Yue. We have received a couple of cards in the past from Rose, but that has been it. I'd almost thought she'd forgotten about her son.

Mary is talking about Mom! "Aahhh!"

46年6月6日 (Thursday, June 6, 1957)

Little Josephine looks like Harrison, and yet she doesn't. She looks more like Rose than Harrison does. You would never know they were siblings unless someone told you. That's probably a good thing. Less questions around here. I can't stop staring at her. Rose named her after Josephine who she owns the bakery with. She has been doting on Harrison all night, and I worry that Harrison will find out because Rose won't be able to hold it in.

My curiosity also took over. I asked her why she'd left Harrison here when he was only five months old. She told me the whole story. I had no idea! I'll never forgive the Wilkens for what they did to her. Thank goodness for fate allowing her to meet Josephine instead of someone else, and that my parents grocery store was down the street from them. But it was my brother's crush on her that sealed our fate. Our lives could have been so different. We would never have become friends. Who knows what would have happened to Harrison?

46年6月18日 (Tuesday, June 18, 1957)

Harrison has instantly taken to Josephine. It was like they knew they were connected. No one can separate them. Watching Rose with Harrison is breaking my heart though. She should never have come. This time it's going to be a lot harder for her to leave without him. I can tell she is torn and wants to take him with her, but his life is here now. He doesn't know any other life, and to tell him that Rose is actually his mama will confuse him and make him not like either of us.

46年6月22日 (Saturday, June 22, 1957)

Rose and Josephine left tonight. I'm back to holding Harrison while he cries himself to sleep. He told me that Josephine understood him better than Mei-Jing did. He wanted them to stay. Why did they have to leave? I couldn't tell him that I had wondered the same thing for many nights before too.

I was starting to get a better idea of why Mary was the way she was. I wondered what had happened to Harrison if he had had such a good life with Mary. I couldn't keep reading though. On that last page, I'd been nodding off every couple of sentences. I decided that tomorrow would be a good day to tackle all these new findings.

CHAPTER 23

Rrrriiinnnnggg.

What in the world?

I somehow found my phone. It had fallen off the bed and onto the floor overnight. I raised the screen and saw that I had already missed a call.

"Hello?"

"Anne?"

"Brian?" Now my eyes were wide open, but my brain was still in a fog.

"Hey Anne." I heard a sigh of relief, and I was confused

"Hey Brian. Something I can help you with?"

"I was just wondering what you were doing today?"

"Um, I'm not sure. I think I'm going to go and find someone who knew my uncle."

"Can I come with?"

"Sure . . . What time is it?"

"It's eleven thirty in the morning."

For a moment I was speechless. *How could it be that late? I never sleep in that late.* "Meet me at the Chiang Kai-Shek subway station in an hour."

"See you there."

He hung up before I could respond, but I didn't hesitate to jump out of bed. I stood in the shower for as long as I could, ran out the door, grabbed a dang bing, and sat down on the stairs leading to the subway station. It wasn't until then that I thought about what I'd just done. Did I just agree to meet with Brian, and on top of that, he wanted to come with me to find someone who knew my uncle? And I'd given Sebastian a hard time with Isabella only yesterday... The irony did not slip past me. I took out my phone to text Sebastian to tell him that I missed him, that I loved him, and that I wished he were here . . . . But I didn't do any of that. Instead, I pocketed the phone and rode the subway to meet Brian.

I could feel my hands sweating when I saw him. It was cold so I couldn't blame it on the heat. He came over and gave me a hug. A really nice hug that smelled and felt right, and I knew that I would forever associate him with the brand of cologne that he always wore.

"You look great, Anne."

"You don't look bad yourself." I took a breath and asked what was on my mind. "Brian, why did you call me?"

"I'm not sure. I didn't want to hang out with my other friends and my first thought was of you. I thought I'd ring you to see if you were keen to catch up."

"How did you get my number?"

"Sebastian gave me both of your numbers so we could get together another time."

Before Sebastian knew who you were.

"You don't mind if we hang out today, do you? Just as friends."

"No, that's fine." It wasn't fine at all, but I didn't know

what to say, and part of me was glad that I wasn't going to go and meet a total stranger by myself. What harm could come to us hanging out today anyway?

"So, where is this person you want to meet? And why are you searching for your uncle?" Brian asked.

"He works near here, and it's a long story about my uncle."

"I've got all day. Why don't we go grab brunch? You can update me. My treat."

"That sounds great. I'm so hungry."

"I know just the place to take you." With a nudge of his head toward the station we rode the subway to Zhong Xiao Dong Lu. He took me through alleyways to the point that I was turned around. The scenery all blended together until I caught the smell of fresh tortillas and fried chips. I hadn't had a taco in forever. Okay, maybe a couple of weeks ago, but the thought that I could get one here made the smell even more tantalizing.

"Welcome to the best and only Mexican restaurant for miles, if not the whole island!" Brian exclaimed.

I was already walking in, following the smell. The menu was not what I thought though. This had happened to me in KFC too. I wanted two pieces of chicken, a biscuit, and a side of coleslaw. I got the chicken, but I didn't see any of the usual sides. There were buns but not biscuits, congee with chicken strips, and stringy pork floss. The food surprised me though, and it ended up tasting even better than what I'd had in the States. Everything was fresher. Not to mention that there were a lot of people in the multiple floor restaurant—and I meant restaurant, not fast-food place.

"Do they have quesadillas?"

"No, but you can get a burrito."

"That's good enough."

Brian ordered me my favorite burrito without even

asking. I had found a table and was wiping it down when he came to join me. He sat on my left knowing I liked having elbow room when I ate, and that I needed the space to reach across and get my drink. I gave him my hot sauce and he tore off his extra tortilla skins and passed them to me. Then, we just sat there and ate, not a word between us, because we both knew we liked to savor our food and not eat it cold.

"Here, you might need these." Brian handed me a stack of napkins, which I used to wipe up the wad of salsa that had dropped out of my burrito. The cheesy goodness was so good, and I realized that during my time in Taiwan, I hadn't had any cheese until now.

"Brian, this is delicious. How'd you find this place?"

"I followed my nose."

I laughed so hard that some food came out, which was disgusting, and yet Brian didn't care. He was laughing with me.

"I forgot how you make me laugh," I said. It felt right being here with him.

"Yeah, you have the best laugh."

"Aw, thanks Brian."

I looked up from my burrito to find him staring at me. His expression was so intense that I had to look away. I refocused on my food and could feel a blush creeping over my cheeks.

"So, who are we meeting?" he asked.

"You're really interested in hearing what I've been up to?"

"Yes, I am." He just sat there, waiting for me to speak. It was the oddest thing. Usually, Brian couldn't stop talking. He always had to be the first person to tell a story and get the last word in. It was one of the annoying things I remembered about him. But maybe he had changed.

"It started with my Ah Po a long time ago." I told him the whole story. Every detail except for Sebastian. He didn't need to know about my love life. Plus, they had already met. "After

Rose left the Wilkens, she worked for a lady named Josephine."

"Who your mom's named after!"

"Good memory!" I said, actually impressed. I continued, "There, she met Charlie and Mary who were siblings, and worked at their parents grocery store down the street. Rose married Charlie and moved to Astoria. Mary moved with her parents to Hong Kong. It was in Astoria that Rose had her baby, Harrison."

"And this is who you're looking for now," Brian said.

"Yeah!" Wow, he was paying attention. "Then some people, presumably sent by Lord Wilkens, tried to kidnap her baby. So they sent Harrison to Hong Kong to live with Charlie's family. They ended up back in Taiwan, and Mary raised Harrison as her own even though she was very young. Something happened during his time with Mary, and she no longer knows where he is. And here we are in 2011 still searching for him."

He'd nodded his head throughout the story. I liked this new Brian. He listened.

"I'm staying at the condo I own through Anthony, and I learned a lot from the security guard who works there. I'm newly motivated and want to go and check out my next lead, which is another address in this little white book." I pulled the notebook out of my purse to show him.

"Wait, what? You own a condo here?"

"Yes, I do." *Was that all he took from the story?*

"That's way cool."

I felt guilty for liking his approval. Then I got back on task and asked him, "Would you still like to meet this person I'm looking for? I don't want to go alone."

"Definitely! There's no hurry though. You take your time," he said, gesturing at my food as he leaned back in his chair. As usual, he had scarfed down his burrito. More like inhaled it while I was only halfway through mine.

"I see you still devour your food like a velociraptor."

"I'd like to think that I like my food hot. When it starts getting warm, I don't want to eat it anymore. It's better to eat it as fast as I can."

"You haven't changed," I said, and I hated myself when I heard a little sigh escape my lips.

"Should I have?"

"No. You were always great the way you were." *Oh wow! Why did I just say that?* I hurriedly tried to cover it up with, "It still baffles me that you want to come along."

"I want to hang out with you. Is that so weird? We used to do all sorts of things together. And beside, I haven't seen you in ages."

"Okay." But something inside me was sounding an alarm. I pushed it aside. It was nice to have an old friend back. Everyone else was gone at the moment. It would be good to have someone with me, especially a boy to meet a man I didn't know.

We walked up and down the street trying to find the place. When we found it, I was amazed—not at the store but at the fact that we'd even found it. It was by accident, too, given we had walked up and down that block probably ten times. The entrance was no more than a body width wide. The sign was about five inches tall, centered over the door frame, and there was no neon sign flashing in all sorts of colors to catch your eye. It was literally a hole in the wall. Brian gave me a little nudge and I moved through the door.

The inside was amazing. There were massive office supply stores everywhere in Taipei. They were usually two to three floors of pens, DVDs, pencils, dolls, paper of all sizes, binders, clips, erasers, stickers, and every cute office thing you could think of. I loved going through them and finding hidden gems on the shelves. But this place—this place was something else. It was like I had stepped back in time. Brown bookcases lined the walls. There were typewriters, paper, old fountain pens, and then there was the big dresser-like block of wood that ran down the middle of the store. On each side were little drawers, just like you would find in an old library catalog or a hardware store, and what I found inside made me giddy. There were pastels of different colors, paints, ink, stamps, stamp pads, paper cut into flowers, ducks, giraffes, monkeys, and a host of other animals. I knew I could stay in this store all day. It was a miracle that there weren't more people here. At least, that was my opinion. I wondered how in the world this store stayed in business.

"Can I help you?" asked an old man with large, wire rimmed glasses and thin strands of hair swept across his bald spot.

"Oh, hi. Yes. I'm here to see Mr. Wang."

"That is me."

"Hi. I already said that. Um . . . do you have some time to talk with me?"

"We are talking right now." I could hear Brian snickering behind me. He wasn't helping.

"Right. I'm Anne. This is Brian. I'm looking for Harrison Lin. I found a letter that said he used to work for you." The guy didn't change expression at all, as if this wasn't a surprise to him.

"Come with me."

"Okay . . ."

"Are you sure you want to follow this guy in?" Brian asked, no longer snickering. "He's a bit creepy."

"I'm sure it's fine," I whispered back, sounding braver

than I felt. The guy was creepy, but I needed answers. "Plus, you're here. You'll keep me safe."

"That I will," he said, puffing out his chest. I laughed and slapped him on the arm. That seemed to break the tension, and we both followed Mr. Wang to the back office.

The office was just as old as the store, frozen in time. Brian and I sat down in wooden chairs that swiveled on wheels. We both looked at each other and tried not to laugh. In college, a group of us had taken a few chairs just like these and brought them to the quad where we'd had chair races for hours. I could tell Brian wanted to say more but I shook my head and avoided eye contact with him before I burst out laughing.

Mr. Wang caught my eyes and said, "You are Anne."

"Yes."

"I've been waiting for you."

"What? I mean, how could you be waiting for me?"

"Mary came by earlier this week to let me know that you were looking into Harrison."

"I . . . I don't . . ." I didn't know what to say. Mary again? Why couldn't the woman just tell me herself! This was getting aggravating.

"Mary?" Brian asked.

"My great aunt," I said through clenched teeth.

"Do not be mad at her. She has kept a secret for a long time . . . just as I have. It's hard to break that even if she wanted to."

"Yes. Yes. I know all that. We met with her when we arrived in Taiwan."

"Oh, so you two have met her then?"

"No. Just me, my mom, and my boyfriend."

He looked at Brian. "This is not your boyfriend?"

"No, I'm not her boyfriend," Brian said, but I thought I heard a hint of annoyance in his tone.

Mr. Wang narrowed his eyes at him and said pointedly. "You. Wait outside."

Brian and I looked at each other, wondering if we had heard him right.

"It's really okay if he stays. I don't mind," I said. "He's giving me moral support."

"No. Family only. That is what Mary wanted. No one outside of family is allowed to know what I'm about to tell you."

"Look," Brian said, "I've known Anne for a long time. I used to be her boyfriend. I'm practically family."

"No. Wait outside."

I cut in. "Brian, I'll update you later. I really need to get some answers."

"Okay. Okay. Don't get all tied up in a wad. I don't think this is right, but okay. I'll be in the store if you need me." He gave me a knowing look.

"Thank you, Brian. This shouldn't take long," I said to him with a soft smile.

"Yes. Yes. Not long. Now leave," Mr. Wang said, waving his hand at him.

"Okay. I'm leaving. Geeze."

Once Brian left, Mr. Wang did not mince words. "I do not like that boy. It is good he is not your boyfriend anymore."

"Um . . . you were saying about Mary?"

"Yes. Mary came to tell me that you were here in Taiwan, looking for Harrison. She made me promise that I would not seek you out myself even though I wanted to."

"You wanted to?"

"Yes. I have been waiting all these years for answers as to where Harrison is. I wanted to see who his family was. The day Harrison left me, I went to look for Mary. Harrison had told me where he grew up, so Mary was not hard to find. I thought she could help me find him, but she was just as lost as I was. The boy did not like to stick around for long. As soon as we tracked him down, he was already on to a new place."

Mary had tried to find him. I felt a tear rolling down my cheek. I needed and wanted to go back to the hotel and read more of her journals. She missed him. She must have been worried about him all these years. I couldn't even imagine. Based on her journals, Harrison was her son through and through. She'd raised him.

"Let me show you something."

He opened a closet behind his desk and inside there were stacks of canvases, all covered in beautiful scenes. City landscapes, country landscapes, portraits, and some that were just swirls of color.

"These are all Harrison's. If you ever see him, let him know that they are here. I would like him to take them. They are taking up too much room," he laughed. Then he got solemn. "He never came back. He was like a son to me. It hurts me that he never came to visit."

I could tell that my visit had hit a soft spot and I felt bad for witnessing him cry. The guy looked exhausted. He had waited all these years on a boy who we didn't even know was still alive.

"I am old. Do you know Mary pays me to keep the store running? I think she gets the money from a man named Anthony."

Before I could form a reply, he said, "One more thing." He rummaged through his drawer and pulled out five notebooks. He handed them to me and I tried not to sneeze at the dust coming off of them. I opened the first one to find sketches— of landscapes, of the store, of Mr. Wang, of Mary's house, of what I assumed was Harrison's school, and of himself. I stared at the self-portrait of what looked like a thirteen-year-old boy. He looked sad and so much like Anthony. There was no doubt the boy was Anthony's son.

"These you can take," Mr. Wang said. "They were his practice books when I was teaching him how to paint. The boy has talent. True talent. Not something you usually see. He was a smart boy, and he was compassionate even though he stood out his whole life." There was some silence before he continued, "Did you know that Harrison made me promise to never tell anyone where he was? He did not want his family to find him. I was once a boy. I knew what it was like to get in trouble. But one person was allowed to visit him."

"Was it Grace?"

"Yes. You know her?"

"No, I've heard mention of her though."

"She was very kind, and the only person Harrison let near him."

"Where did he live?"

"Here. I have two bedrooms upstairs. One is my room so I can take a nap in the middle of the day. He did not have much. He came with just a backpack. Never complained. Helped me with everything."

"How did you two meet?"

"I was talking to a friend about how busy I was in the store. My wife could not help anymore because we had just had our first son. Harrison overheard me talking and asked if he could work for me. I could tell the boy was a good kid. An honest kid."

"You could tell? You had just met him."

"I can tell, just like I know you are a good girl and the boy outside is a bad boy."

"Right . . . so you hired him?" I said, trying to change the subject.

"Yes."

"Do you know where he might be?"

"I told you, he is hard to track down. He always talked about traveling. I don't know why he ran away from a good family. He always liked going to the art district though. Couldn't stay away. I walk by there sometimes hoping I'll catch a glimpse of him, but so far nothing."

"Is the art district around here?"

"Yes. If you find him, tell him he must come back to pay his respects and retrieve his canvases. I will be waiting."

"I will do that." I could tell that I'd been dismissed, and he looked as though he could fall asleep in his seat. I walked back into the store, and Brian accosted me as soon as I came out.

"Are you okay? What did he say?"

"I'll tell you on the way back to the condo. Some of the pieces are starting to come together. I now know where my uncle got his art training from. I have a lot to think about."

CHAPTER 24

THE WALK BACK WAS UNEVENTFUL. BRIAN STAYED quiet while I talked. I showed him the notebooks, and he ooed and aahed at them. He also held onto them a bit longer than I would have liked. I took them back and put as many in my purse as I could fit.

Mr. Wang's talk about Brian must have hit a nerve, but I had known Brian for a long time. We were one person all through college. We did everything together. He understood me in a way Sebastian didn't because he was also Taiwanese American.

"Here we are," I said when we reached the condo.

Brian lingered, seemingly not wanting to leave. I was starting to get confused as to why he was hanging out with me. It had been nice reverting back to some of our old habits, but this was kind of out of the blue.

"Let's have breakfast tomorrow," he said. "I can meet you here. I found a wonderful breakfast spot you'll love. It has all your favorite Taiwanese breakfast food." He picked up my hand and rubbed the back of it.

I was really getting confused now. "Um . . . Brian."

"I know we haven't seen each other in a long time and we didn't end on great terms, but I've missed you."

"I have a boyfriend," I said, just dumping it there.

"And where is he now?" Brian returned.

"Well . . . it's not his fault."

"Look, I just want to have breakfast with you. Nothing more."

We stood like that until I couldn't look him in the eyes anymore. This was getting to be too much. But then a voice I would never have expected to hear came from across the street, loud and clear. A voice that made me so happy that I almost started crying.

"Hey! You get your hand off her! You wait till I get to you. You'll be a puddle on the ground if you touch her again!"

I didn't want to believe she was here, and I didn't know I needed her until I saw her running across the street when the light turned green, swinging her purse like a weapon. I almost yelled in glee, but I didn't want to get whacked by her purse. Brian, on the other hand, was not so fast.

Whack! It landed right on his back, almost toppling him over.

"You better leave right now before you get another one from me," she threatened.

"Victoria, great to see you again," said Brian.

I smirked at the fact that he was cowering a little before Victoria.

"The feeling is not mutual." If her eyes could shoot darts, Brian would have been covered in them. His spell broken, I watched from the sideline, cheering Victoria on. I wanted him to leave so that I could give my friend a huge hug. I needed one back myself.

"Anne, I'll see you later. Think about breakfast and what we talked about," Brian said to me.

I watched as he turned and a part of me wanted to call

him back, but it was a yearning that was starting to diminish. Before I knew it, Victoria had me in a tight hug, and I gave one just as tight back. I started crying this time.

"What are you doing here?" I asked between sobs.

"Talk later. Right now, you need to feed me and get me updated. Brian? Really?" she asked, giving me a stare that I cowered under.

"He showed up. I didn't ask him to be here."

"Uh huh. How's Sebastian?"

But instead of answering that, I said, "Let's go get you fed." I hooked my arm through hers and went in search of some delicious baked goods.

"Why didn't you tell me there was all this delicious food here?"

I watched as Victoria scarfed down pan fried dumplings. This was the third place we had stopped at. There had been no time to talk but I didn't care. My best friend was here, and I felt like a big stress had lifted from my shoulders.

"I did."

"You so did not. And if you did, you should have dragged me over."

"I'm so glad you're here."

"Me too. What is up with Brian?"

"I bumped into him at the National Taiwan University library. He said . . ."

"Yeah?"

"He said he missed me." I couldn't lie to Victoria. She could always call me out.

"I'm sure he did."

"What if he really does?"

"And what if? What about Sebastian? What about what

Brian did to you? He just left, Anne. Poof. It was like college never happened. I bet he's found out that you're rich now."

"Brian would never do that."

"That's what you think."

"What are you doing here though?" I didn't like all this talk about Brian. It was making me nervous and uncomfortable, and I wasn't ready to talk to her about Sebastian.

"Sebastian called me," Victoria said.

"What?"

"You heard me. Sebastian called me. My opinion about him might be changing. He's not so bad."

"Why? Don't get me wrong. I am *so* glad you're here."

"He said you were being a doofus."

"I highly doubt he said that."

"Maybe not that exact word, but I knew what he was trying to say. And I need to be updated on everything that has happened. Sebastian wouldn't tell me, and he pulled me away from a beautiful cabana with Paul in Hawaii. You owe me and you better have a good story."

"You and Paul are doing well?" I hedged.

"We're doing fantastic, but no more getting off the subject. Spill."

I told her everything that had happened since I last saw her. While I talked, we went and got boba drinks, walked to Taipei 101, window shopped, and had dinner from the street stands. Victoria insisted that she did not want to rest because she needed to stay awake and sleep through the night. I was okay with that, and by the time we got back to the condo we were both exhausted.

"I'm assuming you're staying with me?" I asked, hoping she was.

"Where else would I stay? Sebastian asked me to come, but it's not like he planned the trip. And you've been busy."

"Yeah. It's been a whirlwind. I don't know why my family all of a sudden has so many secrets."

"Well, the secrets have always been there. You're just finding them out, is all."

"You're supposed to be jet lagged. Don't make so much sense."

Her smile fell and she asked softly, "What are you going to do now?"

"I don't know. I just don't know. My uncle could be anywhere."

"I'd like to see this store you went to visit today."

"I'll take you tomorrow. You'll love it." But as I looked over, I found that Victoria had fallen asleep on the sofa. I put a blanket over her and sat down next to her to watch some television. Even though nothing had changed, it felt like what I was searching for suddenly wasn't so hard anymore—as long as I had my best friend beside me.

CHAPTER 25

"I LOVE THIS PLACE!" VICTORIA SQUEALED.

"I thought you might."

I watched as Victoria dug through every nook and cranny she could find. Mr. Wang had popped out when we first came in but after seeing it was me, he went back to his office. Victoria didn't seem fazed that he didn't say hi to her, so I didn't push it. She was too absorbed in what she was finding on the shelves and in the drawers.

"You know, I wonder if he went to any of the art galleries?" Victoria asked, pulling out more drawers.

"That's a good point." Why hadn't I thought of that?

I went to the office and sought out Mr. Wang, but he wasn't there. I yelled up the stairs. I thought I heard a muffled reply, so I started up the stairs. When I reached the top, I saw the door was ajar. There was a faint light seeping out and I could hear crying.

"Mr. Wang, are you okay?"

"Oh, Anne. I didn't know you were coming up."

"I tried to call up, but I wasn't sure what you had said."

"Come in. Come in."

The inside was bare to say the least. There was a mattress on the ground, a small stove in the corner, and a lamp that seemed to provide the only light in the room, but it was warm. The blanket on the bed seemed to be of down and new. The chair by the window was made of leather. The bathroom was clean. Was this where he lived?

"I thought Mary was paying you this whole time?"

"I live a very meager life, don't I?"

"Yes . . ."

"Mary does pay me. I never save the money. I use it to pay the bills and then I send the rest to the Living Art Gallery."

"Are you a sponsor?"

"You could say that."

We stood in silence while I soaked in this new information. Mr. Wang did not seem like he was done telling me stuff, so I waited.

"Living Art Gallery was started to give people a place to see art from living artists. It is where Harrison started showing his work. He submitted his drawings to them thirty years ago, and they loved them. They kept asking for more. I found his work there when I visited the gallery one day. He does not know I have been sponsoring him. He only knows it's from a donor."

"You didn't think to tell me this yesterday?" I managed to say. I was so sick of secrets.

"I did not know if you should know. I had to follow up with Mary."

"So, if I didn't come back today, I would never have found out."

"I believe you would have. It just would have taken you longer."

"Ah!" I stomped all the way back downstairs, grabbed Victoria, and hightailed it out of the store. I was going to break something if I remained in there any longer.

"What's wrong? Can you slow down? These heels don't walk as fast as your tennis shoes."

"Sorry," I said, letting go of her arm and slowing down to match her speed.

"Want to tell me what's going on?"

"Harrison displayed his work in an art gallery. Mr. Wang never thought to mention it to me yesterday. I am so mad right now that I don't even know where we are anymore." We had walked and walked until I was in front of what looked like an old stone gate—one of those castle doors that have a drawbridge but with an Asian twist to it.

We both looked at this old monument that was in the middle of a great big intersection in one of the busiest parts of Taipei. The plaque on it said that it used to be part of the border around the city during the Qing dynasty. I curled up on the underside of the tunnel and cried while Victoria just held me.

I thought about why I had come to Taiwan. I still wanted to find my uncle. If only for Mom's sake as I knew she would like to meet her brother. But here I was, sitting under an ancient artifact in the middle of Taipei City, crying on my best friend's shoulder while not knowing what my boyfriend was doing with his ex-girlfriend. At that moment, I did not like my life at all.

Victoria said, "Let's go home. We can explore more tomorrow. I'll make you some hot soup. We'll binge watch whatever we can find on TV, and we'll call it a day."

"Okay."

I let Victoria lead me to a taxi, then upstairs to my condo where I collapsed on the sofa and just stared out into the void, not really seeing anything.

CHAPTER 26

I woke up the next morning to find Victoria still asleep in the other room. I knew that now was a good time to catch up with Mary's journal. I went to the kitchen to find something to eat and found some lonely tea leaves in the back of the cupboard. It was a reminder that I needed to go grocery shopping as this was no longer a hotel where I could call upon room service. But I had money. Apparently I had enough money to pay the bills and salary of an old art shop, fund my uncle's art career, and pay for the cleaner of this condo.

I stomped back into the living room with Mary's journal, then I remembered that Victoria was still asleep. I cuddled under the blanket and opened up the journal to commiserate with another person's miserable life.

50年2月6日 (Monday, February 6, 1961)

I can't believe it's 1961 already. I haven't written in so long. Life has just been too busy. Harrison is thirteen years old and very handsome. He and Mei-Jing are inseparable and I hope they always stick together. She's good for him. I still worry about Harrison, but I have three other kids now and my attention is pulled in every direction. I know he is feeling neglected and I do not know what to do. It's good that he still has a good relationship with Liang-Chun, and they practice Kung Fu every week.

Something happened today that has made me come back and write this entry. I received a disturbing letter from Anthony this morning. It does not have an address on it. I think it was placed in our mailbox by someone who walked by. How did he find us? What if Harrison had found the letter before me? I did not even know Anthony knew who we were. I've taped the letter here. I don't know where else to put it where Harrison will not find it.

Mary

I know you don't know me but I'm aware that Rose has told you our story. You have the right to think badly of me, but I really do not mean anyone harm. I only recently learned about Harrison, and I hope you will let me come and see him. I have bought a place in Taipei where I can stay to allow my son and I time to get to know each other. I want to be a father to him. Please reach me at this address or number at any time.

Anthony

No! He can't meet Harrison. I promised Rose that I would always keep him safe—away from the Wilkens family. But Anthony has found us. He wants to meet Harrison. Part of me knows Harrison has the right to know his baba, but he doesn't even know I'm not his real mama.

50年2月8日 (Wednesday, February 8, 1961)

I found a carved plum blossom in front of our house today. The kids asked me what it was. I didn't say anything. Harrison made mention that it looked like the glass plum blossom I had given him, but I didn't say anything to him either. If Liang-Chun asks, I'll tell him . . . but not the kids.

50年2月9日 (Thursday, February 9, 1961)

A beautiful drawing of a plum blossom tree with Rose and Anthony under it holding a baby arrived today. I hadn't seen Rose for years and I couldn't help but stare at the drawing for a long time. A tear even escaped my eyes and I quickly wiped it away before any of the kids could see me.

50年2月10日 (Friday, February 10, 1961)

I've received a painting of plum blossoms. This man will not give up. I left a note for him today, telling him my mind will never be changed. He needs to go home and leave us alone. Let Harrison live in peace.

50年2月11日 (Saturday, February 11, 1961)

My oldest tore up the painting! She told me she hates Harrison, and that all he does is cause trouble. I have noticed that she and Harrison pick on each other the most. I'd always thought it was just siblings fighting, like me and my brothers did. But this is more than that and it makes me scared. She actually told me that he does not belong in this family because he does not look like the rest of us. Maybe Harrison meeting with Anthony is a good idea. Then he can learn about the other half of his heritage. Rose, please forgive me. I only want what is best for Harrison.

50年2月12日 (Sunday, February 12, 1961)

I am not going to do it. I changed my mind. No. No. No.

50年2月18日 (Saturday, February 18, 1961)

I am so mad. He thought he could just show up and knock on my door? Disturb my family and demand to see

Harrison? I told him he had no right. The yelling got pretty loud. I am sure I will be hearing from Ms. Yang and Mr. Wu soon. Why could he not stay away? Why does he have to come? Rose said he is married. He has his own family now. Leave Harrison here with me. Leave him alone!

50年2月19日 (Sunday, February 19, 1961)

I am worried about Harrison. He has not been himself all day. Dinner is his favorite meal, and he did not join us today no matter how much I tried to persuade him, or how much Liang-Chun yelled at him. The other kids tried to not join dinner too!

50年2月21日 (Tuesday, February 21, 1961)

I am sitting in my room crying while writing this. Harrison skipped school for the first time today. He has never done that before and has always done good in school. He finally came home late at night and would not tell us where he was. He ignored us and went to bed. What is going on?

50年2月23日 (Thursday, February 23, 1961)

Liang-Chun and I sat Harrison down after learning he has not been in school all week. At first, he just kicked his feet around and would not look at us. He is such a big boy now. Not the little one who used to cuddle in my arms when he was sad. I wanted to go and hug him, but Liang-Chun kept a hand on mine. Eventually, he told us what has been going on, and what he said has stunned me. The Saturday Anthony came to find him, Liang-Chun had taken the kids to the beach. No one was home but me. But Harrison had come back early and heard the yelling from the front door. So he hid and heard Anthony say that he was his baba, and what is worse, he heard that I was not his mama. He looked at me with the most heartbroken face and my heart broke with him. I did not know what to do so I just let him walk away. I do not know where he is right now. He is my son. He is my first child. I will not let anyone else tell me differently.

50年3月15日 (Wednesday, March 15, 1961

Harrison has been going to school these last two weeks. I am still holding my breath. I can only hope that Anthony has left, and Harrison will know he can talk to us more if he needs to. Our oldest is not being nice to him though. I have had to keep them apart this past week. I am so tired. But I promised Rose, and he is my son too.

50年3月31日 (Friday, March 31, 1961)

I cannot believe Chi-Yue gave Harrison the address to the condo Anthony bought! She dug through my drawer and found the letter. I cannot believe she would put him in danger! He is not home yet. This is not happening.

50年4月1日 (Saturday, April 1, 1961)

He will not talk to me. He came home after dinner and went straight to his room. What am I going to do?

50年4月5日 (Wednesday, April 5, 1961)

Anthony needs to leave us alone! He has asked Harrison to go back to the States with him! He dared to ask him directly without coming to me first. True, I would say no, and that is what I told Harrison when he asked. He yelled at me that he was going to go even though I said no. I hope those are just words. I really hope they are just words. It scares me so much, thinking of him walking into Anthony's home. A world, according to Rose, that is like no other. I cannot let him go.

50年4月8日 (Saturday, April 8, 1961)

He left! I am so mad! Chi-Yue helped him sneak out of the house last night and he flew to America! I have been wondering why Chi-Yue and Harrison have been getting along recently. Liang-Chun and I sat Chi-Yue down this morning and questioned her till she finally told us what was going on. I have lost him! I need to let Rose know that he is heading over there. I bet Anthony flew with him. I cannot believe this is happening.

The next entry was about a month and a half later, and it seemed Harrison was back in Taiwan. What had happened during his visit? Great! I was in the middle of a riveting tale, one that involved my own family, and now I had to go back upstairs to find it. Knowing what I know about the Wilkens family, I was dreading what was going to happen to Harrison. I took my time rummaging through my room. When I finally found it, I carried Andy's journal back downstairs only to hear a yelp from Victoria. I almost fell down the last few steps. Victoria came running down the stairs after me and stopped when she saw me.

"Oh, you are here."

"Good morning to you too. Was I supposed to be somewhere else?" I asked, trying to catch my breath.

"I had an awful nightmare and then heard some rustling in your room. I thought you were sneaking out to meet Brian for breakfast."

Oh yeah, breakfast. I had forgotten about it. Hmmm . . .

"Well, I'm here safe and sound. No saving needed."

"Good, I'm going back to sleep then."

"You do that."

As Victoria headed back to bed, I snuggled into the sofa and began reading where I had left off in Andy's journal.

Saturday, April 29, 1961

Anthony has been happier than I have seen him in a long time. Even Sally has noticed because he dances with her randomly in the hallway. I had been wondering what was going on, but today we found out and I don't think Anthony thought this through. He was probably acting from his heart and thought no one could do anything about it, but I feel bad for the boy. He's been thrown into the lion's den. Anthony found his son! And then brought him home! I don't understand. Even after everything he went through with Rose fourteen years ago, he still thought it would be a good idea to bring his child to their home where Lord Wilkens and Lady Mary live . . . and also where his wife, Sally, lives. It doesn't help that Geraldine is still here too. She's twenty-four now, and even more trouble than she was when she was ten. This is not going to end well.

Monday, May 1, 1961

Maybe I spoke too soon. Everyone seems to be on their best behavior. Cook has welcomed him with open arms, and he practically lives in the kitchen most of the day, tasting this and helping to cook that. But I can also feel the tension. Lord Wilkens's scowl has gotten deeper and I see him wringing his hands behind his back more and more now.

Tuesday, May 2, 1961

The doctor came—the same one who was supposed to have given Rose an abortion. I let him in and then escorted him to Lord Wilkens's office. I couldn't help but linger for a moment and heard Lord Wilkens say something about the doctor not having taken care of business like he was supposed to have done. This does not bode well for Harrison. He looks a lot like Anthony and there's no denying he's Anthony's son.

Wednesday, May 3, 1961

Geraldine tried to tell Harrison about his mother today and thank goodness I was walking by and could stop her. Who knows what vile things she was going to say about Rose? I won't stand for it! Rose has finally started having a life again. Josephine and her bakery are doing very well. I still order food from there about once a month, and I visit at a set time so Josephine knows I'm coming. I wait till Rose is gone before I come up to the building. Josephine always has our food ready for us. It's only food for Cook and I, but this exercise has allowed me to watch little Josephine grow up. She's beautiful like her mother. She's also seen me a few times, but she doesn't know who I am. I'm just another customer to her. Now that Harrison is here though, I can compare the two, and I have to say that Harrison looks like Anthony's son, and Josephine looks like Rose's daughter. No one would ever guess that they are siblings. Maybe Harrison could stick around and have a life here? No one needs to know he's Rose's son. He could be adopted for all they know.

Saturday, May 6, 1961

I don't know what Anthony was thinking. Was it just curiosity on Harrison's part? Did *he* think it was a good idea to go and visit Rose? And how did they get Rose to agree? So many questions! It's been chaos in the household all day.

Friday, May 12, 1961

I got a letter from Josephine today. No wonder Harrison chose to leave this week and head back to Taiwan.

Andy,

What a wonderful and terrible day. I'm sure you know Harrison is in town, but did you know he came by the bakery? Anthony must have told him where we were. The man just can't leave the past well enough alone. I was getting the shop ready to open when I noticed a taxi stop right outside our store. I didn't think anything of it. Taxis come and go, but then I felt like someone was staring at me. When I looked out of the window, I saw this boy staring at me. I swear I thought it was Anthony at first glance—a younger version of him.

It was creepy, let me tell you. The boy never moved, just stared. I went out to give him a piece of my mind, but as I got closer, I noticed that he was shaking. It wasn't cold but it was windy, so I tried to get him to come in. But he wouldn't budge. Then, a car came up and parked right in front of us and who should come out but Anthony himself! I stared at the two of them back and forth like my head was on a swivel. Then it clicked. I'm getting old, Andy. I don't know why I hadn't seen it from the very beginning. There was no denying the boy was the little boy I had helped raise for his first five months before those monsters tried to hurt him and he had to move to Taiwan.

I told the boys I was going to get Rose, but both of them told me no. Can you believe them? His own mother is right across the street, probably in the back baking up more loaves, and all these two boys can do is stand there and stare at each other. If they were my sons they would have gotten quite a talking to. In the end, I relented and satisfied myself with giving the boy a hug, and a teary one at that. By this time, Rose had come out to the front of the bakery, but the morning customers were starting to pour in so she never looked out the window. Charlie was there, too, helping her, and there was little Josephine, who was not so little anymore. She was bagging pastries for the customers. One look at the scene before me and I knew Harrison would never go and see his mother. The scene was one straight out of a movie. The perfect family, happy with each other, balanced. No room for an outsider. Not even one who had no idea how much he would be loved by everyone.

I watched Harrison, who without a word went to Anthony's car and got in. That's when Anthony told me he'd had no idea that Harrison had come to find his mother. He would have prepared us for their arrival instead of surprising me this morning. I told him to come *back when Harrison was ready. He said he would, but he also told me not to tell Rose. Not yet. He didn't want to break her heart again if he couldn't persuade the boy to come.*

Josephine

To say Anthony is sad would be an understatement. The man is devastated. He's crushed. It's like someone placed a five-ton boulder on him and just watched as it made him sink further into himself. I have to give Sally credit though. She's doing all she can to help him get through this while also not making a fuss. I don't know how she does it.

Anthony had left a note here, too, which read:

I wasn't just devastated. I felt like my whole being did not exist in this world anymore. I had finally found out that I had a son—my own flesh and blood that I had created with the love of my life . . . and he denounced me. Wanted nothing to do with me. I could have given him the world and he wanted none of it. I am glad I was able to keep Rose from feeling the same pain. This hurt has never left me. I hope you never have to feel the pain of losing your own child. This is the end of Andy's story, but hopefully Mary has opened up and is telling you hers.

"I'm awake!" Victoria suddenly exclaimed, wide awake this time as she bowled into the room.

Thank goodness my tea was on the other side of the table or I would have knocked it over. Victoria was way too energetic when she woke up. I quickly ran to the bathroom before Victoria could see me. Why did she have to come down now?

"You need to take me out and walk me around," she called after me. "We need to go and talk to the manager of that art gallery."

"If I didn't know any better, I would think that it was you who was looking for my uncle," I yelled back at her from the bathroom.

"Stop stalling. Let's go. Let's go."

"All right. All right. Let me get dressed first," I said, forcing myself to laugh all the way up to my room. It felt good to be laughing again. This would be a good distraction from the rabbit hole the journal had dragged me into.

When we arrived at the art gallery, I told myself to expect more surprises but to not be surprised. I don't know if that was doable, but I sure was going to try.

"Come on, Anne. You love art. Say you're scouting for your mom."

"That's a good idea. That way, I can scope the place out first. I don't have to talk to anyone."

"Well, eventually you'll have to talk to someone."

"Don't burst my bubble."

"Don't worry, I'll be by your side the whole time."

I took a breath. "Okay, here goes."

A blast of warm air hit us in the face as we walked through the door. I was excited. Even if we didn't find any more pearls of information, I hadn't gone to an art gallery in a long time. I hooked my arm through Victoria's, and we went to explore. Every room contained art from different decades. I was looking at some landscape paintings that looked very familiar and was sure I had seen this painting before.

"Anne, you should come over here," I heard Victoria say.

"One second. I'm trying to figure something out."

"No, you should really come here!"

I walked over to where Victoria was standing and looked over her shoulder at a self-portrait. It was clear as to why she wanted me to come over in such a hurry. It also answered my question as to where I had seen the painting I'd just been looking at before.

"Is that not the exact same drawing you showed me from the art book you got from Mr. Wang? Tell me it's the exact one, because it'd be creepy if there was a doppelganger," Victoria said.

I read the placard next to it and sure enough, Harrison's Taiwanese name 林飛鴻, Lin Fei-Hong, was right there in big black letters. The placard read:

Fei-Hong is a master of his time. He didn't receive formal training until he was thirteen. This exhibit showcases his work throughout the years. His teenage years were about experimentation and sketching. This led to studies in oil, pastel, and watercolor. Taiwan's landscapes and people have been beautifully captured by this native artist.

"It seems he is accepted now," I said.

"I'd hope so. It's the twenty-first century already. Well, it looks like you've found him."

"I want to check one thing." I walked around all the paintings in the room, and sure enough, every single one of them had a plum blossom in the bottom right corner. No signature. Just a plum blossom. I turned back to Victoria. "It looks like I have found him. Let's go find a curator."

I sat there, gob smacked, while Victoria rubbed life back into my arms and back. At one point she fanned me and forced me to drink water. We had found the curator and she was excited to know that I was related to Harrison. But what I thought would be a definitive address for him became quite the opposite. She was hoping I could tell her where she could find him because she didn't know where he was, even though she was showcasing his work!

"I do have an email we correspond by. Let me get that for you."

"Thank you. That would be great," Victoria said. "She's just in shock. She's been meeting different people who keep saying they knew him but don't know where he is. Oh, and would you know a Mr. Wang?"

I was grateful to have Victoria asking the questions I should be asking because I couldn't even work my mouth to talk anymore.

"I'm not sure. Should I know him?"

"He said he funds Harrison's art."

"Oh. Bettie would know then. She's the one who takes care of the money. She's also been here a lot longer than I have, but she's not in today. Would you be able to come back tomorrow? Or can I have your phone number or email so she can respond? I'll ask her as soon as I see her."

"Great! We'll come in person tomorrow then. Thank you," Victoria said.

Victoria lifted me out of the seat and turned us to face the door. Somehow my legs moved, and my feet went one in front of the other all the way to the door, through the gallery, and out the front door. But as soon as the fresh air hit me, I started running. I didn't stop till a few blocks later.

"It's a good thing you don't work out on a normal basis because I could actually keep up with you," Victoria panted as she came up beside me. "You got it out of your system now?"

"I will after I get something to eat," I mumbled, still in shock but not enough that I hadn't noticed an eatery earlier. "I saw a great waffle place when running. Let's go there."

"You don't have to ask me twice."

CHAPTER 27

THE NEXT MORNING WE WERE BOTH UP AND OUT the door by nine o'clock. The gallery opened at ten, and we planned on being outside the entrance, waiting. Victoria had convinced me to chill for what had remained of yesterday. So we went to Taipei 101 and enjoyed the view. We went to Chiang Kai-Shek Memorial again, ate our weight in food and drinks, and just basically caught up on life. I felt like a terrible friend for not having remembered she had gone to a wedding with Paul. But I was so happy to hear that everyone loved her, including his parents, and she and Paul were doing very well.

He had taken her out to different places in downtown Portland to eat, to a Broadway show, and a Winterhawk's hockey game. Victoria hated sports, which meant that she was serious about this guy. This made me a little jealous as I couldn't help but think of Sebastian. What was he doing?

A security guard came walking up to the gallery's entrance. We stood there, both of us ready to hightail it in even though we were all alone; there was no one else waiting outside with us. We walked up to the front desk.

"You must be Anne and Victoria. I'm Bettie," said an old Taiwanese woman about five feet tall with a short bob haircut that was a shiny gray. She had librarian glasses and a back so rigid that I could use it as a straightedge. Victoria and I instantly stood straighter.

"Yes, we stopped by yesterday," I said.

"Yes, I know. Come with me."

We followed her upstairs to the fourth floor where we sat in a relatively old looking office. The rest of the gallery looked like it had just been updated, but the offices not so much. However, her office was nice and neat, not a single sheet of paper lying askew. I felt like I had to sit straight in my seat and not touch anything.

"I've been waiting for you," she said.

"You and everyone else I don't know about."

"No need to be snarky with me."

"Your English is good," Victoria said.

"It has to be. I work with a lot of international artists, such as Fei-Hong. He lives in the States."

"He lives in the States?" I was so excited to finally have a continent to pinpoint him on.

"Yes, but only because all his artwork comes and goes from there."

"Oh . . ."

"How do you know all this when the lady yesterday said she didn't know where to find him?" Victoria asked for me.

"Joy doesn't need to know where to find him. She wants to know every artist we work with because she thinks it builds a connection, but I've worked with enough artists that I know they like their privacy.

"All of his work goes through me. Joy usually handles the work and I handle the money, but in this case, I am doing a favor to Mary and handling everything for Fei-Hong myself. I have been here a long time. I was here when he first showed his work."

"Are you in touch with Mary often?" I asked.

"Yes, Mary comes by sometimes to make sure Fei-Hong is still sending artwork here."

And she didn't bother to tell me this herself! It would have saved us all a lot of heartache. "Would you have a contact for Harrison? I would like to get in touch with him."

"Here's the email that we use to communicate with him but I don't know if he will respond. He only responds if we ask him multiple times."

"Well, thank you for the email," Victoria said, pulling me out of my chair.

"If I can be of any other help, please let me know."

I gave a half-hearted nod and left, Victoria tagging behind.

"Are you going to email him?"

"Yeah . . . but what if he doesn't want to be found? He never came back all these years. He's probably a grandfather by now. I don't want to upturn his life just because we want to find him. I mean, my life got turned upside down and I'm not sure that was a good thing."

"I think it was. You've become more confident and learned so much more about your family. You always complained that you didn't know very much, that your mom wasn't willing to share, but here you are in Taiwan and finally knowing more about your mom, your grandmother, and now your uncle. Heck, your whole grandfather's side of the family is starting to come out of the woodwork. It'll turn out good, Anne. I can feel it. Come on. If you're not going to email him, I will."

"Okay. Okay. But what am I supposed to say? 'Hi, this is

your long-lost niece. I'm rich now and have been spending all my time looking for you even though I didn't know about you until earlier this year?'"

"Everything but the rich part. You don't want him to know that yet until you get to know him."

"Very funny."

We'd found a cute cafe that reminded us of the one back home, but smaller. Much smaller. It was sandwiched between a clothes store and a fruit drink store, and there was a hat shop not six feet away across the street. It was so random that I loved it.

After all this time, I wasn't ready to contact him. I was hoping that Harrison would just appear and surprise me like everyone else had. However, one look at Victoria told me that she wasn't going to let me keep stalling.

I opened up a new email and began typing.

Mr. Lin

"That's so formal," Victoria said.

"Are you going to let me type it?"

"Okay, go ahead."

I carried on typing.

You don't know me, but my name is Anne Huang. I received your email from Bettie at the Living Art Gallery. I know you met a man in Taiwan when you were growing up by the name of Anthony Wilkens. I met Anthony's family last year and it started me on a journey to discover my family. I've since found out that my mom is your half-sister, and I have spent the last two weeks trying to find you and would

love to meet you. I'm currently in Taiwan, but I live in America. I can
meet you anywhere though.

Sincerely,

Anne

There, I thought that was heartfelt. *Groan.* Who was I kidding? The whole email sounded drab, forced, and boring. I had no idea what to say to him. Revealing too much might scare him away and I really wanted to meet him. After going through all these hoops, I wanted to know if he was real. I went to delete the message when Victoria reached across and pressed send.

"Victoria!"

"Well, you weren't going to do it. Now you don't have to overthink it."

"If you weren't my best friend—"

"What? You'd fight me?"

I could see the amusement in her eyes, and as it was Victoria, I gave in and huffed. "Want to go to the zoo?" she said then. "I've read that they have pandas for the first time there."

She knew exactly how to divert my attention. I loved zoos. It was the one place where I could relax, and Victoria knew it. "That'd be fun. It might get my mind off everything else going on."

"That would be the idea."

Bing.

I looked back at my computer and couldn't believe what I saw. At the top of my email was a message from Harrison. He had replied back already! I hoped he wasn't one of those workaholics that was on their device all the time, or was he so busy that he sent auto-replies?

"Are you going to open it?" Victoria asked, and I jumped,

letting out a squeal. Victoria had come up behind me and her mouth was right next to my ear.

"Don't do that," I said.

"Well, are you going to open it? Cos if not, I'm ready to press the button."

I noticed her finger was already on the mouse clicker. "I'll do it," I said, moving her hand away. I clicked and we both read:

I'm sorry to inform you that this email is no longer active. Harrison Lin, also known as Lin Fei-Hong, passed away this month. I'm sorry for any inconvenience this might cause you.

"What? No! No, No, No!" I got out of my seat and started pacing the room. This wasn't happening. Especially after I'd spent all this time and energy finding him! Not to mention Mary's interference, popping into places to warn the others that I was coming. He was supposed to reply that he would love to meet me, that he was glad to hear from me, or at the very least be interested to hear what I had to say. I would even accept a "No, I'm not interested in hearing from you." But not dead!

"I think now is a good time to be going to the zoo. Let's go. I've got your coat," Victoria said, already pushing me out the door.

An hour later we were looking at a map that was four or five times the size of the zoo back home. The place was enormous. I loved zoos. I could spend all day in one. This zoo was divided into continents and it was fascinating. It was the most diverse group of animals I had ever seen.

"Ah, here's North America. I wonder how many we'll recognize," Victoria said, dragging me along. I was reading every placard and stopping at every exhibit. The animals had such a carefree life, sleeping, walking around, eating their food, and just doing what they did. Why couldn't I do that? Why couldn't we all? Why did I have to care so much? These thoughts would cycle around in my head before Victoria would drag me away to the next animal.

"There's all those people staring at something on the ground. What do you think it is?" Victoria asked like I was a three-year-old.

"Don't talk like that."

"You've been mopey, and I'm supposed to be here with my best friend having fun."

Harrison's e-mail had shocked me and I was missing Sebastian. I couldn't help it. "Sorry. I know."

"Let's go check it out."

We walked closer and couldn't see anything walking around or in the trees, or even hidden in some dark corner. There were probably six people grouped around the center of the cage looking down at something. When they finally moved, Victoria and I walked forward.

"A raccoon? They were here pointing at a raccoon?" Victoria shouted, slapping her hand to her forehead.

I couldn't help it. This was the most ridiculous thing I'd seen in a while. I wasn't expecting this at all. A raccoon. The varmint that went through Mom's trash can at home. The one that we were all warned as kids carried rabies. It was here, in a zoo, for all to see. I laughed so hard that I had to find the nearest seat to sit down on before I fell over. Tears were rolling down my cheeks. The stress was emanating out of me. So what if I never met my uncle? Here was a creature that was transported halfway around the world, stuck in a cage, begging for food from the people who ogled at it every day. I laughed even harder.

"Well, if I'd known a raccoon would make you happier, I would have brought one with me," Victoria said.

"Maybe you should have."

"You feel better?" Victoria was looking at me with some relief.

"Yes, I feel much better."

"You think you might tell Mary soon?"

"I don't know. I probably should, but I don't think I've accepted it yet. I've only been searching for two weeks and I feel devastated. Mary will crumple when I tell her."

"Well, think about it. She deserves to know."

"I'll tell her," I said, feeling a bit annoyed that Victoria had better sense than me at the moment. "I just need to wrap my head around it. Let's go find those pandas you were talking about," I said, hoping to change the subject.

"So, you were listening."

"Of course I was. I always listen to you," I said, giving her my most innocent look.

"Yeah, sure you do."

I hooked my arm through Victoria's and skipped all the way to the pandas. I didn't even care that there was a line zigzagging through the lobby and out the front door. It was like the whole world had just opened. I no longer had to care about finding him. He was dead. Dead, dead, dead. I couldn't do anything about that.

"Why are you suddenly so chipper?" Victoria asked.

"The guy's dead. I don't need to worry anymore. I can go on with my life. I should call Sebastian and ask him if he wants to do dinner tonight."

"Uh . . . Sebastian flew back to the States the same day he called me. He didn't tell you?"

"No . . . Oh well. I'm not going to think about it. I'm happy right now and I'm not going to let him burst my bubble." *What? He left?*

"That's my girl. Do you think the pandas are as cute as we see on YouTube?"

I knew Victoria didn't believe a word I said, but she was my best friend and knew when to keep her mouth shut. I was sure she'd be watching me closely for the rest of the day.

"I think so. I hope so. Yay! We're moving. Wow, we're going upstairs." Even my voice was a bit too happy for my own liking. Maybe I was going crazy. "This is quite the place they've built for pandas."

"It's their first one ever. Taiwan has never had pandas before."

"Really?"

"Are you really Taiwanese?" Victoria countered.

"I resent that."

"Don't worry. I just read the sign outside before we came in," she laughed.

I didn't respond. My mind was wandering all over the place. Now that I was free from looking for my uncle, I wondered what I could do with my time. Maybe I could email Sebastian to come back when he was done with the Wilkens family. *That's what I'll do.*

I pulled out my phone and started typing. After all, we were going to be in this line for a while. Victoria had just gotten a call from someone, too, so why not do it now?

I wrote Sebastian a nice long email, telling him how sorry I was for not being more understanding and letting him explain. I updated him on Harrison, and that I was now free to go on that Taiwanese trip we had planned. I pressed send and then, of course, wanted him to respond as soon as possible. I know, totally unrealistic, but I was in line with nowhere else to go and a lot of time to think.

"Who was that you were on the phone with?" I asked Victoria.

"Paul. Anne, I think I'm in love."

"Yeah?" *That was fast.*

"He wants to come to Taiwan and meet me here. Anne, I think I might have found the guy."

"You haven't known him that long. And we're not staying here much longer."

"When you know, you know. You know, like Sebastian. You know? And I'm going to tell him not to come, but it's the gesture. He would come here for me. Isn't that the best?"

"Right . . ."

"Oh, come on, Anne. You're deeply in love with Sebastian. He's not Brian. He's not going to just walk out on you or go back to Isabella."

"You don't know that."

"I don't, but I've talked to Sebastian long enough to know that he has more integrity than Brian ever did. And that's me talking. You know how I felt about Sebastian after the bombing. I couldn't stand the sight of him."

"You never told me you thought that of Brian."

"You loved him. You would have never believed me. Plus, Sebastian flew me out here with his own money. He loves you, Anne. Like really loves you."

"I'm so stupid."

"No, you're just too preoccupied and can't see past the end of your nose."

"Glad I have you then."

"Yeah, me too. I don't know what you'd do without me." It was great to be laughing again with Victoria by my side.

The next thing we knew, we were in front of the exhibit. "They're so cute! Look at them rolling and chewing on the bamboo," I said.

Not more than a couple of seconds later, I was getting

shoved. "Hey!" I said, looking to my right. The older couple didn't even seem to notice me and the other people standing next to them. They just kept on pushing. I turned to Victoria. "I guess we can't stop to look much longer."

Rrrriiinnnnggg. I looked down at my screen.

"Who is it?" Victoria asked.

"It's Sebastian."

"Well, we're headed outside now anyways."

I put the phone to my ear. "Hi Sebastian." *I'm not going to bring up how he went back to the States without telling me.*

"I'm glad you emailed. I wasn't sure if you were still mad at me. And I'm sorry to hear about your uncle, but I have some really important stuff to talk to you about."

"Okay, what is it?"

"Can I meet you somewhere?"

"Sure, come by the condo. We'll head over there now—wait, aren't you in the States?"

"Is Victoria with you?"

"Yes. And thank you for sending her."

"Oh good. Glad she's with you. See you soon," he said and he hung up.

"That was odd," I said, still staring at the phone.

"How?"

"He sounded so mysterious."

"It sounded like he's here."

"Yeah. Like I said, mysterious."

"Only one way to find out why. Let's head home. Glad you're doing better, Anne. It's nice to see you happy again."

"Me too," I beamed. This trip wasn't going to be a total disaster after all.

CHAPTER 28

WE GOT HOME BEFORE SEBASTIAN SHOWED UP, SO I made sure the whole place was nice and neat. I hadn't realized just how much I'd missed him until he had called. It was so nice to hear his voice again and I couldn't wait for him to get here. Victoria helped, and I could tell she was more relaxed with the notion of being in the same room as Sebastian. It made me happy to know that my best friend and my boyfriend were getting along.

Knock. Knock. Knock.

He's here! I rushed to the door and opened it.

"Sebastian, I've missed you . . ."

The man in front of me was not the Sebastian I had left. This man looked like him but also looked like he had been through a ringer. Like someone had pounded on him over and over and over.

"I haven't slept in days," he said in a garble.

"You look awful."

"I feel it. Do you have anything to eat? I need to sit."

"I think that's a good idea."

"I thought you were in the States," Victoria piped in,

coming up behind me as Sebastian took a seat. The two of us looked at each other, both worried by Sebastian's haggard look.

"I was going to. I know that's what I told you. But Isabella said she wanted to stay here to explore while I went back to deal with her mess, and I just couldn't have that. Not with you still here. I can't leave you alone with her when I'm not around."

Aw, he does love me.

"Sebastian, did you want to sleep a bit before telling me what you needed to say?" I asked.

"Oh no, I can't. I need to tell you immediately. Anne, this is very important."

"What is it?"

"There's a storm coming, and you need to be prepared. And I love you, Anne. Brian can't possibly love you as much as I do. I'd do anything for you. I would never leave you."

My heart raced at his response. "Why are you saying this? What does Brian have to do with anything?"

"I know you were with him the other day," he said evenly.

What? "How?"

"Isabella went to talk to a shop owner about your uncle. He said that you were with another guy just the other day."

"Why is she asking about my uncle?"

"I'm jumping around. I need to start over."

"No, please, just tell me what Brian has to do with it."

"I can't lose you, Anne."

I was getting worried now. "You're not going to lose me. Brian came to help me with my search."

"And I scared him away," Victoria piped in. "He won't be bothering Anne anymore. The loser better not show his face again."

"Really?" Sebastian said. The relief that flashed over his

face was like a punch to my gut. I hadn't been treating him very well.

"You were about to mention something important," I prodded.

"Yes. Isabella and her mother wanted me to look into these other properties that Anthony owned."

"I thought you were only working with Jack."

"I am. But . . ."

"Technically, you work for the whole family. Yes, I know."

He nodded. "And Jack asked me to look into it too. Anne, they threatened to hire someone else who could make your life even more difficult." He looked so frazzled that I felt bad for giving him a hard time. "Anyways, the Hawaii house they knew about, but this one in Taiwan, they only just found out about. This was the only property that was not listed as being bought by the trust. Rather, Anthony bought it under his own name, and it's making them mad that they didn't know he had this secret place. And that's not all. At some point between the time he bought it and now, he added a name onto the deed."

"Who?"

"Harrison Lin."

"My uncle?" I shouted, now sitting upright in my seat.

"And he made your uncle the majority owner."

"Who's dead."

"Yeah . . . that's unfortunate," Sebastian sighed.

"It means they can't do anything then," I said, sounding more chipper than I felt.

"No . . . it makes it more complicated. It means that Anthony didn't have full rights to give you the condo. He needed written permission from Harrison. And because he never got that, the house fell under the trust because it defaulted there when he died."

"I don't get it. It wasn't bought under the trust. It was his own private property."

"But he had everything that he ever owned rolled under the trust. He must have forgotten about that or thought that Harrison was still alive. It means, Anne, that they are looking for your uncle too."

"But he's dead."

"They don't know that yet," Sebastian said.

"But they will."

"I told you before, people like Isabella and her mother don't stop until they get what they want. This is the path they're going down now. You need to be careful, Anne. And one more thing—we found your boat."

"You found my boat? It was missing? Wait—I own a boat?"

"Yeah. Anthony wouldn't tell Andy or me where he had parked it, and he wanted me to find it before letting you know. It's not a small one either. It's one of those double decker mini cruise ships. He named it Rose, and the family is incensed. It's parked in a private dock."

"And they've told you to represent them, haven't they?"

"I quit."

"You did?" Victoria and I both asked at the same time.

"I did. I can't work against you. I just can't. I can't lose you again. So, I quit. I'm on your side, Anne. I will represent you in this battle. I want to spend the rest of my life with you." Sebastian seemed to trail off at the end as if what he'd just said had surprised him too.

Did he just ask me to marry him?

"Wow, this is better than any soap opera," Victoria said, sitting at the dining table with her mouth open.

Before I could gather my thoughts to answer him, there was knocking at the door. "Maybe that's the cleaner. He's the only one who knows about this place," I said while I got up to answer the door.

The person outside was not who I thought it would be in a million years.

"Isabella?" the three of us exclaimed.

"Hi, my dears. I hope I didn't catch you by surprise. Oh, it looks like I did," she said with one of her infamous coy smiles.

"Isabella, what do you want?" Sebastian asked, standing up to come between Isabella and me.

"And how did you find this place? Wait, don't answer that," I sighed.

"I'm sure our sweet Sebastian has updated you on everything. I've been learning so much about Taiwan, it's economics, this condo, and the boat. I needed to come and see the place for myself."

"Well, now you've seen it, so time for you to go," Sebastian said.

"Isabella, why don't you stay?" I asked. I could see Victoria and Sebastian boring holes into me. I wasn't going to back down so easily though. *Always keep your enemies close.* "Would you like something to drink?" I asked, heading toward the kitchen.

"I'd love a cup of water, if you don't mind," she said with as much sweetness as she could pour into her words. She was quite the actress.

"I'll go get it for you."

I came back to the three of them having a staring contest.

"Isabella, why are you doing this?" I asked, handing her the drink.

"And what would *this* be?"

"You know exactly what I'm talking about."

She titled her head, pursed her lips, and said, "Because I don't think a person like you should come into my world and get everything for nothing. It's just not right."

The odd thing was that she said this with no malice at all. It was a matter-of-fact statement. She really believed what she was saying. I was a bit shocked but not surprised. Though maybe I was more surprised than I thought because I don't know why the next words came out of my mouth. "I just learned that I have a boat. Why don't we all go for a boat ride?"

"That's the best thing I've ever heard you say," said Isabella. She was already halfway to the door, the rest of us following like she owned the place and not me.

Isabella's first words were, "That is so small."

To Isabella, this might have been a small boat, but Victoria and I had never seen anything like it. It was an eighty-foot motor yacht. At least, that's what Sebastian told me. He seemed to not be fazed either. It had a big deck at the front. The back had a standing area, too, and it was two stories tall. What would I do with something like this?

"Are you coming, Anne? Can't get on board without the captain," said Isabella, standing at the entrance with one hand pointing at the boat and the other on her hip. She looked chic standing there. I could feel myself getting red in the face because she looked like she was the owner, and I knew she knew it too.

"Um . . . I think we forgot that none of us can pilot a boat," I ventured to say.

"Already taken care of," said Sebastian. Then he whispered in my ear, "I still can't believe you invited her. And why are you being so nice to her?"

"I'm keeping my enemy close. You once told me that we had no proof that the bombing was done by Isabella's family." I watched as Sebastian's lips tightened. He looked so cute when he was mad that I wanted to laugh but stopped myself in time.

"Over open water?" he countered.

"Okay, I didn't think that one through," I admitted, "but I just can't shake the feeling that there's more to this than whatever *this* is."

"Okay, if you say so."

I had also been thinking about Sebastian and Isabella. Ever since Sebastian had mentioned Brian, and that he might lose me, I had softened at the thought of him and Isabella. I remembered feeling a connection with Brian when I saw him here the first and second time. It was comfortable and familiar. Something safe I already understood. He was of the same culture too. He understood my background. Why couldn't that be the same for Sebastian and Isabella? Well, at least Sebastian. And he quit his job for me! That was saying something. It was ingrained in me that he couldn't separate himself from the Wilkens. They had done too much for him, but here he was, standing by my side while I invited a Wilkens onto my boat, which used to be owned by a Wilkens. Oh, the irony.

We all went to the upper deck and sure enough, there was a captain dressed in uniform standing there, ready for us to come on board. There were other staff too. And food. Goodness, was this my life now?

Victoria didn't think twice before throwing herself at all the different hors d'oeuvres on the table and accepting a glass of champagne. I hung out at the edge of the boat watching the shore recede as we pulled away. Why did we all have to be against each other? Why were Isabella and her mother so adamant about taking everything away from me? I could give them what they wanted, but would that get them off my back? I had a feeling that getting the property wasn't the point. Making my life miserable was more likely the point.

"This is the life, isn't it?" Isabella asked while she settled herself next to me. "I've been watching you. You don't seem sure about all this."

"And what would all *this* be?" I asked, throwing her own words back at her.

"The house, the boat, being rich. You're still unsure."

"Of course I am. It's all new to me and your family hasn't been very inviting."

"Great Uncle Jack seems to have invited you with open arms."

"He's the only one."

"Doesn't matter. I can take all this worry off your mind. Just sign over the property and money to us. I'll even make it worth your while. You can keep a few million for yourself. Go live your simple life and be done with all of this."

I looked at her. She sure could make all my stress go away, but at the mention of Jack, I remembered what he had said: "Don't let them get to you." And I finally understood what he meant.

"No thanks. I'm happy trying to figure out this new life of mine. It comes with hardship but I'm no stranger to that. It's something you wouldn't understand so I won't go into details." I could see her face contorting, wanting to turn into a scowl, but years of looking composed was keeping her from showing her true feelings. I wanted to laugh, but thankfully kept my composure. Then she did something I didn't think possible. All I could do was stare.

She pulled out a wad of hundred-dollar bills and started throwing them into the water one by one! I couldn't grab them fast enough. She wasn't even laughing or smiling. Just watching me.

"This bothers you, doesn't it? You'll never be a part of this life. You have to own it. Know that you deserve all this. Believe that you have an infinite amount of cash."

"No! That's crazy! I don't ever want to be like that." By this time, Sebastian and Victoria had come to see why I was yelling. They also joined me in trying to catch as many of the hundred-dollar bills as they could.

"It's just paper," Isabella continued.

"There are starving children!"

"And you can create foundations to feed them."

That actually makes sense. Wait—no! I mean, yes! Ah, she's confusing me.

"I'll just write off that money as a donation. Someone will find them, don't worry," she said, and just like that she turned and walked inside the cabin. I watched her sit on the couch, ask for a drink, and just stare outside.

"What in the world just happened?" Sebastian yelled at me.

"Huh?"

"What just happened?" Victoria repeated, coming up to me and placing both hands on my shoulders as she looked me straight in the eyes.

"One minute we're watching you two talk, and the next you're lunging and almost falling into the water," Sebastian said. "Then we come out and see a lot of hundred-dollar bills flying everywhere. What in the world?"

"I'm not sure, but we need to get home. I'm done with this trip."

"Yeah, us too," Victoria said, pointing a thumb at Sebastian and herself.

Isabella left without a word after we docked. She just got up and walked off. The rest of us sauntered back home. I was done. This had all gotten too much for me.

CHAPTER 29

THAT NIGHT I COULDN'T SLEEP. I KEPT HEARING what Isabella had said about owning it. I opened my bedside table and grabbed a few hundred-dollar bills and just held them in my hands. This was nothing. Pennies to me now, but I knew I could never think like that. But what Isabella had said was right. I should use the fact that I have money for the greater good. Well, she didn't quite say that, but I thought that.

I rolled over to look at the clock. Three o'clock . . . Maybe the green onion pancakes we grabbed at the night market were still in the fridge? I got up to look and sure enough, there they were in all their oily fried goodness.

I grabbed Mary's journal and went to the couch with my green onion pancakes in tow, opened the book and began to read.

50年5月26日 (Friday, May 26, 1961)

Harrison is home. I am so relieved. He looks in bad shape, but I am so happy he is home. Liang-Chun is worried about him because he is not himself, but I told him to give

Harrison some time. He needs to readjust. I remember how bad the jet lag was when we arrived from America. I was down for a whole week.

50年5月28日 (Sunday, May 28, 1961)

He hasn't said a word to us. He joins us for meals, sits with us in the living room to watch a show, but he still hasn't said one word. Even Liang-Chun can't get through to him. What happened in America? What did Anthony do?

50年6月3日 (Saturday, June 3, 1961)

Harrison left again! It's been two days and he hasn't come home. Where could he have gone? I went through his whole closet and noticed his favorite shirts and shorts are gone. I only just washed them, so I know they are not somewhere else. He always had the plum blossom I gave him in his drawer, but it is no longer there. Did he leave forever? Without telling us? He's still so young. Where will he go? Why would he leave? He knows we love him. He is my son. Where did my son go?

50年8月6日 (Sunday, August 6, 1961)

Liang-Chun and the others are telling me that I should stop looking for him. But what mama stops looking for their child? I will always look for him. He's somewhere and he needs me.

50年11月17日 (Friday, November 17, 1961)

Even I am getting discouraged, but I'm still not giving up. I had heard there was a boy who had wandered out to Yilan. New clues will come. I know it.

51年8月6日 (Monday, August 6, 1962)

I found the contact at Yilan, but I was told that the boy

had left a long time ago. Harrison's still not at home. He's so young and I can't hug him or wipe his tears. Where are you, my son?

52年4月1日 (Monday, April 1, 1963)

Anthony has persuaded me to work with him. I'll help maintain his condo and let him know if I ever find Harrison. In return, he'll provide the funds to continue the search. This secret of Rose's has caused more hurt than anything else in my life. It stops here. Harrison, wherever you are, know that you are loved. I will never give up looking for you.

I flipped through the rest of the journal to find it was more of the same. Mary started making connections between the people Harrison had been with, but no one could pinpoint where he was at any given time. He seemed to appear and disappear out of nowhere.

This was absurd. Mary was still alive and I knew where she lived. I should go to the source. I'd read enough, and she had been going behind my back talking to everyone about me, but yet I wasn't allowed to ask questions and get answers from her directly? And as much as I didn't want to be the bearer of bad news, Mary deserved to know that Harrison had passed away.

I went back upstairs and dressed as quietly as I could so that I didn't wake Victoria and Sebastian. I was pretty sure that Mary woke up early. She was older than Mom, and Mom and her friends all got up before the sun rose.

I left a note for Victoria and Sebastian, so they wouldn't freak out when they woke up, and snuck out to find Mary.

Breakfast places were starting to open up so I grabbed a half sandwich with pork meat, an over easy egg, cucumber, margarine, and three slices of bread with no crust. I scarfed it down while I navigated the subway.

Would Mary even talk to me? She had been adamant about not sharing information with me the last time I was there.

When I got to her apartment block, I took the stairs this time. After having walked all around Taipei, I was pretty fit, easily able to walk up five flights of stairs. When I got to her door, I knocked quietly, hoping she wouldn't come to the door. Now that I was here, I was afraid to face her. She didn't want me to know about Harrison, and yet she had provided me with her journal. Maybe she didn't want me to come back and ask questions? I had so many questions in my head though. Someone had to answer them.

"I've been expecting you."

In my self-absorbed thoughts I hadn't realized that the door had cracked open. Someone was busy getting the chain off the inside of the door. I heard Ming-Yue come and help, and then there she was—Mary, standing right there in front of me. But what was that on her face? Actual joy on seeing me? At a closer look, I grew concerned. Mary seemed to have aged ten years since the last time I saw her.

"Come in. Come in," Mary urged. "Ming-Yue, make us some tea."

We settled ourselves in the same place where we had first started this discussion two weeks ago. I couldn't believe it had only been two weeks.

"I heard that you have been visiting sites that Harrison's been to," said Mary.

"I've heard you have too."

"Yes, I have. I'm not going to apologize for keeping you in the dark, but I'm sure you have a lot of questions."

"I do."

"Go ahead."

"Just like that?"

"Yes."

"You've hidden everything from me and now all of a sudden I can ask questions?"

"Do you want to know more answers or not?"

I did a couple of deep breaths so that I wouldn't start yelling. Yelling at an eighty-year-old woman didn't seem like the right thing to do, especially if she was the only one who could tell me more about Harrison. And I still had to find a way of gently telling her the bad news.

"Why did you send me on this wild goose chase?" I began.

"You read the journal I assume?"

"Yes."

"Then you know how rough Harrison's life was, and how much Rose wanted to keep him a secret. I made a promise—"

"Yes, I know the promise."

She gave me a look like an elder would give a youngster for cutting them off. I wasn't backing down though. Not today.

"Let's start over. Where have you gotten to in the journal?" Mary asked.

"You couldn't find Harrison anywhere."

"Ah, so you've got through it. Your Chinese is pretty good."

"Lots of Saturday classes, Chinese competitions, Chinese camps, and talking at home. Mom prepared me well."

"She's a good mama."

"Yes, she is, and she would have liked to have known her brother."

"Yes, that was the request when you first came here. I am ready now to answer whatever questions you have. You know now that I do not know where he is. I went to all the same places you did and searched for years. I received a wedding invitation from him about ten years after he left, but I couldn't get myself to open it. And when I did open it, I realized I had missed the wedding. They had sent it to me very last minute. Did you find it in the safe?"

"Yes," I said and almost broke down. Watching Mary get quiet as she told me about the wedding invitation, and the fact that she looked so much older than two weeks ago almost did me in.

"I acted like a child," she continued. "I was still so young, and there were a bunch of other little ones in the house who depended on me. But Harrison always had a special place in my heart. I always felt guilty for allowing Anthony to get so close to him after promising Rose that I would always take care of him."

"I don't think anyone blames you."

"That's what I've been told. But I will never forgive myself. He ran away because he was lied to."

"Is that why you still maintain Anthony's condo, and keep in touch with everyone who ever knew Harrison?"

"Yes."

She didn't say anything more and I didn't want to push. This was the most I had heard from her own mouth since we had first met. I wasn't about to break the streak.

"I threw myself into opening a school to teach English," she continued. "It was the only way I knew how to survive. Mama and Baba were starting to retire, and they were going to move in with Oldest Brother in Taipei. They didn't need to tell Liang-Chun and I that if we wanted to stay in Hualien we'd be on our own. I knew that already. We had our daughter, the one in Australia. The one I never get to see anymore, and who has two grandchildren who I never get to see either."

"Mama, keep going with your story," Ming-Yue said.

"But she is part of my story," Mary retorted.

"The story that Anne would be interested in."

"I want to hear everything though," I piped in. I didn't want to miss a thing. She was talking now.

"You will. You will. But Ming-Yue is right. I got off track. Where was I? We had our daughter and three boys already. Ming-Yue came later. Liang-Chun found us a small apartment in Taipei to start our new life and still be close to my parents."

"Were Liang-Chun and you estranged from Liang-Chun's family?

"We were for awhile, but over time that got mended. We saw them on holidays when we needed to go back for New Years and other festivities. Both Liang-Chun and I grew up in loving families who taught us that family is the most important thing in the world, and that is how I raised my children too."

"She did," Ming-Yue said, nodding along to what her mama was saying.

"Where was I? I think that is about it. There's not a lot to say because you read it all in the journal, and Harrison never came back."

I should probably tell her that he's dead. But it would break her heart. Yet she needs to know. Why am I the one that needs to tell her?

"Ah Goo, I have something I think you should know."

"What is it?"

Her eyes bored into mine. All of a sudden, I felt very uncomfortable. *Should I tell her?* She'll blow up and die from sadness. I'll be the cause of her death. *Snap out of it, Anne. Just out with it already. She needs to know.* Maybe it'll allow her to start healing, even at her old age.

"Well, what is it?" asked Ming-Yue, sitting on the edge of her seat. Had I been thinking in my head for that long? I took a breath and said, "I got Harrison's email address from Bettie at the art gallery. The one you still fund through Mr. Wang."

"Yes. I have that email. I've never gotten a response from it."

"Oh." Of course Mary would have it. She's in touch with everyone.

"Is that all?" she asked with a hint of annoyance.

"No."

We stared at each other for what seemed like forever before I finally broke the silence with, "He's dead."

I didn't think the room could get any quieter, but somehow it did. Mary's face did not show a single sign of surprise, which made me unsure of what she was thinking. Was she no longer surprised by any news about Harrison? Even his death? If anything, she looked mad. I was ready to comfort an old lady and her daughter while trying to hold it together myself.

Mary broke the silence and said the last thing I thought she would say. "That's not possible."

"I got an automatic response from the email I sent. It said that he had passed away this month."

Mary's face was set. "The gallery just received new artwork from him this week. They are supposed to get something new soon—an artwork that he has been working on for years. And Bettie has been trying to persuade him to come here. So if he's not working on these paintings, then who is?"

"That's a good question," I murmured.

"That was rhetorical," Mary said without a trace of a smile. "Do you think I like jokes played on me?"

"No, this wasn't . . . I wasn't . . . I think it's time for me to leave."

"I think so too."

I walked to the door feeling her eyes boring into my back. But before the door shut, I saw Ming-Yue's face and I could have sworn she said, "Thank you."

CHAPTER 30

"DID YOU LEARN ANYTHING NEW?" VICTORIA ASKED as soon as I walked in the door.

Victoria and Sebastian were waiting for me when I got home. They had a smorgasboard of food on the dining table and looked like they were going to eat everything in front of them. I joined them.

"I found out that Mary thinks he's still alive, which is preposterous. You two saw the email. It said he was dead."

"Did she say why she thought that?" Victoria asked through a mouthful of radish cake.

"She said he's supposed to be working on a painting that will be the culmination of all his life's work, and Bettie has been trying to persuade him to bring the artwork to the gallery in person."

"Then this is very simple. Let's go visit the gallery and ask Bettie what she thinks," said Sebastian.

"Yeah, maybe Mary is starting to get delusional," said Victoria.

"You guys are delusional. You saw the email!"

"Don't believe everything you read on the web," Sebastian cautioned.

"Ha. Ha. Ha," I said, rolling my eyes at Sebastian.

"You just don't want him to be alive because you'll start worrying again and the search will continue," Victoria said.

I glared at the two of them because I knew they were right. We packed up and left for the art gallery.

I was hoping Bettie wouldn't be in, but sure enough she was.

"How can I help you today?" she asked.

"I was hoping you could clear up a misunderstanding," I said as I was pushed forward by both Sebastian and Victoria.

"Come to my office. This looks like a private matter."

We followed her to her office and when we sat the silence was deafening.

"I went to see Mary today and she finally told me what she knows about Harrison." I hoped Bettie would say something. I didn't know what. Just anything so I didn't have to keep talking. "I sent an email to the address you gave me and I got an auto response saying Harrison had passed away this month. But Mary said that wasn't possible. She thinks Harrison is still alive."

Bettie started laughing. Not the reaction I was expecting.

"Why are you laughing?" Sebastian asked.

"Fei-Hong is very much alive. He is a prankster. The best I've ever seen. You really have to know how to work with him and gain his trust, which is hard to do before he treats you with respect."

"What?" I could feel my hands shaking, they were gripping the arm rests so hard. Sebastian and Victoria both had a hand on my arm, trying to keep me steady. I thought I might scream.

"Harrison is supposed to be delivering his artwork to the gallery tomorrow. Why don't you come by? I cannot promise that you will meet him. I'm wondering myself if he will actually come."

"Why didn't you tell us this the first time?" Victoria asked with some annoyance.

"Because I only just found out this morning. The artwork was supposed to be delivered just like his other ones. There wasn't anything to tell you because that's how we have done it since he started. He never wants to come here, no matter how much we try to persuade him. We were willing to pay for his flight, hotel, food, transportation—anything he wanted, but he never wants to come. I don't know what's changed his mind this time."

Is it because he got my email? Does he want to meet me? Then why tell me that he died? I could have flown back to the States already. Then again, maybe it doesn't have anything to do with me.

"Sure, I'll come by tomorrow to meet him."

"That would be great. I'll call Mary and see if she wants to come too."

"Sure . . ." *Was this how I was going to see Mary again? In front of Harrison? And after she thought I'd played a joke on her?* But what was I supposed to say . . . no? Mary's been looking for him for decades. She would never forgive me if I didn't include her.

"Do you not want to include Mary?" Bettie asked, kicking me out of my thoughts.

"No. No. I think that sounds great."

"Mary probably will not come. The couple of times he had said yes to coming, I called Mary and she got excited, only to have him cancel at the last minute," Bettie said as if to reassure me. Was my anxiety on meeting Mary that apparent?

"I think we've taken up enough of your time. Thank you for having us," Sebastian said hurriedly, pulling me and Victoria out of our seats.

Sebastian led us out the door, through the gallery, and into fresh air. Once outside, it felt like I took my first breath in a long time. Then on its release, I said, "He's alive! I can't believe he tricked me. But what if he doesn't show up tomorrow?"

"He will. He probably received your email and now he's curious," Victoria said, but even her voice wasn't filled with confidence.

"Let's go get some food. I found a great bakery we should try," Sebastian said. He appeared to be the only one holding himself together.

"I'm so done," I groaned while stuffing myself with a cream filled puff pastry.

"That's what you keep saying and yet you're still here," Sebastian said. He wasn't eating anything, just looking at me, which was a bit unnerving. Victoria had gone 'shopping.' She said she wanted to leave us alone. I saw her and Sebastian talking while we walked to the bakery, but I'd been too preoccupied by my thoughts to focus on their conversation.

"You don't want to admit it to yourself because you keep getting disappointed, but you really do want to get to know your family better. That includes finding your uncle, getting to know Mary better, knowing her kids, and understanding where you come from," Sebastian continued.

"You're making too much sense."

"I don't like seeing you discombobulated. You need

closure after all this searching, and the only way you can do that is to keep going until you find your answer. There's no point in moping here with me in the bakery while you could be out there getting answers."

"Well, what do you want me to do? You heard Bettie, he's not coming until tomorrow. That's the earliest I can do anything."

"There's another way."

"And what would that be?"

"Now, don't get mad at me."

"Why would I get mad at you?"

"Isabella—"

"What does she want?" I shouted, cutting him off and at the same time getting some dirty looks from a few of the customers next to us. I quieted down and now understood why Sebastian had taken me to a public place.

"Just hear me out," Sebastian said, holding up his hand. "Isabella called me yesterday. I wasn't going to pick up, but she kept calling until I did. She wanted to talk to you but she knew you would never pick up, no matter how many times she called."

"And of course you would."

"Don't get started, Anne. She's just another person. I'm with you now."

"Sorry, I'm all bent out of shape."

"I think she can help you."

"Really? Like she's helped me in the past?"

"This time it's different. She wants to tell you in person. She's leaving tonight and wants to meet up with you before she leaves."

"And where would this meeting be taking place?"

"Here."

"Here? This is why you brought me here and Victoria is out 'shopping?'"

"I just want you to talk to her."

"And why should I?"

"Because she's trying to make up for being snotty."

"She said that?"

"No, but she implied it. Look, I know you don't like it, but I have a history with her. I know her better than her own mother does. Her father has been out of the picture for years so there's a reason she acts the way she does. Just give her a chance."

"Fine. This is ridiculous though. You know that, right?"

"I know this seems like it's all twisted, but I think that what she has to say will help you, and that's all I care about."

"Okay."

"Yeah?"

"I said okay."

"Okay then. I'll let her know." He commenced texting and I commenced calming myself down. I didn't want to lunge at her in public.

Within minutes, Isabella was walking through the door.

"What, was she waiting around the corner?" I sneered.

"She was, actually."

I glared at him so hard that I hoped his head would get a hole in it.

"I really believe this will help you," he added.

"Hi, Anne. May I sit down?" Isabella's voice sent my heart racing and I had to hold onto the table to stop myself from bolting.

"Like I have a choice."

"Anne . . ." Sebastian started. I glared at him again, and he got up and left us alone.

"I see we've gotten off to a great start," Isabella said with sarcasm dripping from every word. I didn't respond. "Anne, I'm here to help you."

"So I've been told." *More than once.*

"I have a private investigator."

Surprise. Surprise.

"I think he can help you," she continued. "He's very good at what he does."

"Is that what you came here to offer? Harrison is supposed to be here tomorrow, so I don't need a private investigator. Great to see you, Isabella, but no thanks." I started getting up to leave.

"Sit down, Anne. Listen to what I have to say."

I saw Sebastian looking over at us and I sat back down.

"He's never shown up before," she continued. "What makes you think he's going to show up this time? If you really want closure on if he's dead or not, I can help you. Hire the private investigator. Find out what you need to know about this guy—who none of you really know."

She had a point there and I hated her for it, and hated myself for starting to consider her proposal.

"Why are you doing this? You don't like me at all."

"That's true but believe it or not, I do love Sebastian. If he wants to be with you, he deserves to be with someone who is stable and not trying to find her family. Plus, I have a vested interest in finding Harrison too. I'm sure Sebastian explained that to you."

This wasn't the first time I had heard Isabella say that she loved Sebastian, but it didn't really hit home how much until now. I looked over at Sebastian, who was sitting on the bench facing the street, and thought how lucky he must be to have two women love him this much.

"Okay, I'll do it. Send me his information."

"I already have."

"You have, have you?"

"I knew you would hire him. You've been on this family search since you inherited my great uncle's money. It's nice to have all this time to do what you want and not worry about money, isn't it?" And there was the Isabella I knew and hated. "Well, I've got to run. My flight leaves tonight."

I didn't bother getting up but watched while she gathered her things and sashayed out of the door, and hopefully out of my life.

CHAPTER 31

THE GALLERY WAS BUSY TODAY. WE MEANDERED around looking at the art pieces before asking for Bettie. She had told us that Harrison was going to be here at eleven o'clock, so we showed up at ten-thirty, and I hoped that looking at the artwork would calm me down before I met him.

"Bettie, we're here," I said when I saw her walk down the stairs. I wanted to meet my uncle. This was it. I was really going to meet him.

"Oh, hi Anne, Sebastian, Victoria."

All four of us stared at each other for what seemed like minutes. An air of awkwardness was starting to settle when Bettie said, "You just missed him."

"Wait. You said he was coming at eleven. We're early. How could we have missed him?" Sebastian asked.

I'm glad he asked because I was too shocked to talk. After all this time.

"He came early this morning. You can see his work in my office if you'd like."

"Come on, Anne. You should at least see this," Victoria said, trying to put a positive spin on it.

"He's not here," I said in a daze.

We walked to Bettie's office. Leaning against the wall was an oil on canvas. There were mountains, just like the ones I had seen at Taroko lining the background. In the middle was Skyline Mansion, the very one I had inherited. And in the foreground was the lady in the fountain running with her son, a happy look on her face. It was the same fountain that adorned the front of the mansion, but this time they weren't in stone. This time they looked as real as if they were standing right in front of me. Looking at the little boy was Ah Po. The happiest I'd ever seen her. And the little boy was Harrison. In the bottom right was Harrison's signature plum blossom.

"What do you think?" Bettie asked.

"It's beautiful," I said. I didn't bother wiping away the tears that were flowing down my cheeks.

"He really captured the strength of the mountains and the movement."

"Yeah." That wasn't all he had captured. This was the most important work of his life, not because of the art itself, but of whom he saw himself as. I needed to meet with him.

"Have you seen the rest of his exhibit?" Bettie asked.

"We've only seen a little," I said, embarrassed that I hadn't spent more time looking at his art. Somehow my feet wouldn't gravitate back to his work.

"Let me show them to you. I think you will like them."

"Come on, Anne. Let's get to know your uncle a bit more through his work," Sebastian said.

"All right." I reluctantly let them lead me away, although I could have stared at the painting for a lot longer. As we headed toward the stairs, something made me turn to look once more at the painting. When I did, I saw a man standing at the doorway of Bettie's office who looked exactly like what I'd pictured Harrison would look like—a Taiwanese man in his sixties with sad green eyes, wire rimmed glasses, and a balding head. He was looking right back at me.

"Wait, you guys! Look, he's here." But when we all turned back around, he was gone.

"Anne, please come with me. I think you'll learn quite a bit about Harrison through his paintings. Take it from me, you cannot rush the man," Bettie said, and this time her tone seemed to have become gentler and more understanding.

CHAPTER 32

Sᴇʙᴀsᴛɪᴀɴ ʜᴀᴅ ᴛᴏ ʙᴏᴏᴋ ᴏᴜʀ ʀᴇᴛᴜʀɴ ꜰʟɪɢʜᴛs home the next day. I was in too much of a daze. That had been Harrison. I would swear in court that it was. But why hadn't he come and said hi? Why had he appeared like that if he didn't want us to meet him? Had he known I would turn around? The questions kept circling in my mind, and I spent the rest of the day lying on the couch.

Bettie had been right. The exhibit had started with some sketches and then moved into paintings that were dark: grays, blacks, and swirling madness. It was disturbing, including the feeling of dread that came over me when I walked past those paintings. But then, the rest of Harrison's artwork portrayed a man who had traveled the world, someone who was coming to terms with his past, as well as paintings of his own family, his grandchildren, and beautiful portraits of him and Grace from different points in their life. There had also been a beautiful painting of Mary with him and Liang-Chun.

I had called Mary when we returned from the exhibit, wondering if she had seen the painting. The only answer I got was a yes, but I could hear her breath quicken as if she was trying to hold back tears.

The more I learned about Harrison, the more I didn't think he was a crazy person. I'd found him. I had brought him out of whatever hole he had hidden himself in. Maybe he wanted to be discovered but didn't know how. Like Mary, he was too entrenched in his past.

"Anne . . . Anne," Sebastian whispered. "It's time to go. Everything's in the taxi."

"Okay." I reluctantly left the couch and followed him.

Victoria and Sebastian tucked me between the two of them, each holding one of my hands. I rode the one-hour drive to the airport with my head on Sebastian's shoulder. The last two weeks had taken a toll on both of us. I didn't think I could love the man more. With everything going on, Sebastian and I never got to dwell more on our future. But having gone on this journey with him by my side, I knew my answer would be yes.

"Are you ever going to read the letter that you found in the bank?" Sebastian asked after we were safely in the air.

"I have it here with me," I said, taking it out of my purse.

I opened it to find it was only one sheet long.

Harrison,

I wish I could have been in your life for every minute since you were born. I wish I could take away all your pain. I loved meeting you, and I understand why you never want to see me again. I need you to know that I love you very much. I do not mean to do you any harm and I will always be here for you.

I have made you majority owner of the condo in Taipei. Please use it as you wish. It is yours. I will keep it maintained and will never expect anything from you.

You are always welcome in my home. No harm will come to you. I promise.

Love,

Your father

"It doesn't really provide you with anything new," Victoria said.

"It just confirms what others have said," I replied.

"I have a feeling we're going to meet him soon, Anne. Your family is more tight-knit than you thought," Sebastian said, squeezing my hand.

"I do too, Sebastian. I do too."

EPILOGUE

ISABELLA

"SHE FELL FOR IT," I SAID.

"Of course she did. You know her better than she knows herself. Do you think she'll have a problem with the private detective being me?" Nick said, hanging onto the side of the pool.

"What she doesn't know won't hurt her. Plus, you're one of the best. She would be crazy not to hire you. Anything you find out, you let me and Grandma Geraldine know first. Anne will be on a need-to-know basis. I know I can win Harrison over. We'll get the Taiwan condo, and we'll get our money back."

"Only if I don't have to talk to Grandma Geraldine directly."

"Are you still scared of her after all these years?" Nick never needed to know that as much as I loved Grandma Geraldine, she still scared me too.

"I swear the woman is a witch," Nick said. "You've said so yourself."

"All right. All right. You only have to report to me then."

"You're a genius, Isabella, but you know that. You know

I'd do anything for you."

"I know," I said, clinking my wine glass with his. "We make a good team."

"Did you call Brian back?"

"Brian is worthless. He couldn't even win back his ex-girlfriend. I've cut ties with him."

"I thought you said he contacted you the other day."

"He did and I've blocked his calls. All he had to do was win Anne back and get her out of our lives. I would have Sebastian back, and then I could focus on getting our inheritance back. But the blockhead couldn't even do that. I even promised him a hundred grand if he could pull it off. I could hear him salivating over the phone at the thought of getting the money. It was disgusting."

"Good riddance to him. I think the private investigator will work wonders," Nick said, giving me a knowing smile.

"I'll drink to that."

Will Anne ever meet Harrison? Does Isabella get to Harrison first? Join Anne as she navigates the sea of family secrets and realizes enemies aren't who they seem.

Visit this link to continue Anne's journey in *Secret Blossom*: Skyline Mansion Book 3. Or read on for a sample.

Join Nola's newsletter to receive a FREE story and be the first to learn about new releases and giveaways.

newsletter.nolalibarr.com/skylinemansion

WHAT'S NEXT

Secret Blossom
Skyline Mansion Book 3

How many secrets could one family have?

After failing to find her uncle in Taiwan, Anne is back at Skyline Mansion and wants life to be quiet for a change. But when Harrison suddenly makes an appearance, only to disappear a few days later, her life is once again turned upside down.

When Anne receives Harrison's journal with a note requesting her to read it before she decides to search for him again, Anne takes the mission to heart. She once again forsakes her family and friends as she delves into her uncle's past, unravelling a history of more secrets, pain, and loss.

At the same time, another Wilkens family member has reached out to her. The girl is charming, but she wants something, and Anne suspects her true intentions, especially when she learns that she is best friends with her arch nemesis—the same woman who still has eyes on Anne's inheritance.

Secret Blossom is the third book in the Skyline Mansion women's fiction series. Filled with soul-searching heroines, paths to self-discovery, and stories of perseverance, Secret Blossom shows how love conquers all.

Visit this link to continue reading *Secret Blossom* or read on for a sneak peak

SNEAK PEEK

Secret Blossom
Skyline Mansion Book 3

As a country, Taiwan is not one to be missed. You can cross it from tip to tip in less than seven hours if you're driving, but this journey can be as fast as ninety minutes if you take the high-speed rail. The variety of people, culture, and food are never ending. Taoyuen Airport is an hour away from Taipei. A bus or taxi ride will get you from the airport to Taipei in an hour. I prefer the bus because you get a cushy seat and you're one of many travelers. It's also cheaper, and you can get lost in the scenery without having to talk to anyone.

Taipei is a mini NYC. There are people, cars, yellow taxis, buses, and subways everywhere. The only difference between Taipei and NYC is that there are hundreds of mopeds. At first, it's disorienting to cross the road when a mass of mopeds are turning in your direction, but over time you will come to realize that if you keep moving they will go around you, and that it is when you hesitate that an accident is more likely to happen. It is like Dory says in *Finding Nemo,* "Just keep swimming, just keep swimming."

Oh my goodness, now I'm referencing Disney movies? This wasn't going to work. *International Travels* wanted the first revision of my article on Taiwan within the next two days, and all I could focus on was my uncle. I swear I saw Harrison in the office at the gallery, but maybe it was just an office worker . . . ? But the man didn't look Taiwanese, and he didn't have jet-black hair. And he was tall—too tall to be a Taiwanese person. Then again, I did see a few tall Taiwanese people while there. Okay, maybe more than a few as I'm tall for a Taiwanese person. *Ugh, I'm getting way off track again.*

"Anne?"

I looked up to find my best friend standing in the middle of my bedroom. "Oh, hi, Victoria."

"Oh, hi? You're still reminiscing over the guy you saw in the office, aren't you?"

"Yes, and so what if I am? Don't you and Paul have a date to go on?"

"Don't change the subject. I'm not against you. You just don't know who that guy was. For all we know, he worked there and probably went into the office to grab a pen and left."

"Yeah . . ." But I couldn't tell her that the feeling he was who I thought he was wouldn't go away.

"Have you unpacked from the trip yet?" Sebastian asked as he came and joined us in the bedroom. His dark brown hair was wet, and a few short strands fell across his forehead, making me smile. He had complained about the heat in Taiwan, saying his thick hair was absorbing too much heat. He'd almost went to a hairdresser and shaved all his hair off, but I persuaded him otherwise, thank goodness.

"Earth to Anne?" he said now, standing right in front of me. I could smell his cologne and wished Victoria wasn't here in this moment, but I also knew there was no way she was going to leave. I could sense she had something on her mind.

"Yes, what did you ask me?" I asked Sebastian with a sweet smile.

A hearty laugh came out of his mouth, making my lips

widen. "I asked if you had unpacked from the trip to Taiwan —which I can see would be a no."

"Almost." I looked around the room. My stuff was strewn all over the bed, dresser, and floor. Lady, my cocker spaniel, started barking right then.

Sebastian raised a brow. "It seems Lady agrees it's a mess."

I made a face at him. "I'll get to it when I get to it."

"Are *you* unpacked?" Victoria asked, pointing at Sebastian.

"Of course. I did it all on the first day."

"Sebastian likes things orderly," I said. "It's one of the reasons he's such a good lawyer."

Victoria's eyes grew big at my acknowledgement. "Wow! I'm with Anne. Things will go where they need to when it's time to put them away. For example, I am in search of my flat iron and I think I put it in one of your bags, Anne."

"That's my cue to leave then," Sebastian said, raising his hands. "Anne, I'll let you know when I'm on my way home." He came and gave me a kiss that made Victoria turn away and suddenly busy herself searching for her flat iron.

I remained standing there, following the sound of Sebastian's footfalls all the way out the front door before I turned to look back at Victoria. She was now looking flustered that she couldn't find the flat iron. "You can just borrow mine, you know," I suggested.

"Yes, I know, I know." Victoria turned and looked at me with her head slanted to one side. "But you know something?"

"What?"

"I never understood why you needed a flat iron. You have perfectly straight Taiwanese hair. You wake up in the morning and don't have to do anything to it."

"That's a misconceived perception," I said, walking to one of my bags to retrieve the coveted item. "I have waves under all this straight hair, you see. I have to brush it and flatten it if I want it to look nice."

"If you say so," she said dubiously. She took the flat iron from me. "Thank you. I will not be returning this until I find mine, so you'll have to deal with your so-called waves unless you come to my room to use it."

"Oh no, I can only deal with one messy room at a time."

We both started laughing, breaking the lingering tension in the room. I knew this conversation was never about the flat iron. Sobering, I said to Victoria, "Just spit it out already. I know you want to ask me something."

Her smile slipped and she asked quietly, "So . . . have you thought more about what Isabella said?"

"I knew you were going to ask that!" I burst out.

"Well, I agree with Sebastian. I think it's your only hope of finding your uncle. We need a professional."

"I know."

She looked relieved at my response. "If it makes you feel any better, I asked around about this Nick guy and heard that he's a pretty good detective. So, don't take it from Isabella, but from me that I want you to hire him. We spent weeks looking for him in Taiwan and all to no avail. I really think you need closure in order to move on."

"You make good points," I mumbled.

She didn't smile. "I make the right points and you know it."

From the look on her face, I knew I wasn't getting out of this one. "Fine, I'll give him a call."

Victoria promptly held out her hand. "Here, use my phone."

I raised an eyebrow. "I have a perfectly good phone."

"Of which you have no idea where it is and will hence postpone this call to another day."

I sighed. "Okay, fine."

I took her phone and dialed Nick's number. It wasn't like I hadn't thought about Isabella's offer to hire the detective over and over again. She had sent me his number and I had looked at it every day to the point that I had it memorized by heart. Victoria was right, I didn't want to be taking any favors from Isabella, but there didn't seem to be a way out of this.

The phone was picked up on the other end.

"Hello?" a low voice said, sounding kind of sleepy. I looked at Victoria, who was listening quietly as I had the phone on speaker. Was this the right person? Maybe I should have gone looking for his number before dialing.

"Hi, is this Nick?"

"It is. Who is this?"

"This is Anne. I got your number from—"

"Anne! I've been expecting your call. Isabella has said so much about you." I heard a distinct splash and some expletives and wondered again if this was the right choice. "Sorry about that," Nick continued. "I was just sleeping next to the pool when you rang, and my niece thought it would be funny to splash me." I heard giggling in the background. "Hold on a second, Anne. Let me move into the house."

Victoria and I exchanged glances.

A moment later he came back on. "Sorry about that. Yes, Isabella had mentioned that you were looking for your uncle."

"Yes, that was—"

"I could come by today if you are free," he cut in quickly. "We could discuss your case."

I felt I had no choice but to agree. "Sure . . ."

"Great! You're at Skyline Mansion, right?"

"That's right. Do you know how to get here?"

"I've been there loads. Done a lot of work for the family. One note, though, can you make sure it's just you and me when we meet in person? I like to keep my identity hidden from as many people as I can. My job depends on me being discreet given the society we're in is very small."

"I'm going to be there too," Victoria interjected before I could stop her.

There was silence on the other end of the phone for a second before Nick said, "Who is that?"

"It's Victoria; she's my best friend."

"Um . . ."

Victoria jumped in before he could say more. "I don't know anyone in your society except Anne, and for her sake I won't be telling anyone who you are. I cross my heart and hope to die. Stick a—"

"All right, all right, all right. She's okay." Nick seemed to be letting out a lot of air in a drawn-out sigh. "I need to go. I'll see you this afternoon about twoish." And with that, he hung up.

Victoria looked at me. "Well, if anything, he's not going to be boring—nothing like those television shows we used to watch."

"No kidding. I have no idea what just happened."

Visit this link to continue reading *Secret Blossom*
nolalibarr.com

MORE FROM NOLA LI BARR

Skyline Mansion Series

Forbidden Blossom
Hidden Blossom
Secret Blossom
Family Blossom

Companion Stories to the Skyline Mansion Series

Summer of New Love
Summer of Second Chances
Summer of My Dreams

ABOUT THE AUTHOR

Nola Li Barr writes family sagas with a touch of mystery and sweet romance. When she's not writing she can be found reading, making photo books, and navigating the path of motherhood.

Receive a FREE story when you join Nola's newsletter. Be the first to know about new releases and giveaways.
newsletter.nolalibarr.com/skylinemansion

www.nolalibarr.com
@nolalibarr